THE

Lauren Silva and

THE
CHARMED
BRACELET

by

Best wishes,

Jordin Everrey

With illustrations from the sketchbook of Keri Kirby

A CIP catalogue record of this book is available from the
British Library

ISBN: 1-905006-31-4

Cover design by The Digital Canvas Company, Scotland

Location photographs, more information about the true
history behind the stories and the opportunity to e-mail the
author and pre-order the next volume in the series can be
seen at:
www.thestonespear.co.uk

Printed and bound in Great Britain by
Antony Rowe Ltd., Chippenham, Wiltshire

Thanks to all my friends and relations who read, listened to, commented on, or otherwise inspired the writing of this series of books.

Apologies to the National Trust, who will not know that the Silva family has owned the site of Longstone Cottage, Mottistone, for centuries!

Apologies to Southampton City Council for rebuilding the end of a terrace of town houses beside the old cellar excavations.

This series is dedicated to the children of St. Margaret's Primary School, Ventnor, Isle of Wight 2002—2004, who inspired its beginnings on a wet Friday morning.

The Bracelet Timeline by El Silva

European Time Line	probable location of Silva family	Events
Bronze Age	? N. E. Europe?	1500 — Lori & Axiel defeat Thor
		1400 — Lori the Healer
		1300
		1200
		1100
	Eastern Mediterranean	1000 — Lori the Horsebreeder
		900
		800
		700 — Lori Friend of Wolves
		600
		500
Iron Age		400
		300 — Loriel the Scholar — Lori and son assassinated c. 120BC
		200
		100
		BC.
Roman Empire		A.D. — Loriel the Seafarer
		100
		200 — Lori the Silk Trader
		300
		400 — Lori Dolphin-Rider
		500
Dark Age & Medieval Europe		600
		700 — Lori the Wine Grower
		800
		900
	Rome, France, England	1000 — Lori the Farmer
		1100
		1200
		1300
		1400 — Laurielle friend of Louis XIV of France — 1515 Alessandro di Selva burned as sorceror
		1500
		1600
Modern		1700 — Laura b.1787 — 1791 De Silvères guillotined
		1800 — El born 1789
		1900
		2000 — Lauren Ella Silva given bracelet

v

Prologue: 1500 B.C.

In the darkness the sudden silence was deafening; only the wind hissed eerily around the mountainside where the three survivors huddled together under an overhang of the unclimbable cliff face, waiting dumbly for whatever the silence would bring them: death or victory, slavery or freedom. The woman, her heart already dead with her husband and children, fingered her last bronze-tipped arrow, the last arrow that she had saved either for her enemy or for herself if their last desperate hope failed. It was terrible to think that in this world where the natives thought so much of war and aggression it had been one of their own people who had brought them to near-extinction. Of her two companions, she was sure that whatever happened one would not survive the night. Despite the tight binding she had tied around his leg she could still see the blood pooling beside his feet, dark against the moonlit snow.

The silence continued, and she slowly managed to free herself from her angry bloodlust and sent her mind probing gently into his body. It had been so long, so long since she had been able to think of healing instead of killing. Perhaps even now he might be saved, but for what? Perhaps it would be kinder to let him die. Her other companion clutched at her arm, even in the darkness somehow aware of the change in her.

"There is always hope," he whispered urgently.

"Lori," she murmured back. "Our only hope."

Chapter 1
The
Bracelet

Lauren Ella Silva had managed to reach the age of twelve years and three days never doubting that she was just about the most ordinary person in the world, that her life was quite possibly the most boring and depressing life in the world, and certainly never doubting that she was just as human as everyone else.

Until this day, Saturday May 6th 2000, a date that would fix itself in her memory for as long as she lived. For a significant, historic, amazing day it had started badly.

"Lauren! You are not going out to lunch with your grandmother in your jeans!"

"Oh, Mum!" Lauren started to get up but had to sit down again while her mother attacked her mane of black hair with a hairbrush. "Grannie won't care."

"Well, I do." Her mother's voice took on the rhythm of the brushstrokes as they hit a difficult tangle. "She hasn't seen you since this time last year. I can do without her thinking I've let you become a ragamuffin."

"She's always more interested in what I do than what I look like," Lauren objected. "Anyway, she never looks really smart herself."

"That's got nothing to do with it. If you have to wear trousers all the time, wear your new black ones. Do you want a plait?"

"Ow! OK Mum." She was secretly surprised she had enough hair left for a plait and sat patiently with her head throbbing while her mother finished the styling. "If you're going shopping could you get me a new gel pen for school?"

"Black or blue?" Heather Silva stood back to view the results of her handiwork. "You'll do. Now hurry up and get changed. She'll be here soon."

"Blue please," Lauren replied, reluctantly pulling off her jeans. "Did you wash my black sweatshirt?"

"I don't know when you think I've had any time to do the washing," her mother snapped. "You know I haven't even been home before six once this week and then I had to get that case together in the evenings that I took over when Robert Ellis was taken into hospital. You'll just have to wear your thin one. It's not cold. Here." The ringing of the doorbell interrupted them and in relief Lauren grabbed it and ran downstairs to open the door.

"Hello Grannie." She always expected to feel shy when her grandmother came to pick her up once a year for her birthday lunch but somehow her awkwardness could not survive the old woman's easy friendliness. Old? Lauren thought. In some ways she seemed older than her friends' grandparents and her other granny, her deep, dark eyes full of wisdom as if she knew everything worth knowing and had read everything worth reading. In other ways she seemed ageless, her hair a dark greyish black always trying to escape from a rather old-fashioned clip and the lines creasing her narrow, tanned face those of kindness and humour rather than old age. She seemed a country person, always a bit out of place in the bustling centre of Southampton; the sort of person who would never be shocked at anything. Perhaps it was because Lauren saw her so seldom that she always found herself telling her grandmother things she would never have shared with her mother.

"Happy birthday." A friendly squeeze on the shoulder and a smile that seemed to wrap Lauren in a warm glow were enough to break the ice. "Mmm, you look very striking in black. Have you decided where you want to go this year?"

"How about Italian?" Lauren asked. She had no fear that they would not do whatever she suggested; Grannie had cheerfully taken her anywhere she wanted to go ever since she was five. There had been three years of McDonalds before her tastes had begun to be more sophisticated, since when they had sampled the varying delights of out of town pubs that had been recommended by friends who went out more than she and her mother. "Keri says the pasta place in the City Centre's pretty good."

"Fine by me. Are you ready?" Lauren nodded.

"Bye Mum!" she called. Her mother called out a muffled goodbye from upstairs, they hurried into the waiting taxi and Lauren told the driver their destination.

"Did your mother mind you coming?" Grannie asked abruptly as they fastened their seat belts, her eyes piercing into Lauren's. Taken by surprise, Lauren had to think for a moment. Mum had seemed even more moody than usual.

"She didn't say so," she ventured. "She never talks about you or Dad or anything." Her grandmother nodded, a quick dismissive action that killed all the words on the tip of Lauren's tongue that she had wanted to ask for years. Where had her father gone? Why had her father gone? Lauren could not even remember what he had been like.

"It's not easy for her, you know." As usual, Grannie seemed to sense what Lauren left unsaid and to sympathise. "It's a demanding job, being a solicitor, and it's hard being a mother on your own." Lauren made a little face. It wasn't that easy being a daughter on your own.

"Maybe we can do something about that," Grannie murmured as if she had heard.

The meal was delicious; Lauren ordered all her favourite dishes without having to think about whether they were healthy or not, or whether she should suck the garlic butter off her fingers or drink two huge glasses of coke or speak with her mouth full. She was able to talk about how boring and miserable school was at the moment, and even enjoyed some funny stories Grannie Laura told her about her cottage in the Isle of Wight and her seven cats, but all through their lunch something seemed different. Something about her grandmother was even more alert and birdlike than usual. Lauren had often wondered what kind of bird she reminded her of. A blackbird perhaps, or a thrush, she thought: very bright-eyed and constantly watchful. Or perhaps something a little more dangerous like a hawk, with her piercing deep-set eyes and fierce thin nose. If she'd been a teacher, Lauren thought, not much would get past her. She even ate a bit like a bird, sparingly, but Lauren made up for that and sat back at the end of the meal feeling full and happy. It was not until they had paid the bill and were ready to go that her grandmother stopped her friendly talking and gave her a penetrating stare.

"And now for your birthday present." She leaned across the table until their heads were almost touching, her voice low, eyes glancing round the room once again. Suddenly, tension throbbed between them and the noise of the busy restaurant seemed to fade as if their small table was cocooned in a bubble of privacy. "It is time for me to pass it on now you have reached your twelfth birthday." She slipped a small package from her pocket. "This has been in our family for a long, long time, passed down from mother to daughter. You will be its thirteenth keeper, so you can guess how old it is." Lauren took the present that was wrapped not in the usual birthday paper but in a soft, shining fabric tied with a white ribbon, and held it for a moment in one hand where it settled heavily into the shape of her palm. She carefully pulled away the ribbon, reached inside and drew out a silver chain hung with charms, every one a perfect miniature sculpture. For a moment she could think of nothing to say, and could not drag her eyes away from it as she pulled it through her finger and thumb to look at every silver model.

"Oh Grannie," was all she could whisper.

"It is very precious. Irreplaceable." Her grandmother's voice was a murmur. "Will you let me fasten it for you?" Lauren looked up, eyes shining with wonder and thanks that she could not express, and found her grandmother staring at her with a mixture of sadness and solemnity that seemed to pierce her soul. Without taking her eyes away from that hypnotic gaze she held out her hand. She jumped. As her grandmother touched her wrist to fasten the bracelet an inexplicable tingle shot up her arm like a small electric shock.

"Lauriella Silva, this heirloom of our people is yours until the day when you will know that it is time to pass it to your own descendant. Guard it well."

"Thank you," Lauren whispered, awed by the formality of her grandmother's words. "I will."

As they got up to leave, a man sitting near the door smiled at her and lifted a hand in greeting. Lauren thought with slightly possessive pride that he was easily the best-dressed man in the restaurant, his pale grey suit looking casual but expensive. Everything about him seemed perfect, even his slightly over-large nose simply making him look more aristocratic. Lauren waved back, secretly enjoying the bell-like tinkle of the charms as her hand lifted.

"It's Uncle Daniel, Mum's boss," she told her grandmother. "Looks like he's brought his mother out to lunch today. He's frightfully rich and always gets me the most wonderful birthday presents. He got me a portable CD player this year, but nothing'll be as good as this."

She felt the weight of the bracelet on her wrist all the way home in the taxi as she sat leaning companionably against her grandmother instead of chattering as they usually did. She kissed her goodbye on the doorstep, giving her a swift but fierce hug.

"It's the best thing I've ever had, Grannie," she said again. "Thank you. I will take care of it."

Her mother opened the door attempting a smile, and Lauren slipped inside and ran upstairs to her room. Through the banisters she could see that instead of closing the door behind her she opened it wider and Lauren strained her ears to hear her words.

"Have you seen him?"

"Not these seven years. Believe me, if I knew he was alive or dead I would have told you."

"I'm sorry." Lauren was shocked that her mother's breath was like a sob, and pressed her face through the banisters to hear better as she continued. "You know I've blamed you, and him, for being so different. It's hard to move on, not knowing."

"Of course." Lauren saw her grandmother's hand reach through the doorway and rest gently on her mother's shoulder. "He did love you, Heather, both of you, more than anything."

"Then why?" Her mother's voice broke, the first time Lauren had ever seen her cry, and bright tears rose too in her grandmother's eyes. She suddenly felt like an eavesdropper witnessing something she should not have seen, an emotion she could not share for the father she could not remember, and slipped into her bedroom.

The bracelet felt heavy on her wrist and Lauren turned it to look more closely at the finely crafted charms that hung from the silver chain. She counted. Twelve, all different. A little bird reminded her so strongly of Grannie that she smiled, turning it between her fingers, and all of a sudden she thought she could see her blowing her nose defiantly in the taxi that was taking her back to the Isle of Wight ferry. She dropped the charm in shock but slowly and warily touched it again, holding it between her finger and thumb. Her grandmother was paying the taxi, then turned and smiled straight into Lauren's mind.

Our secret. Our heritage, she seemed to say.

"Have you finished your homework this weekend?" Her mother's voice floated upstairs, clearly under control again. Lauren made a face. There was never any peace; it was always 'Lauren have you done this?' or 'Lauren have you finished that?' or 'Lauren, you should really get on with the other'.

"I've got to find out something about life in France at the time of Louis XIV," she called back reluctantly, hoping her mother wouldn't offer to help. The only thing worse than no one helping with her homework was her mother trying to get her to do it properly. Nothing Lauren ever did was perfect enough for her. "Can I use the computer?"

"Give me half an hour to finish here. Anything else?"

"Maths." Definitely not her favourite subject but even that was better than the vague history assignment. She couldn't even sort out one Louis from another and just hoped that the internet or their encyclopaedia would be able to tell her something.

By the end of the evening her brain felt in a total whirl with Louis XIV and she wished devoutly that the Sun King would appear in her sitting room so that she could tell him what a pompous poser she thought he was. Putting his face in the centre of the sun for a motif! She was sure she'd seen that design before somewhere, but she was too tired to think where.

"I'm going to have to finish tomorrow," she yawned, for once not waiting for her mother to tell her it was bedtime.

"I used to rather like Louis XIV when I was younger," her mother said rather dreamily. "His period was part of my history A-level."

"Yuk!" Lauren exclaimed.

"Actually, this ring was supposed to have been given to one of your ancestors by King Louis." She waved the large sapphire she always wore under Lauren's nose. "It was a family heirloom your Grannie Laura gave to your father for me when we got engaged. Here." Heather searched the bookshelves and pulled out a battered looking book. "The Three Musketeers. Why don't you see if you enjoy it? It's quite true to history and fun. There's a series, and I should think you're probably old enough to enjoy them. We could borrow the films on video but they're not as good once you've read the books."

"Thanks." Surprised to find that her mother had once liked something as impractical as adventure stories, Lauren said goodnight and started reading on the way upstairs. By the time her eyes started to close she had established that firstly she liked the mad young hero d'Artagnon and secondly it probably wasn't much use for her project as it wasn't Louis XIV at all but Louis XIII who was the king at the time. She went to sleep with her assignment whirling through her brain into her dreams, which were somehow full of French lords and ladies in ornate costumes dancing in a huge ballroom, and dinners and hunting parties. She was dressed like the others in a rich silk gown, laughing secretly to herself at the way all the other courtiers were trying to get King Louis to notice them. They weren't even allowed to sit down in the presence of the king unless he gave them special permission! Then all of a sudden he was there behind her, lifting his amazing feathered hat to her and kissing her hand while sliding a jewelled ring onto her finger. Partly herself, Lauren recognised the ring as her mother's engagement ring. She laughed at him, surprised, and almost felt the jealous stares of the others as he walked next to her through the beautiful gardens.

All at once in her sleep she began to feel a great fear, knowing that somewhere someone was hunting her. She was hiding under the rocky shelter of a cave mouth, watching as lightning flickered across the horizon and thunder rumbled like the insane chuckle of a giant. As a long flash lit the world outside, Lauren saw with a shock that she was kneeling by the body of what looked like a child, only a weak moan showing it was still alive. A woman ran in, her breath panting in short gasps, and as another flash lit the scene in front of her she fell to her knees beside them, tears wetting her cheeks as she cradled the child in her arms.

"Thank you," she whispered, and picking him up she ran back out into the darkness. Lauren, or whoever she was in that dream, stared after her, grief and pity flooding through her as she somehow knew that child would not live to grow up. All at once, lightning stabbed again and again like a spear aiming for the running figure and Lauren screamed a useless warning as the woman managed to swerve and duck away despite her burden. Then she was running too, beyond terror as she was swept with the two fugitives, knowing without being told that rain of death was seeking them. They ran on until her chest was sore with gasped breath across a grassy plain studded with the skeletons of burned trees, peals of thunder ringing in their ears, a crowd of others joining them in that desperate flight. She dodged madly as a bolt of lightning earthed close by and her scream as another hit one of their companions was drowned by the most immense crash she had ever heard.

She woke to find herself sitting up in bed, shaking with fear and in a bath of sweat, clutching her wrist and the bracelet with her other hand, panting in the orange glow of the street light that filtered in through the weave of her bedroom curtains. As she fuzzily began to realise she was awake and that it was only a dream she tried to tell herself that she hadn't been afraid of storms for years, but this was not any ordinary thunderstorm. It was a thunderstorm with malevolent purpose. The wail of a police siren in the distance made her jump; it was as if she had to remember who she really was and where she lived.

"I'm Lauren. Lauren Silva," she muttered to herself. But somehow she wasn't just Lauren Silva any more. She knew that she had lived through terror and loss and grief beyond the understanding of her twelve years and she would never again be the same person who had gone to bed so normally the evening before.

After a while she managed to calm down enough to lie back on her pillows, but dared not let her eyes close again until the first glimmer of dawn had banished the dark shadows from every corner of her room.

Chapter 2
Dream or Reality?

"Do thunderstorms ever kill people?" Lauren was pushing her food around her plate, so tired after her sleepless night that she was finding it hard to eat the Sunday roast that they had cooked for her mum's boss, Daniel Torsen.

"Hardly ever," her mother replied.

"What makes you worry about that?" Daniel looked up from his plate and gave her a quizzical look.

"I had a really awful nightmare," she confessed. "It was as if a storm was chasing me." She felt silly as she said it, expecting them both to laugh at her, but her mother looked concerned and Daniel nodded slowly.

"Well, that's pretty unlikely," Heather tried to reassure her. "You know about not standing under trees and unplugging TV sets and computers of course."

"Have you had nightmares like that before?" Daniel asked her. She shook her head.

"I've never had a dream like that before, that I've remembered so much of the next day. It was so real." She blinked hard, and he gave her a sympathetic smile.

"There's usually a reason for a nightmare," he advised. "Something you're worried about maybe?" She shook her head. No way was she going to discuss her problems with him over the dinner table! It was bad enough having him there with them like one of the family and she wished she had never mentioned it. "What did you eat for lunch at the restaurant yesterday?" he asked.

"I had the four cheese pizza."

"Cheese? Always used to give me bad dreams when I was small," he laughed. "Actually, I used to have terrifying dreams when I was a child, so I know just how you feel. I was like you, my father died when I was too young. It's a great loss. I hope you know that if you need me I'll try to fill the gap a bit." For a moment she didn't know what to say. He was very kind, but she couldn't imagine confiding in him like a father. And her father hadn't died. He had left them. Her mother kicked her foot under the table and she stammered,

"Th-thank you Uncle Daniel." She didn't feel thankful at all. She felt suddenly sulky and cross and hated the warm smile her mother gave him.

"Do you wear that bracelet to bed?" he asked her suddenly. "I should think if that was spiking you all night you'd be bound to have bad dreams!"

"Oh, Lauren!" Her mother joined in. "Make sure you take it off tonight. You looked so awful this morning. You've still got great purple circles round your eyes."

"Mum!" Lauren protested, so embarrassed at the way they were both staring at her that she wanted to shrink under the table. She suddenly felt she had to lie, to protect the bracelet as if it was her friend. "I didn't wear it last night. I expect it was just the cheese." She put down her knife and fork. "I really can't eat any more. Shall I clear the plates?"

Daniel had planned a surprise for them that afternoon and after coffee he made sure they were wrapped up well in warm coats, ushered them mysteriously into his car and drove out of the city. They soon left the main roads, winding through wooded lanes until he turned left through a huge archway topped with the carving of a stag into a private avenue leading through wide meadowland studded with huge old oak and chestnut trees. Lauren could see some kind of stately home in the distance at the end of a long avenue of beech trees but they turned off the approach and drove around the back of the building.

"Where are we?" her mother asked, mystified. "This isn't your home is it, Daniel?" He shook his head.

"Much grander. It belongs to a friend of mine. We share an interest in carriage driving and his grooms look after my horses for me." Lauren peered curiously out of the window as he drew to a halt in a cobbled courtyard and caught her breath in surprise as she saw the vehicle waiting for them: a fairytale open carriage with four shining white horses harnessed to the front, a groom holding their heads and a coachman in a top hat holding a long whip sitting on the box seat at the front. One of the horses stamped a hoof impatiently.

"Well?" Daniel asked Lauren, smiling down at her as she scrambled out of the car. "Grand enough for you?"

"Where are we going?" she asked.

"Oh, only round the estate," he replied. "But if you enjoy it, perhaps you could come with me on one of our events. It can get to be a very competitive sport when we're racing."

"You're not driving us today then?" her mother asked mischievously as he held the door open and tucked a fur rug around her.

"The company in the back's too tempting." This time there was no mistaking the warm look in Uncle Daniel's eyes as he took the seat next to her and Lauren suddenly felt like refusing the treat as the groom helped her up next to the driver at the front and jumped up beside them. At least she didn't have to look backwards and she was soon distracted as the driver let her have a turn at holding the thick cluster of reins. It took all her concentration to try to keep them the same length and stop them tangling and somehow the horses refused to keep walking straight when she was in control like they did for him. He laughed at her when she complained, but kindly.

"Don't worry," he said. "You're pretty good for a beginner." They arrived back after about an hour with her face glowing from the fresh spring wind and she jumped down feeling almost like her dream self from the court of King Louis of France.

"I don't think she'll have much trouble sleeping tonight," her mother said fondly as Daniel dropped them back at home. "Thank you, Daniel, for a lovely afternoon."

"Yes, thank you. It was really great." Lauren tried to make up for her earlier moodiness. "I can't wait to tell my friend Keri all about it tomorrow."

"Next time, why don't you ask her if she'd like to come too?" he suggested and she smiled her thanks at him. Perhaps if her mother was thinking of getting her a new father she could do worse. She knew she wouldn't talk about him even to her best friend, though. It would make it seem too real to say "my mother's boyfriend" instead of "my mother's boss". And she would never admit to anyone how much she had enjoyed herself.

That night when she went to bed she felt afraid to put out her light and fingered the bracelet nervously. Could Daniel's remark about it spiking her be nearer to the truth than he could have imagined? Her hand went to her wrist to unfasten it, and froze. Somehow it felt wrong to take it off. She remembered her grandmother's expression as she had clasped it on her wrist and her hand fell away from it. Rubbish. As if jewellery could give her nightmares. She switched off the light and tucked herself resolutely under the covers. No more nightmares. But she could not stop her mind drifting back to the court of Louis XIV, so much more real to her than the books she had read even if it was just a fantasy. What would that woman have been like at her age, Lauren wondered. Had she always been rich and spoiled, the darling of a king?

She drifted into gloom. A smell of new-kindled wood smoke hit her so sharply that she almost woke, every sensation so real, so unlike a dream. The crowd around her was shouting and jeering, pressing forwards, and she could feel their bloodlust like an angry cloud filling her mind. Cries of 'Kill the Sorcerer!' filled the air. Desperation made her push harder, squirming her skinny body through the press of smelly people, the precious bundle of jewels and money tied under her skirts weighing her down and almost tripping her.

Get away from here now! Save yourself! Her father's voice was urgent in her mind, his fear for himself submerged in his fear for her.

No! Together we can kill the flames! she shrieked. She tried to link minds with him, failing as she felt the push of another mind against them, laughing and triumphant, fanning the fire to an inferno. She fought back, her inner struggle finding voice as she screamed with the effort, but her shouts were drowned in the roaring of the crowd and the roaring of the flames as they devoured the man who had been her father.

She wept and screamed helplessly, some rational instinct knowing that it was only a dream and that if she screamed enough she might wake herself up. Then before she woke, a feeling of warmth and comfort seemed to flood through her.

You're safe, Lauren, it's only a nightmare. I'll be here with you if you hold my charm when you go to sleep.

Grannie Laura. She turned over drowsily, almost feeling her grandmother's arms protecting her as the fear fell away and she drifted back into a cosy dreamless sleep, the bird charm warm beneath her finger.

The faintest scuffle next to her bed woke her with a jump. Her breath froze in her throat as she opened one eye and saw a dark shape silhouetted in the glow from the street lamp outside her window and her heart began thumping as loudly as a drumbeat.

"Mum?" she whispered. The shape jerked suddenly in surprise and knocked the glass of water off her bedside table with a crash. Lauren did the only thing she could: opened her mouth and screamed as loudly as she could. She heard her mother's door fly open and in a moment her bedroom light flooded the room with brightness. It was empty. There was no one there, only the water glass smashed on the floor.

"Whatever's the matter?" her mother asked, standing in the doorway.

"There was someone here. In my room," she whispered, feeling herself shaking.

"There's no one here." Heather checked that the window was shut. "No one could have got out past me. It must have been another nightmare. Go back to sleep." Lauren stared at her, dark eyes flooding with tears while her mother bent down to pick up the pieces of broken glass and put them on Lauren's dressing table for the night. She pulled the duvet back over her daughter. "Come on, pet, you must have woken up and knocked it off yourself." Lauren nodded, and managed to lie back on the pillow. It was the only explanation but as soon as her mother had left and gone back to her own room she turned on her bedside light, too frightened still to lie in the dark alone. She lay there holding the bird charm between her finger and thumb until she stopped shivering and began to warm up, but it was nearly daylight again before she managed to get back to sleep.

She could not bring herself to leave the bracelet at home on Monday morning and decided to risk wearing it to school.

"What's that you've got on?" Tania's sharp voice made half the corridor turn and look, and Lauren felt her cheeks burning.

"Nothing," she muttered.

"Yes it is. You're wearing jewellery. Let me see."

"No." Lauren pulled away. "It's only a birthday present from my grandmother." She was used to Tania getting at her, but it didn't make it any easier.

"Hey! Amy, Jessica! Come and see what wussy jewellery Lauren's got from her gran!"

"Ow!" Lauren's head jerked back as her ponytail was seized in a vice-like grip that felt as if it was tugging her hair out by the roots.

"What, this old clip?" Jessica dragged her new hair bobble off with a large tangle of hair and gave the remains of the ponytail a tug for good measure that sent Lauren staggering against the wall.

"No, this!" Tania made another more successful grab for Lauren's arm. "Ow! What've you got on that thing? Razor blades?" She snatched her hand away, rubbing it. "Oh, come on you two. We don't want to be seen hanging around here. People might think we liked her or something." Tania tossed her blonde head and flounced off with her friends flanking her like bodyguards, Jessica scrutinising the hair clip ostentatiously and then tossing it back over her shoulder. Lauren fiercely blinked back the tears that had sprung to her eyes as she scrabbled for it on the floor of the crowded passageway, determined not to show anyone that she cared.

"You all right Lauren?" Her friends Kim and Keri came running through the school doors shaking the rain off their short hair. They were as alike as bookends, both with light brown hair and round faces although Kim was what Lauren had always thought to herself as more knobbly and a lot scruffier than his neat and precise twin sister.

"Yes," Lauren smiled wanly. "I should be used to them by now."

"They're just a load of losers. What were they after this time?"

"Oh, nothing." Lauren was strangely reluctant to mention the bracelet, even to her friends. She wished she had left it at home but she had felt a tug of panic at the thought of it being out of her sight. "It was just a present from my grandmother." She showed them quickly and then tucked it under the cuff of her sweatshirt.

"It's beautiful," gasped Keri. "Can I see?"

"Later. I shouldn't have brought it. It's a sort of family heirloom. Very old."

"Perhaps you should hide it somewhere." Kim suggested, his eyes mischievous, his wide mouth curling up at the corners in a grin. "Sew it into your underwear or something." Lauren giggled.

"Oh Kim!" Keri gave her brother a long-suffering look. "We don't all live in one of your fantasy adventures!"

"Wish we did!" he laughed. "Come on, we'll be late for registration." They pushed past the crowd into the classroom taking care to avoid Tania and her cronies who were busy flirting with Lewis and Reese, the football stars of Year 7. Lauren and Keri sat down together while Kim found his friend Matt, another computer games fanatic. Lauren found herself thinking about his idea. Perhaps it wasn't so silly. She carefully slipped the bracelet off her wrist and tucked it into her shoe, where it made a warm lump along her instep.

"We've got something to tell you," Keri whispered as the class quietened for the register. "Dad might've got a job in America."

"America!" Lauren's reply was a startled squeak that earned her a fierce glare from Mr. Brown their teacher. Kim and Keri were her best friends, probably her only real friends. How could she cope with Tania and co. without them? They couldn't move. It seemed like hours before breaktime and she could ask Keri about it properly.

"He's applied for it at the moment," she explained. "It's with the same company he works for already. We don't know if he'll get it. But if he does, it'll be for a year, and we'll all have to go. Mum's dead excited, says it'll be a great adventure."

"Oh Keri, you can't go. I'll really miss you," Lauren whispered, near to tears.

"I'll miss you too," Keri smiled, "but it's not like we can't e-mail each other, every day if we want. And maybe your mum would let you come over for a holiday. Imagine what fun we can have in Florida. I can take you to Disneyworld and the film studios and everything." Lauren tried to enter into her friend's excitement, perhaps enough to fool Keri, but all she could think about was how on earth was she going to survive at school without her.

The rest of the day passed like a miserable dream and she almost forgot the bracelet until she was changing for PE in the afternoon.

"Unfortunately it's stopped raining." Keri made a face; she was no sportswoman. "What do you think they've got lined up for us this afternoon?"

"As long as it's not cross country!" Lauren hadn't forgotten the last time.

"Don't worry. Josie and I'll stick with you this time if you don't go so fast. It's all about survival rather than winning when Tania and Jessica are about." Lauren rubbed her head, remembering vividly the three stitches she had needed when Jessica had 'accidentally' tripped her over a stile. There was also the problem of what to do with the bracelet. To leave it in the box of watches and other valuables that the teacher left on the shelf in her cupboard was unthinkable. In the end she replaced it inside her sock and hoped that it wouldn't bruise her if she landed on it.

"Hey! Come on you two!" Josie shouted from the door. "Guess what we're doing today! Javelin!"

"Javelin?" Lauren grinned, the first time that day. "Stick Tania in the target and I could hit anything!" Perhaps it was only the fantasy of aiming at Tania in the distance, but Lauren picked up the new sport really quickly. She brought her arm back and threw, straight and true, as if she had been doing it all her life. At the end of the lesson she ran back to the changing rooms excited by her success, and locked herself into a toilet cubicle before she pulled the bracelet from her sock again. She was sure... yes, there it was on the chain, a little silver spear. She held it between her finger and thumb and closed her eyes. The dark eyed face from her dream swam into her mind, fierce and wild, hair as long and black as Lauren's own swirling behind her. She shivered and fastened the bracelet back on her wrist. If only she had someone to tell. She guessed that even Kim, who lived in the fantasy world of Middle Earth most of the time, would find it hard to believe her. And they were moving.

"Class! Everybody come here please!"

Lauren opened the door to see the rest of the girls standing in a silent group facing Miss Reynolds, looking shocked.

"Right," the teacher continued. "Did any of you go into my cupboard or see anyone around?" They all shook their heads. "Someone must have. Someone has tipped your valuables all over the cupboard." The silence held. They all shuffled their feet and looked down at the floor. "Well, I suppose the best thing is for you all to come and claim your own belongings, and see if anything has gone missing."

"Your bracelet!" Keri hissed, scrambling for her watch. "It's not there!"

"It's OK." Lauren pointed to the slight bulge in the sleeve of her sweatshirt. "Has anyone lost anything?"

Nobody had, but Lauren was left with a feeling of great uneasiness as she walked home that afternoon.

When she reached her road she saw that there was a police car outside her house.

Chapter 3
Burglars

"Mum!" Lauren began to run up the street, through the gate and open front door into the hall where her mother was talking to two uniformed officers.

"Mum!" she cried again. Her mother turned a worried face to her and waved her arms helplessly.

"I'm afraid we've been burgled, Lauren. We don't know how they got in but Mrs. Cleaver found the mess when she came to clean at lunchtime and phoned me. I don't think we've much to steal so I can't find anything gone, but they've left a dreadful mess." Lauren inched round the group in the hall. She could just see into the kitchen and gasped with shock at the sight of the floor covered with what looked like rice, pasta, flour and dried beans that had just been emptied out of the storage tins.

"I think we've done all we can, Mrs. Silva," the older constable said, smiling in that gooey way that men always seemed to when they talked to her mum. "If you discover anything missing, give us a call would you?"

"Of course." Lauren's mother moved to the door with them. "It's all right if we start to tidy up now, is it?"

"Fine. If they left any prints, we'll have 'em. If you and the young lady would come down to the station tomorrow we can take yours and eliminate them. But frankly I don't hold out much hope. Usually in cases like this the thieves are looking for something very specific, something so valuable to them it's not worth wasting time with anything else." He looked her in the eye for a moment, but she just shook her head helplessly.

"Nothing. Nothing like that. My engagement ring, but I always wear that." She waved her hand with the antique sapphire ring vaguely in front of him and he nodded wisely. Lauren with difficulty suppressed a gasp and clutched at her wrist. Surely it couldn't be? First at school, then here? She opened her mouth, suddenly desperate to tell her mother about Keri leaving, the bullies at school and most of all about the bracelet, but one look at her face as she walked to the door with the policemen stopped her. She was wearing that closed off expression she usually had that somehow made it impossible for Lauren to tell her all of her little worries and upsets.

"Granny'll be round soon," said her mother, shutting the door and heading purposefully for the vacuum cleaner. A great sense of relief flooded Lauren and then died away as she realised she meant Granny Lloyd, her mother's mother and her usual after school minder.

"I'm just going upstairs Mum," she called and bolted for her bedroom. It was a complete mess. Lauren slid to her knees on a small pile of soft toys, clothes and papers that had been ripped from all her cupboards and drawers, pulled her sleeve back from the silver charm bracelet and clutched at the tiny bird charm.

Grannie! Oh Grannie, please, she thought desperately. *I need your help!* The image of her grandmother's face, startled and with what looked like a paint smudge on her nose, floated into her mind.

Slowly, slowly, she soothed, as images of the day all flooded into Lauren's mind at once. Lauren took a deep breath and tried to make her thoughts as slow as words. Her grandmother's face grew grim.

I'm so sorry, she breathed. *I had no idea anyone would be watching us, or that it would be important to anyone. I should have told you more. You need friends, and you need knowledge. I'll ask your mother if you can come to me for your half-term at the end of the month, but in the meantime, have you friends you trust?*

There's Keri and Kim, she thought doubtfully. *But I don't think they'd believe me.*

If they are true friends, trust them. You need not be alone. Your mother would probably not understand. Your father's disappearance has made her so resentful towards our family, and despite her great love for your father, she is still hu... ordinary. Children have more flexible minds. They find it easier to accept the impossible.

But why is this happening? Who wants it? And what is it? Lauren could not keep the tears from her eyes as her brain whirled with questions.

No more than I told you, a bracelet that has been passed down our family for many generations. Everyone who has owned it has added a charm: a charm that sums up her character, or main talent, and holds the history of her life. They give you the strength or skill, in a small way, of them all. I can't think why anyone else would want it, except maybe to obliterate the memories of our family. I can't tell you about it now, like this. Be strong, trust your friends, and don't fail to contact me whenever you need to. She blew a kiss to Lauren, and faded from her mind. Lauren moved to the top of the stairs and watched her mother attacking the floor using the business end of the cleaner like a weapon, an unbelievably fierce energy from someone so small and delicate-looking.

"Mum! Can I phone Keri?" she asked as soon as the floor was clear again and the angry sound was switched off. Heather looked up, refusal in her eyes, but her hard expression melted slightly as she recognised the distress in her daughter's face.

"Go on then," she nodded. "As long as you get your room tidied before Mrs. Cleaver comes to clean tomorrow.

I need to get back to work for a while as soon as Granny gets here. I've a client to see at half past five. It was the only time she could get in after she'd finished work." She gave a small snort of tiredness and frustration and went back to her clearing up.

Keri and Kim were round almost as soon as Lauren had put the phone down.

"Wow!" Kim's eyes were as round as gobstoppers. "What a mess!"

"You must feel awful," Keri wailed, automatically starting to fold up some of Lauren's clothes that were still littering the carpet. "Strangers doing this to your things."

"Did they steal anything?" asked Kim.

"No." Lauren explained what the police had said. "I think this is what they were after." The three of them sat down in a circle on the floor with a tray of biscuits and drinks that Lauren's mother and Granny Lloyd had provided, and inspected Lauren's bracelet while she told them everything she knew.

"Wicked!" Kim breathed when she had finished. "I wasn't far off with my underwear idea."

"What are you going to do?" Keri asked.

"Hide it I suppose."

"Travel belt?" suggested Kim. "One of those things you can hide stuff in when you're abroad. Got any money?"

Lauren emptied out the piggy bank, untouched by the burglars, and counted out a few pounds.

"If we go now we can catch the shops before they shut." They gabbled a hasty explanation to Mrs. Silva, promising to finish tidying when they returned, and scrambled on a bus to the city centre.

"We've got to find out who's behind it." Kim's mind had moved on. "The police will never find them. And you won't be safe till you know."

"Ooh." Keri was not so sure. "It could be dangerous."

"Cool," said Kim, his eyes glittering with excitement. Lauren looked at him doubtfully.

"Keri could be right. I'm not sure that they would be quite ordinary."

"Cool," he repeated happily. "I know just what to do, and I've got some money here if you haven't enough."

"What are you up to?" Keri asked suspiciously.

"Aha." Kim waggled his finger in front of her nose. "Wait and see."

"I don't trust you one bit when you look like that," his sister muttered darkly. "It usually means just one thing. Trouble with a capital T." He laughed at her.

"You go and find that belt. I'll see you back at Lauren's."

Back in Lauren's bedroom an hour later he pulled a small package from his pocket.

"Look. When you put the bracelet into that belt, you must wear this."

"What?" his sister asked. "You've bought another bracelet?"

"It's only a cheap one, £4.99p from Argos. It's got dolphins or something on it but it might fool them—whoever they are. What we have to do is set up an opportunity for them to steal it when we can watch them and find out who they are." Lauren and Keri looked at each other warily, having experienced Kim's wonderful ideas before. Keri in particular had been grounded more times than she could count after adventures that had begun with Kim saying 'hey, I've just had a brilliant idea'. "Come on. It could work!" Kim's eyes were sparkling with enthusiasm, his words tripping over each other in his eagerness to get them out. "And I've just got the best idea! The swimming pool. You'd have to take it off when you got changed, they burgle your locker, and we follow them back to wherever they live. We've both got mobiles, so we can keep in touch." The girls looked at each other.

"We couldn't get into too much trouble as long as we do keep in touch I suppose," Lauren said slowly.

"I don't like it." Keri looked worried.

"Why not?" Kim said impatiently. "Lauren can't go on being robbed. They might go for her next time. They must know she's had it on her each time they've tried so far."

"But they're criminals," said Keri. "And we're just kids." Kim snorted scornfully.

"All the better," he said. "They won't take any notice of us. Come on, Lauren, what do you think?"

"Well, OK," she said eventually. "I think it's worth a try."

She wore the fake bracelet semi-openly until the next Saturday, allowing glimpses of it under her sleeve and for once not minding Tania's attempts to tease her about it or get her into trouble for wearing jewellery to school. All the time she tried to imagine who could be after it; was it the man who stepped aside for her in the street, someone at school, even someone she knew? She felt horribly scared all the time, as if unseen eyes were watching her every move. Keri did her best to stick with her, but even so, she felt very alone. Someone might be trying to obliterate the memory of her family. That sounded so vicious.

Kim had planned Saturday like a military operation. At 9.30 they met, on bikes, outside the swimming pool. With his phone in his pocket he was due to loiter around outside, waiting for directions. Keri and Lauren paid for a swim and went straight into the changing rooms. Kim tried to memorise the faces of everyone entering after the two girls, a hard task as the pool was getting crowded. Lauren changed, keeping a towel wrapped round her to hide the fact that she still wore the belt over her costume, shoved her clothes, watch and the fake bracelet into a locker and pulled the rubber key band onto her wrist.

"You know what would be worse than someone stealing it?" Keri whispered as her friend prepared to go out to the poolside area. "Me sitting here for hours shaking like a frightened jellyfish and no one even trying." Lauren gave her a nervous grin. Keri pulled her feet up onto the slatted seat in the changing cubicle so that it looked empty and Lauren left the door a little open so that she could just see the lockers. Her hand was shaking slightly as it poised over the 'send' button of her mobile phone and her heart felt as if it was thumping in her throat. Lauren disappeared out into the noisy pool followed by a group of chattering girls and the changing room began to quieten. A mother and child came in and shut themselves into the cubicle next to Keri's; she let out a relieved breath when they didn't choose hers. There were only three people left in the room: two children and a woman who was combing her hair by the basins. The children left, their swim finished, and the changing room was suddenly silent. Like a flash the woman was by the lockers opening Lauren's. Breathlessly, Keri pressed the button on the phone and heard her brother's voice answer. She waited and watched. The woman slipped the bracelet into her jacket pocket, pushed the locker shut and walked swiftly out of the changing rooms.

"Woman, tall, dark shoulder length hair, blue trousers, white jacket," Keri said quickly, trying not to let her voice squeak. "Flat shoes."

"Got her!" Kim's voice was quietly excited. "She's met a man. They're walking down towards the main road. Get Lauren and I'll follow them." Lauren came flying into the changing rooms as soon as she saw Keri's face at the opening and began to pull on her clothes.

"It was unreal!" Keri gabbled. "She opened the locker—she didn't even have a spare key or anything! She just seemed to stroke it with her finger and it opened!"

"Don't be daft," said Lauren as she tied her trainers. "She must've had a skeleton key or something."

"She didn't." Keri was definite. They ran out through the entrance and Keri phoned Kim again.

"They're walking along towards the Royal Pier," he gasped breathlessly. "Ride down and you might catch us up. They're fast walkers though." He rang off again; the girls unchained their bikes and steered carefully into the busy road. Lauren suddenly thought of her grandmother catching that ferry back to the Isle of Wight. Could these people be some secret enemies of Grannie Laura's?

"Oh no!" she gasped over her shoulder, getting a fierce hoot from an alarmed motorist at the wobble her bike gave as she turned round. "What if they're going on the boat? We can't follow them there."

"What if they've gone to find their car?" Keri yelled back. "I always did think this might be a stupid idea."

Kim was trying to keep the couple in sight without getting too close: a difficult task as they strode swiftly along the straight road and he was pushing his bike with nowhere to hide. He let them get almost out of sight, mounted and rode on until he had overtaken them, then stopped and pretended to fiddle with the chain of his bicycle until they had passed again. As he bent over to hide his face he heard the man's voice muttering triumphantly to his companion.

"The Master will be pleased with you Erin. No one would have guessed it would be so easy in the end."

"Too easy, Ed. I only hope the old woman…" As they passed out of his hearing, Kim heard no more. He kept kneeling down for a while until they had a good lead again, and then pushing his bike he followed them along the road. Like Lauren, his heart missed a beat as they reached the ferry terminal, but instead of crossing the road they turned left up towards the town. Kim began to feel more conspicuous as he peered around the corner by the old town wall and he let them get a long lead. They stopped at a dark door in a small block of old town houses and disappeared inside. His phone was out in a second.

"Keri! They've gone into a house, down the bottom of the hill just past the old city walls. First on the left. I've put the phone on silent ring, but don't call me unless you have to. I'm going to try to get closer and see if I can find out any more. I don't want them to hear me."

"O.K.," Keri replied. "But BE CAREFUL. And DON'T forget Rule 1." She rang off.

"Rule 1?" Lauren asked.

"Mum and Dad's rules. Never go into anyone's house or car, even if we know them, without asking Mum or Dad first."

"Sensible," Lauren replied. "Are we nearly there yet?"

"A bit further. Past the old guard tower, he said." They pushed their bikes round the corner and up the hill past the medieval city walls until they came to a derelict set of diggings revealing old cellars and tunnels surrounded by scaffold poles and mesh fences. Keri suppressed a shudder.

"I always think they look really dirty and creepy," she muttered.

"They're only old," Lauren objected. "Shame they can't make them a bit smarter and easier to look at. I'm sure they're just falling apart worse every year with all those weeds growing on them."

"That must be the house he meant." Keri pointed to the dirty front door in the short terrace of houses that looked almost as scruffy as the excavation. "Where do you think he's got to?" Lauren felt suddenly as though a cold worm was creeping up the middle of her stomach. For a moment she froze, and then she rushed up the road to the corner looking in every direction. Keri followed, punching the buttons on her telephone as she ran. She held it up to her ear and listened, willing her brother to answer. There was no sign of him or his bike up the side road and Lauren sprinted back down the hill towards the house, panting more from anxiety than exertion.

"He's switched the phone off!" Keri moaned. "He'd never do that even if he didn't want anyone to hear it ring. He said he'd put it on vibrate or something. And I've got the most horrible feeling. I just know he's in real trouble."

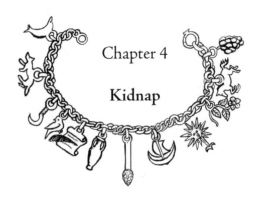

Chapter 4

Kidnap

"Go back down the road a bit," Lauren whispered, trying to force herself to hope. "He may be hiding in the park." They shoved their bikes against the railings and sprinted frantically into the little garden by the ruined turret that was part of the old town walls.

"Kim!" Keri called. "Kim!"

"Look!" Lauren pointed with a shaking finger to where she could just see the back wheel of Kim's bike shoved under some bushes, half-hidden. They ran across and dragged it out; the handlebars were twisted and the security chain was hanging limply from the front wheel.

"Oh no," Keri gasped. "Look here. He'd never have gone off without this." She had scrabbled under the bush and found the crushed remains of his mobile phone. Lauren pulled open the zip of the money belt and touched the bracelet.

Grannie, Grannie! she thought in a kind of scream. *Something terrible's happened. We were trying to track the burglars. We bought a fake bracelet for them to steal, and Kim was following them to this house, and we think they must have kidnapped him!*

You stupid, brave children! Lauren could see her grandmother's eyes screwing up as if in pain. *You must get the police now, at once, before you move or tell your parents or anything*

32

else. Tell them the whole story. And don't go near the house until they are with you. It's too dangerous.

"Dial 999—quick!" Lauren whispered to Keri. "And come back to the road."

Keri dialled the emergency number and in a few seconds had gabbled out the story to the police. To her relief they believed her and within minutes they were flagging down a squad car. Keri, her voice choked with tears, told the officers what he had said in his last call, showed them Kim's bicycle and phone under the bushes in the park and pointed out the house where he had said the thieves had gone.

"He would never have gone inside without telling me," she insisted. "Not unless he was forced or something." By this time, a second police car had drawn up with a screech of tyres.

"Wait here with me." A policewoman broke away from the group of uniformed officers clustered in front of the door and put an arm around Keri's shaking shoulders. "We'll soon find out if anyone's in there. You're quite sure that was the house he said?" Keri nodded.

"This is the police!" one of the men shouted through the letterbox. "Open the door!" No one answered. They conferred and then knocked again, louder. There was still no response.

"He's got to be there," whimpered Keri. "He's got to be." Lauren had clenched her fist around the bracelet in helpless fear. If only she hadn't involved her friends. If only she hadn't agreed to Kim's mad plan. His ideas had always got them in trouble. She began to hear her grandmother's voice in her mind again.

Tell me what's happening Lauren! Is that the police with you?

They're knocking on the door but no one's answered. Oh Grannie, it's all my fault!

No point blaming yourself, it just wastes time. Grannie Laura's mindvoice was brisk and businesslike, and somehow calmed Lauren's hysterical panic. *You've got to get into that house fast. Concentrate on the door,* she continued. *Feel the lock in your mind. Feel the catch and push. No—not like that— gently, gently...* Suddenly, as the police began to knock for the third time, the door clicked and fell open. They exchanged glances and pushed inside.

"This is the police! Is there anyone in here?" Lauren heard them shouting. Their feet as they ran through the house pounded on uncarpeted floors and stairs. Lauren and Keri, still outside with the policewoman, could hear snatches of shouted conversations amid the bangs and crashes of slamming doors.

"Nothing here!"

"Upstairs is clear!"

"Try that door!"

"No good. It seems to be empty." The heavy footsteps slowed as they began to walk back down the stairs again.

As soon as he had seen the couple disappearing inside the house Kim had dodged into the small park in case anyone was watching and propped and chained his bike to the railings. He sidled along the pavement to the doorway where he had seen the two people disappear, excitement making his heart beat faster as he heard voices inside, raised angrily. They had discovered the trick then. He grinned to himself, thoroughly enjoying the adventure, crept up to the door and flattened himself against the wall, listening. He could not catch the words. Perhaps if he could just get closer... all his attention was on the dirty brass letterbox, when suddenly both his arms were pinned to his sides in a tight grip, a hand pressed over his mouth and nose. He bucked and kicked, unable to breathe, but before he could do more the door opened and he was inside.

"We have a spy," a voice whispered, as if his captor was hissing through clenched teeth. Kim could not tell if it was a man or woman. He or she was very strong; all his struggles were like the wriggling of a mouse in the jaws of a cat. His head began to swim as he desperately tried to suck in air through the suffocating hand. The more he tried to struggle the tighter the grip became, the hard band of a ring cutting into his lip. Desperate, he let himself go limp in his captor's grip.

"One of the friends. They've tricked us." Kim could just see the glint of the bracelet he had bought as the woman held it out. His captor moved the hand from Kim's mouth, still holding him firmly with the other, and struck it to the ground before grinding it angrily underfoot. Kim sucked in a great draught of air, and knew at that moment that he could never watch a fish gasping on the riverbank again. When he felt his lungs belonged to him once more he opened his mouth to shout but the man he had been following was ready with a raincoat, flung it over Kim's head and shoulders, and began to fasten his wrists together behind his back with the belt. He squirmed violently, felt a few kicks land successfully and yelled, his voice loud even under the coat.

"Enough!" His captor did not even touch him again but Kim felt his legs turn to jelly and his throat seize up, as if the freezing command in the still whispering voice could order his body without his will. As he collapsed to the floor he felt his pockets being ransacked.

"Erin, take this," the voice ordered. His phone. They had his phone. Cold panic gripped Kim as his last link with his sister was taken. "Dump it with a bicycle you'll find outside."

There was what seemed like an endless wait. He could hear the woman whimpering softly and apologizing over and over again and then suddenly he was lifted, his ribs crushed painfully across someone's shoulder: the first man, he guessed. He heard a scraping, squeaking sound. He was swung round and let out a yelp as his anklebone hit hard against something. They were climbing down. Where his bound hands were free of the coat they felt chill and damp, and the sound of their feet when they reached the bottom echoed on stone. He still took deep and thankful gasps of breath although even under the muffling coat the air smelt mouldy and stale. He heard other feet climbing down the steep steps and a dull thud: the door being closed, he guessed, or perhaps a trapdoor. He must try to remember every detail.

"Would the girl exchange the bracelet for her friend?" the man asked.

"Possibly. But if this one called for help it will be too late. We can't risk the other being seen. We must leave at once." The whispery voice was obviously in charge.

"Shall I get rid of the boy?" Kim felt a violent stab of terror as the grip moved from his body to his throat.

"Leave him here. If he's found, he's seen nothing of importance. You fools have made this house unusable again. And if he's not…" the voice hissed in a laugh. "Serve him right. If we see you meddling in our business again, boy, you will not be so lucky. Get the other."

Kim slumped back to the ground, relief making his legs feel even more shaky than the strange command in the voice of the gang's leader. His heart was thumping in his chest as if it was trying to escape and he started shivering as his terrified sweat chilled in the cold darkness. He found he could move his head again and tried to push his face free of the coat, scraping and wriggling until he managed to make one small hole through which he could glimpse a dark, stone-vaulted cellar. The two he had been following were returning, huge shadows thrown behind them by some unseen flickering light. They were carrying something between them, something large and heavy, human-shaped. They dragged it round past him. He couldn't turn to see where they had gone but all of a sudden there was a hissing and scraping sound, the dim light disappeared, and Kim was alone in silent blackness. He wriggled and twisted, trying unsuccessfully to free his arms from their tight bindings, sobbing with the effort, not daring to shout in case the thieves were still within earshot and came back to finish him off. After a while he decided that he was wasting his energy and lay still in helpless misery, listening hard for any sign that he was not alone. In the silence he began to hear little scuffling noises and froze, praying hard that rats would not attack him while he could not move, the first relief that he was still alive giving way to a hopeless certainty that he would never be found.

The girls inched nearer to the front door, desperate to help with the search, followed by their guardian.

"It seems safe," she said. "I can't see any harm in our going in. You may see something of your brother's." They stepped inside and peered around the dim hallway. The only door on the ground floor was open; the room inside was furnished with a sofa, table and chairs, and a small television set. There were no books, no curtains: nothing that would have made this house look like a home.

"What's that?" Lauren knelt down on the floor and picked up a crushed silvery object. "Look, it's my bracelet. The fake one." The policewoman crouched down beside her and held out a bag for it.

"Evidence. At least we know they've been here."

Keri stared around, looking for anything that could prove that Kim had been there inside the house. She closed her eyes and tried to imagine her brother. Lauren hardly dared to breathe, shutting her eyes and willing her friend with all her might to sense where he might be. It had always worked in games of hide and seek when they were younger, as neither Kim nor Keri had been able to hide from their twin for long. Keri suddenly looked down at the floorboards under her knees.

"Wait a minute, this looks like a trapdoor!" Her voice was breathless with nerves and came out in a little squeak. The policewoman bent lower, and felt around the floorboards with her fingers.

"You're right." She straightened, calling up to the others, "There's a last place to look here, but we'll need a crowbar!" The men came clattering down the last flight of stairs and looked where she was pointing.

"Must be a cellar!" the sergeant exclaimed. "Who'd have thought it? Mike, go and get the toolkit out of the car. And the torch."

"This is a strange place. Obviously lived in, but not a clue to tell us anything about the residents." The oldest policeman took off his hat and scratched his head while one of the younger ones went for tools. The policewoman gave Keri a hug.

"If he's here, we'll find him," she said. "And we have the whole city force on alert. They've put up road blocks on the motorway approaches so no one will get far with a young boy. You did well to phone us so quickly." The young policeman returned with a wheel-changing kit.

"Hold on while I get this down the crack." He worked the tool for getting off hubcaps into the joint between the trapdoor and the floorboards. "Here we go. Get the edges now—heave!" A flight of rickety wooden steps was revealed in the beam of a torch.

"It's huge," he marvelled. The old tunnels and cellars must go right underneath here." He turned and began to climb down, flashing the torch around stone-built vaults, damp with groundwater. The others crowded after him, blocking the girls' view. Lauren clasped her hands around the bracelet muttering "please be there, please be there," over and over to herself. She felt Keri's hands gripping her arms so tightly that it hurt, her eyes squeezed tight with fear.

"Over here!" came a shout.

"Is he O.K.?"

"Tied up. He's alive."

"Thank goodness!" Lauren let out a huge breath that she hadn't known she was holding, clutched at Keri, and for the first time burst into tears. One policeman helped a dishevelled and blinking Kim up the steps. He looked white and strained but managed not to cry in front of the little group of sightseers that had crowded around the two police cars.

We've found him. Thanks Grannie, Lauren thought as they were helped into one of the vehicles. She felt a great wave of relief through the bracelet that connected them.

Promise me, promise me you'll never do anything that stupid again, her grandmother said fiercely. *Whoever these people are, they're obviously more dangerous than you could imagine. I will only be able to help you as long as you tell me everything.* Lauren silently promised, shock and guilt making her promise heartfelt. She could have been responsible for killing Kim and she never wanted to feel like that again. The policewoman slammed the car doors and started the engine. A rattle of voices sounded over the car radio.

"Cheer up," she called into the back. "Your parents are waiting for you." While the others carried on searching the cellars for clues she whisked the three of them away to the police station.

Chapter 5

Mind Powers

"QUICK THINKING SAVES BOY"

Class 7B whooped as Jason paused for effect after reading the headlines in Saturday evening's paper. He continued, making the report sound like a melodrama.

"Twelve year old Kim Kirby's life was almost certainly saved by his twin sister's quick thinking and his mobile phone. Following thieves he had seen stealing from the Swimming Pool, Kim was taken prisoner. Only his foresight in telling his sister on the phone where they had been heading, and her quick thinking in informing the police, might have saved him from being entombed alive."

"What a hero!" Tania mocked.

"What a photo!" laughed Matt. Keri blushed, embarrassed at the babyish pose of the two of them with their faces close together, separated by her mobile.

The headlines in the Daily Echo were the only topic of conversation at school that Monday morning. The group around the paper moved away reluctantly only when Mr. Brown had cleared his throat several times.

"You may as well tell us all about it, Kim," he smiled. "It might save you from having to do it 40 times over in the playground. You did well. Do you feel like a hero?"

"To tell the truth, I feel a right idiot," Kim said ruefully, blushing with so many eyes on him. "I'd always thought if anything like that happened I'd be strong enough not to be grabbed. You know, I could fight and stuff. I thought only a real wimp could be caught. But I was grabbed from behind and there was absolutely nothing I could do, not even breathe. It wasn't like I'd thought at all."

"Will the police be able to find them, d'you think?" asked one of their classmates. Kim shrugged.

"I gave them a description of the two I saw, Ed and Erin, but their photos weren't on the computer or anything. I never got a glimpse of the one who grabbed me and he never spoke properly so I couldn't even recognise his voice."

"Were you scared?" asked Josie. Kim hesitated, not sure whether to bluff it out, but in the end decided in favour of blunt honesty.

"Terrified. That man had his hand over my mouth and nose and I thought I'd never breathe again." Kim blinked hard, trying not to remember that feeling of suffocation too clearly. "It's not too pleasant hearing people discuss whether to kill you or not..." he tried hard to keep his voice from shaking. "Like deciding whether to step on a bug. He would have strangled me if his boss had told him to. I guess he just didn't think I was important enough to bother with. And it wasn't too nice when they left me in the cellar and I didn't know if anyone would ever find me. But now it's all over and I'm safe and home, it was the best adventure that's ever happened to me." He caught his sister's eye with a grin. "Thanks to Keri."

"Yes, well done to you too Keri," Mr. Brown smiled. "Without your quick thinking there might have been a completely different outcome."

"Well," Keri muttered shyly. "He might be a right pain sometimes, but he is my brother."

Lauren smiled too, sitting quietly, glad that her part in the drama was being hidden. The reporters had left her alone, concentrating on the story of the twins, and Kim and Keri had been glad to leave it that way once she had asked them. There were too many questions. Why were they after her bracelet? Who were they? Who was their hidden prisoner and who was their mysterious leader, the Master? And how had they disappeared from the cellar? The police were sure that Kim must have blacked out while they climbed back up the steps and left through the house because they had found no hidden exit. Lauren was sure they would not have had time. She and Keri would have seen them. The thieves were obviously not ordinary. But neither, Lauren was beginning to realise, was she. The woman thief had opened her locker with a thought; she had done the same to the front door of the house. She tried to remember how she had done it—a small push with her mind, a click...

"Someone's locked the door!" Tania's whining voice cut across her thoughts. She was pulling at the handle of the classroom door. The rest of the class tittered.

"Don't be silly." Mr. Brown looked up briefly. "I expect it's just stuck." Tania pulled harder, grunting with the effort. Lauren guiltily reversed the push she had just made. The door flew open and Tania landed heavily on Jason's lap. The class erupted in gales of laughter.

"Squashing your boyfriend, Tan?" hooted Kim happily. Jason rolled around the floor pretending to be crushed. Even Mr. Brown chuckled and Keri was laughing so hard she was crying until she noticed that Lauren was finding it hard to join in.

"It wasn't you, was it?"

"I didn't mean to. I was just trying to remember how I did the door yesterday and it sort of happened."

"Can you move anything else?"

"What sort of anything?"

"Try Tania's trainers. Untie the laces." The class was beginning to calm down. As Tania began to flounce angrily back to her seat her laces slid out of their knots and she almost tripped. The laughter started again.

"Falling for someone else?" Kim gurgled, his ribs still hurting. Enraged, Tania went for him only to be brought up short as her laces seemed to tangle themselves together and she fell against the nearest desk.

"That's quite enough!" Mr. Brown snapped. "Pull yourself together Tania, and hurry up and get the register back to Reception. The rest of you get out your books ready for your first period."

"Telekinesis, that's what it's called," Keri whispered under cover of the rustling bags. "It's fantastic. Think what fun we can have."

"I don't think I should." Lauren was suddenly sure that this new ability should not be used for games. "There's something bad going on here. I need to keep this a secret until we find out what it is. You won't tell anyone, will you Keri?"

"Of course not," her friend assured her. "Well, only Kim."

"He's O.K.," replied Lauren. They all had to split up until breaktime as Kim, Matt, Josie and a few others stayed for Set 1 maths and Lauren and Keri followed Tania and Jessica to another room to meet up with Set 2.

"You've got to practice," she whispered to Lauren as they walked along the corridor. "This could mean that you'll be safer if those people try to get the bracelet again. Do you think you could move anything really heavy?"

"Like what?" Lauren hated to be conspicuous and only wanted to forget about it until she got home. "Jessica, maybe? She's big enough."

"Well, not without her noticing," Keri conceded. "Wait till break and we're outside. I'll find something. Wish you could move old Dragon Breath Cooper right out of the room before she gives out her usual detentions!"

"Oh Keri!" Lauren moaned. "You're getting as bad as Kim!" They were last into the room and she sat down glumly in the only spare seat at the back not expecting to enjoy the lesson, especially as she had to sit next to Jessica. Maths was definitely not her favourite subject and her brain was in too much of a whirl for her to be able to concentrate today. She felt even worse when Mrs. Cooper told them that they would start the lesson with a mental arithmetic test. She made a face at Keri across the room.

"What's up, little Lauren lost her friendy?" Jessica hissed. Lauren ignored her and concentrated on writing her name and 1-20 on the piece of paper. She put the pen down when she had finished and gazed out of the window wishing she could be anywhere but in school. Outside, a beautiful warm spring day was wasting, a little breeze wafting the smells and sounds of freedom through the classroom window. A sudden movement beside her made her look back, and she just managed to see Jessica snatching her pen off the table in front of her. She made a swift grab, missed, and sent her pencil case flying across the room with a great clatter as everything in it spilled across the floor. She felt her cheeks heat with embarrassment as the whole class pivoted in their seats to see what the noise was, and out of the corner of her eye saw Tania scrape a few of her possessions towards her with her foot and slip them into her lap while she crawled red-faced around the room trying to retrieve her property.

"When you've quite finished wasting all our time?" Mrs. Cooper said sarcastically, tapping her fingers on her desk like the rattle of drums at an execution. Lauren slid back into her seat and searched the reduced pencil case for something to write with. "This test will be timed today, so if you miss a question go on to the next one. Yes, what is it now, Lauren?"

"Please Mrs. Cooper, I can't find my pen," she stammered, knowing full well that her new gel pen was under Jessica's books. The teacher sighed loudly and shook her head so that her cheeks wobbled.

"Can someone lend her a pen so that we can get started this week?" she asked impatiently. Keri jumped up and brought one across, and Lauren took it quickly and bent her head over her paper, trying to hide the hot tears of anger and frustration that had sprung to her eyes, blinking hard so that she wouldn't make a complete fool of herself by crying. She hardly heard the first few questions, and could only see Tania peeping backwards to give her sneering glances and fingering the new compasses she'd been given for her birthday. Jessica was giggling silently at her empty paper and all at once Lauren felt her temper snap. She sent a burning glance at Jessica's pen and felt a great wave of exhilaration as the tip exploded and scattered ink all over the paper and Jessica's hand. She grabbed with her mind at her pencils that were on Tania's lap and sent them rolling towards her across the room, she pushed at her pair of compasses and Tania yelled as the point bit into her leg.

Mrs. Cooper began to swell with rage, and as she opened her mouth to shout a burst of smoke seemed to shoot from her lips and she screamed with shock. Lauren took advantage of the chaos to gather as much of her equipment as she could. She pulled her pen back towards her with one tug of her will. Jessica's test paper was smouldering, and suddenly burst into flame. She screamed and jumped up, overturning her chair, and led a sudden stampede for the door. Mrs. Cooper was shouting, trying to restore order, and hit the fire alarm button. Lauren guiltily smashed at the flaming paper with her pencil case until the fire was out and joined the now orderly evacuation of the room. The whole school was filing out to the field and in the distance the wail of a fire engine began to sound. Keri joined her, choking with suppressed laughter.

"Oh Lauren! How did you get the dragon to breathe fire?"

"Don't ask me!" Lauren was shivering with shock and the aftermath of her sudden rage, and her eyes were still pricking with tears. "I just got so mad. Oh Keri, you don't think I'm turning into some sort of monster do you?"

"Well, as a way of getting out of a maths test, that was a bit O.T.T.," Keri said lightly, but her arm was round Lauren in a friendly hug. "I don't blame you a bit. I saw what Jessica and Tania were up to and Dragon Breath is so mean. Ask your grannie what she thinks if you're worried." Lauren did touch the bracelet, still in the belt around her waist, but when she told her grandmother about the incident all she felt was a great wave of laughter and she had the same from Kim when they told him what had happened. By the end of the day, she was feeling a lot better and could almost see the funny side herself.

Her mother was likely to be much more difficult. Since she had found out about the bracelet, and the incident with the thieves, she had not wanted Lauren to leave the house except for school. Why was it, she wondered to herself, that mothers never seemed to fuss when you would have liked them to, but always seemed to fuss when you didn't need it. Lauren would not dare to tell her about her new talents. She had upset her enough by refusing to put the bracelet into a safety deposit box in the bank. That would have been really disastrous, she had thought, and Grannie had agreed. People who had managed to open a locked door with their minds and disappear from a house with no trace wouldn't have much trouble with a bank.

She returned home from school that day feeling more cheerful than she had for a long time but her good spirits were quickly dashed when she saw her mum just sitting at the kitchen table in front of a cold cup of tea, in almost the same position in which Lauren had left her that morning. The breakfast crockery was still unwashed and the phone was ringing. Lauren answered it. It was Daniel Torsen from the office.

"Lauren? Is your mother all right? It's not like her to take a day off without ringing."

"Oh, hello Uncle Daniel. No. She's not well. I've just got home," Lauren replied.

"Do you want me to come round?" The concern in Daniel's voice made her prickle with sudden anger again.

"I don't think so," she said stiffly. "Can I ring you back if I need to?"

"Of course. Any time. Your mother's very important to us you know. Look after her." Lauren rang off, and worriedly turned back to her mother.

"Mum, are you all right?" Heather turned round, and tried to manage a wan smile.

"Oh Lauren, I just couldn't face anyone today. I needed to think. I'm sorry." Her face suddenly crumpled. "I'm so sorry for everything."

"Mum, you've been wonderful since Dad left. You've looked after me, you've worked, we've got a good home."

"That's not what I mean. Put the kettle on, there's a love. I should have talked to you. Especially since you got older. It's just... I tried to shut everything out you see. Don't ever love anyone too much, Lauren. It makes you feel so betrayed when anything goes wrong." Lauren, feeling awkward, poured a cup of tea for her mum and opened a can of coke for herself.

"It's all right Mum."

"Do you know how I met your father? I was still a student, only 21, just about to take my Finals, and he was a lecturer in the archaeology department. But we didn't meet there. It was one night when I was walking home from a party on my own. I think I'd had a row with the person who'd taken me and this gang of boys started to threaten me. And he was suddenly there beside me. He never moved—he just looked at them—I thought they would make mincemeat out of him when a couple of them drew knives but they suddenly screamed and dropped them and just turned and ran away. And then he smiled at me. That smile. She paused for a moment, remembering.

"D'Artagnon rushes to the rescue?" Lauren asked suddenly. Her mother gave a little self-mocking sniff.

"Oh well," she shrugged. "Athos was always my favourite. The quiet, honourable one with a secret past. Your father was always quiet; I never heard him raise his voice once in all the time I knew him. But he had this tremendous inward energy. If you ever saw him in a crowd, you would never notice anyone else."

"You didn't, anyway," Lauren teased, greatly daring, desperate to learn more about her unknown father.

"Before I met him I was always so serious. I wanted to be a lawyer—not just any old lawyer, but the best. Granny Lloyd and my father were never well off, they didn't really understand about university so I had to do everything for myself; I was always working, studying. Even though he was older than me, he didn't seem old. He made me laugh at myself, and take time off just to have fun and do silly things. And I've never seen anyone as proud as he was when you came along." Her mother sipped the tea, a little sad smile touching her lips as she reminisced. Lauren suddenly couldn't remember when she had last seen her mother smile a real smile when they'd been on their own. "He was directing an excavation that summer and we were staying in Cornwall with a crowd of students and all through the dig he carried you everywhere in a little sling. He said it was never too early to start training a new archaeologist. We had such fun and all the students used to make a fuss of you. Do you remember our summers when you got a bit older?"

Lauren thought for a moment, and had vague recollections of pits and trenches and being taught by someone to scrape gently with a little trowel. She nodded slowly.

"But then, one day," her mother continued, "he just vanished. He left work and never arrived home. He took nothing with him, there was no gossip about another woman, and I never heard anything from him again."

"And neither did Grannie," Lauren murmured. "He never even told his mother where he was going."

"Your grandmother's right. He loved his job so much he would never just have walked away. I've tried so hard to hate him all these years." Heather Silva murmured the words so softly that Lauren had to strain her ears to hear. "And I tried to forget but every time I looked at you, with his eyes and hair, it brought it all back. Oh love," Lauren's mother turned and gave her daughter a rare hug. "I think I must face the fact that he's dead. Almost better than feeling he abandoned us. Daniel wants me to have him declared dead officially and spend more time with him. But I can't forget. He was so... so..." she paused, trying to find the right words. "so extraordinary. He always knew exactly how I was feeling or what I was thinking without ever having to ask. Sometimes I thought he could even hear things I couldn't but I tried to pretend. Do you think that's why he never told me?"

"Oh Mum." Lauren couldn't think what to say.

"And you're so like him. You turned into a bit of a wild child when he disappeared. You were so young, you'd been his shadow; you couldn't understand why he wasn't there any more. My mother and I never thought you'd settle in school but you did in the end, even if you've never really liked it. But now you need help I can't give you, Lauren. I couldn't bear it if anything happened to you too. Your Grandmother has asked if you could stay with her on the Island next week at half term and I think you should go." Lauren nodded slowly, though her heart had leaped in relief and anticipation.

"Will you be all right Mum? On your own?"

"Of course. I'm all right now really. I just needed to think. I've got a big case on next week, a trial, and there's the Law Society dinner dance on Friday so at least I won't have to worry about not being here with you. Grannie Lloyd or Daniel will be here if I need them." Lauren fought down a pang of jealousy. After what her mother had just confided, Uncle Daniel felt like an intrusion. Her mother caught a glimpse of her expression and sighed.

"I do wish you'd try to be nicer to him. He does his best to include you. Do you know, I met him the very first time your father took me out to lunch. He was at the next table, and when your father went to pay the bill he introduced himself and said he was sorry that he'd overheard our conversation but that he was looking for a student like me to sign on as a trainee and would I be interested? Of course I was. One of the best firms in Southampton."

"I expect he just fancied you," Lauren growled.

"Yes, he did," her mother replied fiercely. "But I had taken all of five minutes to think that Alex was the most wonderful person in the world, so I wasn't the least bit interested. Daniel's waited for me for sixteen years! Don't you think that deserves something?" Lauren pressed her lips together, feeling almost sorry for him.

"Are you going to marry him then?" She forced the words out.

"I don't know." Heather turned away. "Not if you're unhappy." She turned back, almost pleading. "I'm very fond of him, and he's helped us so much. He is a little like your father was, you know. Oh, not to look at, but he's got the same energy underneath that quiet, polite manner. Promise me you'll try to give him a chance?" Lauren thought for a moment and nodded reluctantly as she got up to find her hated homework.

"OK," she mumbled.

"Oh—" her mother called after her. "I almost forgot. Grannie said your friends would be welcome next week too. Do you want me to phone Mrs. Kirby?"

"Oh Mum!" Lauren ran back and gave her a hug. "That would be really great!"

Chapter 6
Grannie's Cottage

Grannie had met the three of them at the Red Jet terminal on the Isle of Wight and a few minutes later they had left the main roads and were bouncing erratically along foggy country lanes towards the South West of the Island in her ancient Land Rover. She had insisted on Kim sitting in the front with her and over the roaring of the engine she was questioning him hawkishly about every detail of his captivity. Under this treatment Kim remembered things he hadn't even realised he had noticed.

"What **exactly** did they say again about **the other?**" she asked, her eyes leaving the road for a second and boring into him like an apple corer.

"Um..." Kim thought, feeling like the apple and closing his eyes as he tried to relive those terrible moments in the cellar. "We can't risk the other being seen. That was it. They must have meant whoever or whatever they were carrying." Grannie's smile was like a sunbeam.

"And that gives me more hope than I have had for seven years," she murmured to herself.

They turned off the road onto a track that bumped uphill into the clouds. Darkness was gathering and startled rabbits ran from the glare of the headlights as they stopped at a gate. Lauren's grandmother glared at it through the windscreen and it swung open and then closed again behind them. A large rock loomed in front; the track lurched right and then left around it.

"You can explore that in the morning. It's an ancient monument of your mother's people, Lauren! Started your father's interest in archaeology!" Grannie yelled backwards over her shoulder. "Here we are—good job I left the lights on." The friendly yellow glow of windows shone blurrily through the mist ahead as they drove through a tumbledown gateway. It was wonderfully quiet once the noisy engine had been cut and the children jumped out onto the gravel drive. The wind driving the mist uphill blew Lauren's long hair so that it streamed in front of her like weed in a river current and Keri clutched her coat around her, staring, while Kim went round the back to take their cases.

"Thank you, Mrs. Silva."

"Laura. Call me Laura," she ordered. "Lauriella, like Lauren really, a family name, but I was always called Laura in England. Here you girls, don't leave everything to Kim. Start letting men think you need them to carry things for you at your age and you've no hope." Keri and Lauren stared for a moment, not sure whether she was joking or not, and then as she twitched her eyebrows at them ran round to collect their own bags. In a moment they were indoors, coats piled on the wooden coat hooks, cases stacked by the stairs.

"Come on, food first before it spoils and then I'll show you your rooms."

The house was really nothing like Lauren had expected. She had been half-afraid that it would be as dilapidated as the gateway but the kitchen they all crowded into was gleaming with polished copper and smelt of beeswaxed pine. They sat round the long table while Laura pulled a large enamelled casserole pot from the Aga oven.

Three or four cats dozed peacefully around the room, one on the back of the range. Lauren supposed that if it started to bake it would jump down.

"Dig in. You'd better make the most of it, I'm not always the greatest chef in the world," Laura laughed. "I usually put food on to cook and then get busy with something more interesting and forget all about it until the smoke comes out and reminds me." She helped them all to a plateful and for a while there was little conversation as they did justice to the tasty offering. Wonderful syrupy baked apples followed, washed down with home made lemonade. By the time supper was over Keri and Kim felt as if they had known Laura for ever and they happily curled up in the sitting room with cats warming their laps while Lauren and her grandmother cleared the kitchen.

"We only have a week, Lauren," she said seriously when they were alone. "There's a lot I have to teach you, and some things your friends should know too. If they are unhappy about anything, please tell me."

"Of course," Lauren promised. "But you do know they'll be moving soon. To America."

"Once a friend, always a friend. And half a world away's not so far these days. You said it was only for a year; you'll keep in touch." She guided her granddaughter gently into the next room with a hand on her shoulder.

"Oh, wow!" Lauren couldn't help exclaiming in delight as she entered the other room. Her mother had told her she'd see some of her Grannie's paintings at her home but she hadn't been expecting this. All around the room watercolours hung on the walls, mostly portraits of various cats, each of whom showed real character in different positions and locations. "They're lovely!"

"Did you paint them?" Keri asked in surprised admiration. Lauren had never told her what Grannie Laura did for a living. Art was one of her favourite subjects at school and she suddenly had a wild idea of asking Lauren's grandmother if she could paint with her one day.

"Is that one of yours too?" Lauren asked before she could voice the thought. The painting over the mantelpiece was very different, a smiling young man in an old-fashioned flying jacket with helmet and goggles held in one hand walking towards them across the hillside, an old plane with double wings in the background. Laura nodded and replied gruffly,

"That's your Grandfather. I don't usually paint in oils, but I wanted to do something special to remember him just as I first saw him."

"Is this him too?" Lauren picked up a black and white photograph in a silver frame and compared it to the painting. "He's got the same smile but his hair looks darker."

"That's your father. Now Lauren." Her grandmother changed the subject a bit too quickly. "Keri's already seen your fire-raising abilities, but Kim and I haven't." Lauren gave her a quick guilty look but her grandmother's expression was amused. "It's a chilly, damp evening. A fire would cheer us all up." Logs were laid ready in the old brick fireplace and Lauren looked around for matches. *You don't need them.* Lauren jumped. Her grandmother's mouth had not moved. She was mindspeaking. *Think of the flames, gentle warm flames, and push with your mind.* Remembering that day in the classroom, Lauren imagined the logs bursting into flame and all of a sudden with a roar, they did. Kim jumped so that the cat, alarmed, leapt from his lap and Keri let out a little scream. Laura was laughing. "Not bad for a first attempt," she chuckled. "You'll get better with practice." She sat comfortably in the chair nearest to the fire and Lauren sat rather sheepishly on the sofa with Keri. Laura leaned forwards, the firelight flickering strange shadows across her face.

"And now," she said solemnly, "I must tell you all a story, a true story, of our family and our people. You must promise me not to repeat it to anyone." They nodded wordlessly.

"Our people have lived here for many thousands of years. No one remembers where we came from or how we came here but we were not originally from this world. Since humans first inhabited these lands we have lived amongst them, or in the woods and the hollow hills. We call ourselves the Elder People. Our abilities help us to remain unknown. Even those of us who live among humans do not seek fame or power. We dislike ruling or being ruled. We have always sought to live simply, in harmony with nature and those around us, hiding our mind powers from humans. Until one was born in the far North more than three thousand years ago who was different. His parents called him Thor." Keri and Kim exchanged glances, remembering old history lessons, and Laura nodded slowly.

"Yes, everyone has heard the name. His evil passed into legend, and even two millennia later his memory inspired the religion of a warlike people. From an early age he learned to enjoy inflicting pain in order to control first small creatures and then, as he grew in age and power, the primitive humans around him. His parents were horrified but afraid of him. He killed them both, slowly and in agony, when they tried to stop him. His mind was strong, stronger than any of ours, either before or since that time. He gained power not only over some of our people and the humans but over the elements themselves. Lord of Storms was one of his titles. Slowly he gained rule over vast areas of the North and began to move south, causing starvation, misery and war wherever his feet fell. His ambition was to slaughter all of us who would not follow him, to leave himself and his small band of people as the only non-humans on earth, and he attacked us wherever we hid from him. Hundreds of us were killed without ever being able to fight back. He could not be allowed to continue. Against our nature, those of our people who were left banded together in a desperate Alliance. Our family was amongst them. There were terrible wars that sucked in humans as well on both sides. The first wearer of our bracelet was one of the leaders of that Alliance."

"The spear thrower?" Lauren asked. Her grandmother smiled at her.

"You have seen her in your dream." Lauren's mouth dropped open as she realised that Grannie did indeed know about those strange nightmares. "She became dedicated to defeating Thor after he killed her husband Alix. Their son Axiel decided to disguise himself as one of Thor's human slaves and act as a spy in the enemy's own mountain stronghold. He lived with them for years, enduring terrible suffering so that when his mother saw him again she could hardly recognise him. But he discovered the Enemy's weakness, and some of his secrets, and made a plan that could defeat him. Axiel managed to get word to his mother and our people attacked Thor's mountain. During the fighting, he was terribly burned and his mother was killed. But in dying, she destroyed Thor. Axiel saved the spear charm from around her neck, and when many years later he had a daughter grown past her childhood years, he made it into a bracelet for her to wear that his mother and her great courage should never be forgotten. Would you lend me the bracelet, Lauren?" Lauren unclasped it and handed it to her grandmother; as she passed it through her fingers it shone golden in the firelight, reflecting little flecks of light over her face. "That girl turned all her power to healing and made this flower charm to hang beside her grandmother's."

"Then each charm is for one of our family?"

"Only twelve girls have been born into our family from that time to this. The healer, the scholar, the horse breeder; most of us have lived quiet lives and have only the effigy of something we have loved, like my bird."

"But who wants to steal it?" Keri interrupted. "Were those people some of your... the Elder People?" The others laughed with a welcome release of tension as she waved her hands about trying to explain herself.

"Almost certainly. Thor had a wife. He may have had children. Our ancestors could not bring Thermselves to destroy all the family and servants of Thor; we thought we were safe. But the memories of our ancestors I shared in the bracelet are full of fear, and hiding, and moving secretly to new lands. I never learned who they were fleeing. The disappearance of Lauren's father seven years ago was my first warning that someone was still working against us. And now this." They were silent for a few minutes, thinking about what she had told them.

"Why would they suddenly decide they wanted the bracelet?" Lauren asked. "You must have worn it for years, so why now?"

"I have no idea," her grandmother said wearily. "Something must have changed; they may have only just found out where we are, or someone could have discovered something about its powers."

"What powers?"

"Well, only gentle ones. You've already discovered some of them yourself. It holds the memories of all of us who have worn it before you. You can speak with me, because I'm still alive, or I was last time I looked." Kim and Keri tittered politely, but Lauren's face had whitened.

"You mean..." she faltered, "that all those nightmares, all the dreams I've had every night since I had it.... all the things I saw were... true? The storms really were Thor? And the man who burned?" Her grandmother nodded sadly.

"My grandmother had an unhappy life. Somehow the superstitious humans found out that her father could do things they could only believe proved he had help from the devil. She was only your age when she saw her father die and fled to France." Lauren shivered, and Laura moved quickly to sit between her and Keri, putting a hand on her granddaughter's shoulder. "I have seen what you saw. It is not a sight I would have wished you to see at your age. History is full of terror and sadness and ignorance." There was a long silence. "She warned me it would not be easy, to be a holder of the Bracelet."

"That's why you all try to live quiet lives, so no one notices you're different," Keri said uncomfortably, feeling as though her own ancestors were responsible for that terrible execution that Lauren had described to her.

"It could be that you are the first humans trusted with our secret for thousands of years." Laura gave the twins a long, searching look that made them both shift nervously on their seats.

"So you had the bracelet from your Grannie too?" Lauren asked. "Do most of our family have boys?"

"My parents were killed during the terror after the French Revolution when I was two and my brother was still a baby," her grandmother said shortly. "My grandmother escaped here with us, and brought us up." Lauren's eyes widened but as she had no idea of the date of the French Revolution did not manage to calculate her grandmother's age, and Laura obviously did not want to talk about it. Something nagged at the back of her mind, something wrong, and she let Kim and Keri keep asking questions while she racked her brains to think what it could be. Suddenly she realised.

"Grannie!" she interrupted. "If all those dreams and nightmares were real, but just memories, what about the person I thought I saw in my bedroom?"

"What?" Laura's attention was suddenly all on Lauren, and her eyes bored into her like lasers. Lauren could almost feel her memory of that night being ransacked and watching, Keri thought not for the first time how whenever she thought her friend's grandmother was reassuring and cuddly she did or said something to make them all completely uncomfortable.

"Mum said no one could have got out of the door between me screaming and waking her up and her getting out of her room so I thought it must have been another dream."

"This is worse than I imagined," she muttered eventually. "Don't worry Lauren, I will do something to protect you." Lauren felt cold shivers trickling down her spine as she realised that her grandmother totally believed that what she had seen that night had been real. Kim and Keri exchanged looks, both feeling the need to fill the awkward silence.

"Can you all do things with your minds?" Kim asked. Laura raised her eyebrows.

"We're not the only people who can use our minds the way they were meant to be used. It's more difficult for you humans, but not impossible." She stared fiercely at them both. "You must know that I won't do anything to you without your full knowledge and permission. But I would like to help you to do some of the things Lauren can. They know you now. All three of you need to know how to protect yourselves." Kim and Keri both nodded, trying not to look too eager, fully aware that this was not a game. She looked solemnly at them for a long time, and they both waited nervously for something to happen. Instead, Laura stood up suddenly.

"Well, time for a cup of hot chocolate and then bed," she said briskly, and disappeared into the kitchen.

Kim and Keri looked at each other, and Kim grimaced, disappointed.

"Do you think we'll feel different?" he asked his sister.

Well, you tell me. Do you? Keri, startled, looked around to see who had spoken. Laura had stuck her head back round the door, her deep-set eyes bright with mischief. *Try shaking Lauren's hand.* Her lips had not moved. Her mouth open and feeling a bit silly, Keri held out her hand to her friend and gasped as she felt the soft tingling that Lauren had noticed when her grandmother had held her hand that day in the restaurant. Kim tried as well.

"Wow. It's like electricity. Did you feel that Lauren?" Lauren shook her head.

She won't, the older woman explained, still using her mind rather than her voice. *She has felt it with me, but before this year she assumed it was just static electricity and I was able to brush it from her mind. You are still human. I have raised your awareness, so that you can feel the energy within our people. You will be able to recognise one of us when you meet us, and to speak to us silently, if you need to. As for the rest, we will just have to wait and see what your minds are capable of. Tomorrow.*

Chapter 7
Attack in the Night.

Lauren and Keri were woken next morning by a rhythmic banging coming from outside their bedroom window.

"Whatever's the time?" Keri yawned sleepily and looked at her watch. "Quarter past eight? Who's being murdered outside?" Lauren pulled open the curtains and looked out into the sunlit garden. Her grandmother was perched up the top of a wooden step ladder with a huge metal post rammer in both hands, banging it down steadily on a tall wooden stake.

"Morning!" she called when she saw Lauren's startled face peering down at her. "Trellis repairs! I've just got to put in a couple of these. Help yourselves to anything for breakfast!"

"What do you want us to do today?" Lauren asked.

"Enjoy yourselves!" Grannie shouted, waving one arm in the air while hefting the rammer with her mind and bringing it down heavily on the post. "I've got a few jobs to get on with this morning and a painting to finish in the studio. Come and find me when you've had breakfast."

"Wow," said Keri, finally waking up enough to drag herself out of the cosy bed. "Let's wake Kim up. I'm starving."

The Studio turned out to be a wooden building at the bottom of the large, tangled garden and they found Laura sitting on a tall stool in front of an easel, already with a smudge of paint on her cheek. There were paintings stacked on every surface, framed and unframed, and all three children paused in the doorway in a moment of silent admiration. The paintings were not friendly like the portraits of the cats. They were all of British birds or wild animals but they looked really wild and made them all realise that nature was a cruel thing. That bird singing on the top branch of a winter tree that Laura was colouring was a fragile creature, the only splash of colour in a ragged, wind-torn landscape.

"Wow!" Keri was beginning to wonder if she had forgotten all her other vocabulary. When Laura glanced at her she wriggled uncomfortably but her friend's grandmother just smiled.

"If your friends can spare you for an hour or so one day this week, why don't you come and have a paint with me?" she asked, and Keri went pink with pleasure. Lauren looked at her and raised her eyes to heaven, never understanding why anyone would want to do anything indoors on a beautiful day.

"What shall we do?" she asked for the second time that morning.

"Enjoy yourselves. Explore. There's the forest that way down the track and the Downs that way." She pointed up at the green hill behind the house. "Take your pick."

"Wow," Keri said again.

They chose the forest first: down a track, across Strawberry Lane, and uphill again through a huge field of cows. Kim paused to get his breath and looked back across the valley to where the trees around Laura's house looked like a little square on a patchwork quilt.

"I think I've still got my Town legs," he laughed. "They should definitely call these the Ups and not the Downs. And I'd never have believed it would get so hot after yesterday. It's like summer. Pass us some of that lemonade, Kes."

"Come and get it," his sister replied, sitting down and pulling a plastic bottle and three cups out of her rucksack.

"Too lazy!" Kim sprawled on the grass on the other side of the path and held out a hand; after a moment's wobbling the bottle flew to it.

"Hey! Give that back!" Lauren yelled, laughing, and used her mind to grab it before he could take a swig. "This is a polite picnic, if you don't mind!"

"Neat!" Keri said admiringly, and then collapsed in giggles as she tried to send him a biscuit and accidentally let it drop into the middle of a cowpat. Kim tried to look disgusted but ended up rolling around with laughter.

"You should've practised in bed last night like me," he snorted.

"Shame we can't teleport ourselves up this hill!" his sister complained.

"Hey, let's see how far apart we can talk to each other in mindtalk," Kim suggested when they had got their breath back. "You two wait here till I've got up to those trees at the top of the hill."

Keri and Lauren watched him until he was almost out of sight.

What's it like up there? Keri asked.

Wicked. I reckon we could build a great den in the forest here.

"I can't hear him now," Lauren admitted.

"He wants us to build a den." Keri made a face, but Lauren grinned.

"Great!" She began to run up the hill to catch up with Kim. "Come on, Keri." Keri plodded after them but got her own back by proving she was by far the best at distant communication, especially when she was talking with her brother. They found an excellent spot in the forest to build a hidden den and determined to return the next day to start construction.

They all thought that week was the most fun they had ever had in their lives. Of course they never forgot the real purpose of their visit and practised using their minds in every conceivable way all the time, but somehow managed to enjoy themselves twice as much because of it. They were very proud of their little house they'd built in the forest. In the evening they had found an old kite of Lauren's father's that had been fun for Lauren and Kim on Wednesday when it turned windier, while Keri joined Grannie Laura in the studio and under instruction produced a fine painting of a rabbit, and then on Thursday when it became too hot again for the end of May they had managed to drag Laura away from her painting to take them down to the beach. The sea was freezing but they all managed a little paddle mainly so as not to be put to shame by Grannie Laura who had plunged straight into the little white breakers while the three children were still quivering on the shoreline. She stretched out on the beach like one of her cats while the girls helped Kim make a harbour in a stream that waterfalled from a little gorge in the sandy cliffs, and then when the tide had gone right out she surprised them all by sculpting a sleeping sand mermaid that looked real from a distance and attracted a little straggle of admirers from amongst the dog walkers and early summer visitors. They finished the perfect afternoon by collecting driftwood and lighting a small fire. Laura pulled a battered frying pan from her bag, sausages and some rolls followed, and soon the delicious smell of smoke and cooking was wafting across the sandy cliffs.

Keri phoned home in the evening to tell their parents how much they were enjoying themselves but returned with a solemn face.

"We've only got two more weeks," she said sadly. "Mum and Dad already have the plane tickets." The news cast a cloud over them all at supper, despite the good food and Laura's trying to cheer them up by talking about all the exciting things they would be able to see and do.

"We'll be so worried about Lauren," Keri explained slightly tearfully. "She's been my best friend since Infant school and now we could really help we've got to go away."

"We don't know whether they will try for the bracelet again," Laura said. "But I'd already decided that Lauren needs more protection. My brother moved to Canada. I phoned him on Monday night and he's coming over with his son Max, your father's cousin, Lauren. He's going to apply for a job teaching Science at your school from September but they'll be coming over sooner. I hope that your mother might let them stay with you."

"Oh, I hope so." Lauren felt as if a great weight had been taken away at the thought of someone being there for her after all. Keri and Kim tried to feel pleased as well but in reality it felt so wrong having to leave. Kim felt a gnawing of jealousy that someone else would take his place and soon made an excuse to go up to bed. He hunched himself under the covers and played with his Gameboy, taking out his frustrations in getting his highest ever score. Eventually the other noises of everyone talking and going to bed died away, the fresh air and exercise of the day took their toll and he slept.

He didn't know for a moment what had woken him. It was pitch dark. He reached out sleepily for his bedside light, then remembered he was not at home and gingerly began to slide his feet out of bed.

"Hush. Don't switch the light on. Come to the girls' room, quickly." Lauren's grandmother's voice whispering urgently in his ear made him almost jump out of his skin and he had to choke back a shout. He fumbled for his slippers, barked his shin on something on the way to the door and felt his way along the landing to the room Keri and Lauren were sharing. Someone gripped his hand and pulled him through the door. His eyes were beginning to get used to the dark and he could just make out the white, startled faces of the girls sitting up in bed. Laura pulled them all close together, whispering so softly that they had to strain their ears to hear her.

"It may be nothing, but Wards I have put on my boundaries have been broken. Mostly they just keep the rabbits and foxes out of my garden. This must be something larger. Hold hands and don't mindspeak. If anyone's listening, I don't want them to know we're awake." They held hands in a huddled circle round Keri's bed, ears straining. Everything was silent outside; only the rising wind rattled the ivy against the walls. Lauren realised she had been holding her breath and let it out gently, feeling Keri's hand trembling under hers. Her grandmother's fingers pinched hard as her head whipped round towards the window in answer to a sudden rustling of the bushes below and they all jumped as a beam of light flashed across the window. Darkness and silence flooded back as they sat tensely waiting for something—anything—to happen. They began to hear a quiet scraping below from somewhere near the back door.

"Police?" whispered Keri, an unpleasant hollow growing in the pit of her stomach.

"No good. It would take them at least half an hour to get out here," Laura whispered back. "We must defend ourselves. Concentrate on the wall. Feel the air around it and push back. They tried, so hard that Kim felt breathless as if he was really pushing an intruder away. There was a muffled curse, then the tinkling of breaking glass. They felt Laura's mind snap away from their pushing and from outside came a shout of pain, the sound of running feet on the gravel and angry whispering voices.

"Can't expect a broken window not to fight back," Laura muttered with satisfaction. "They know we're aware of them now so don't stop pushing, whatever you do. I'll deal with the rest." For what seemed a long time there was nothing else. The wind rose to a howl, whistling in the broken downstairs window like the eerie howling of wolves. Suddenly, a force like a suffocating blanket seemed to hurl itself at them: they couldn't move, couldn't speak, couldn't breathe. Even the faint light of the stars was blotted out by a darkness thicker than night that stole their sensations and numbed their every thought, as if a voice deep inside their bodies was telling them that hope was gone, life was gone, that they would never see light again, that there was no such thing as light, that the only thing they could do was sink, dissolve, into the enveloping blackness. Through her terror Lauren heard her grandmother gasping,

"Hold together, together." Her voice was like a beacon of hope that gave her some small grip on reality and she slowly began to feel the presence of her grandmother's mind, willing her to be strong, to fight. Taking strength from her friends' hands clutching hers she began to feel her will like a vast umbrella pushing up and out until slowly the pressure began to ease and they took great gulps of breath, blinking as they realised the darkness and hopelessness was ebbing away. Then it was gone and they were left wondering if it had ever really happened.

"We were lucky. They are few, perhaps only two of them, certainly not ordinary humans." Laura stretched out her arms in the darkness and gave the children a hug. "Well done. But they will not give up so easily, I think."

Keri relaxed a little, the tight knot in her chest beginning to ease. Perhaps they had gone. She really felt she had done little to help push away that stifling attack; it had mostly been Lauren and Grannie Laura whose minds had kept them together. Little thoughts began to drift into her head. No one really wanted to hurt her. It was only the bracelet they wanted, only a thing. Not worth risking lives for. Lauren would be happier without it... suddenly realising that someone was trying to manipulate her mind she felt an uncharacteristic rush of anger. Letting go of the others' hands, she ran to the window.

"She's my friend!" she screamed as loud as she could.

"I really need to know why they are so desperate," Laura murmured. "Perhaps we could lure them closer. Hold hands again. Try to be aware of each other's companionship in your minds but relax your thoughts if they try to attack again. Wait until they come close, wait till I tell you and then strike out, hard, as if you were using a weapon." They waited, hearts thumping. It was too silent outside; even the wind seemed have stilled, waiting. Then they began to feel it, a crawling sensation that prickled up and down their spines like the presence of pure hatred.

"Grannie... Grannie..." Lauren whispered, feeling herself begin to panic again. There was a sharp bang from downstairs and Keri gave a little scream as a sudden howl of wind blew the back door open with a crash and whistled through the house. A flicker of torchlight shone through the open door of the bedroom. A stair creaked. Then another, closer. Kim was stiff with tension. How long would they have to wait before Lauren's grandmother thought those burglars were close enough?

"Now!" Laura snapped. To Kim it was just like attacking in one of his computer games. He struck out, his subconscious mind amazed that his body was not in motion too. He felt the others in unison with him, a force that was stronger than anything he had imagined. There was a crash from the stairs, a shout, and the noise of something heavy tumbling down into the hallway. Laura was outside the room flicking the electric light switch before the children had recovered their wits, not like an old woman at all. They crowded out behind her and peered through the banisters, blinking in the light. Two men were lying dazed on the floor. Kim immediately recognised one of them, the man from Southampton. The other was a stranger.

"Now's the time to phone the police I think." Laura was speaking to her granddaughter who obediently went to find the telephone extension in her grandmother's bedroom. Keri went with her. "By the time they get here, I should be able to find out a thing or two," she muttered. She went down and touched the two unconscious men's hands, one at a time. "This is one of us, but not the other." She glanced up at Kim.

"He's the man I was following when I was kidnapped," he said.

"I should think the other is a human burglar. The police will know what to do with him. But I doubt they'll be able to keep this one under lock and key." She shook him roughly by the shoulder until he stirred and moaned. Her eyes seemed to bore into his soul. Kim sat near the top of the stairs, shivering slightly, fascinated. It was like watching a play.

"Answer me," Laura said commandingly. "Why is it so important to steal this bracelet from my granddaughter? Is it revenge?" The injured man's eyes opened to a slit and he spoke, his voice slurred and so quiet Kim had to strain his ears to hear.

"Revenge? Paltry."

"Then why?"

"You will suffer old woman. You will suffer when Thor returns. We already have the sacrifice so now we only need the record of time to turn back the years." Kim heard a muffled gasp from Laura and saw her hand fly to her mouth. His attention was so riveted by the scene in front of him that at first he did not recognise the other sounds for what they were: the softest creak of the back door and a scuffle on the hall carpet. His head flicked round. Every detail of the sight that met his eyes imprinted itself on his memory and developed like a slow motion sequence in a film. The woman from Southampton, a bloodstained scarf bound tightly around her arm, was advancing from the shadowy kitchen into the pool of brightness cast by the landing light, a shotgun in her hands pointed directly at Lauren's grandmother at the bottom of the stairs. He must have made some sort of grunt or mindshout, enough to make Laura twist around suddenly and throw herself sideways. There was a deafening explosion, a burning smell, and a sudden burst of red on the neck and shoulders of the injured man. With a cry, Laura was spun away from him, pellets hitting her arm and side. With horror, Kim saw the barrel of the shotgun follow her around and then still, taking careful aim. He even noticed the immaculate nail polish on the woman's hand gleam as her finger tightened on the trigger.

"NOOOOOO!" he yelled and struck out as hard as he could with his newly strong mind, instinctively, not at the woman but at the gun itself. There was another deafening explosion. The blast was so close to Kim that he was rocked back on the stairs; the woman crumpled slowly to the ground. He shrank backwards, staring blankly at the ruin he had caused as the gun exploded in the woman's face. Shock began to set in as spots of blood settled on the arm of his pyjamas. His ears rang. Keri came flying down the stairs closely followed by Lauren and Laura crawled upwards towards them, her right arm and leg dragging behind her. They all clung together, too stunned for tears but unable to move.

"You are the best, the bravest friends anyone could have." Grannie Laura forced the words through her teeth, looking as though only willpower was keeping her conscious. "Kim, not many people would have the speed or the strength of attack that you have."

"Years of playing silly computer games." Kim tried to joke, but in reality his mind was screaming, "I killed her. I really killed someone".

"You saved my life," she replied urgently, her fierce eyes staring straight into his. "You may have saved all our lives and those of many others. Lauren, your bracelet is more important than any of us realised. They have terrible plans. I think they have your father and if they get hold of the bracelet as well, they will kill him. His life will depend on our keeping it safe."

"But… but surely, they're dead now," Lauren faltered, trying not to look down at the ruin in the hall.

"They won't have been working alone. We know there was another, in charge, who captured Kim. But they wouldn't have a plan like this and have been prepared to murder each other rather than let them talk without a bigger group to carry it through. We can't relax." Her voice died away as pain from her injuries began to set in. "Lauren, if you could bear it, I think we will need an ambulance as well as the police." Reluctantly, Lauren went back upstairs to the telephone. Keri, very aware of the horror in her brother's mind, put her arms around him, as she had not for years. No one could face going down past the bodies.

They were still on the stairs when the police arrived.

Chapter 8
The Arrival of Cousin Max

The fuss after Kim's kidnapping was nothing compared with the fuss now and by the time the three children were allowed to take the boat back to the mainland they were exhausted. Kim and Keri's parents had rushed over the next morning as soon as Keri had been allowed to phone them, horrified that their children had once again been the focus of criminal activity. Laura had limped back with them in order to have a long talk with Lauren's mother. She had concealed nothing about the mind powers or her hope that Lauren's father could still be alive or the dangers of letting the enemy get hold of the bracelet. When they were finally alone Lauren could tell that her mother was still unhappy about many things.

"I've relied on Daniel for so much since your father disappeared," she sighed. "But I couldn't tell even him about this. He'd think I'd gone mad. He already thinks I've taken on too much inviting your father's uncle to stay."

"You asked Uncle Daniel about that?" Lauren gasped.

"I spent a lot of time with him last week." Her mother rested her chin on her hands. "He wants me to marry him, you know."

"But Mum! If Dad's not dead…"

"Of course. It's unthinkable now. But I don't know how to explain it. He's been such a good friend, your father's and mine, since before you were born. I really have no idea how I could have managed these last seven years without his help, letting me work flexible hours when I've needed to and paying for Mrs. Cleaver to clean every day."

"If he's really a good friend, he'll understand." Lauren tried to be wise.

"I don't think he'll understand anything, because I can't tell him anything!" her mother exclaimed in frustration. "I'm almost looking forward to your uncle and cousin coming, even though I don't know how I'm going to find the time to look after them. At least we won't have to pretend."

The two weeks until the twins were due to leave passed like a flash. There was so much to do: sorting, packing, just deciding what to take. Their house in Southampton was being let out while they were away for the year and Keri and Kim were determined that all their best possessions would not be used by strangers. Lauren already had a box full of their things to look after and on the morning they were leaving they appeared on the doorstep with their father, laden with their cherished computer.

"Dad says we can't take it and it won't do it any good to be packed up for a year," Keri explained. "And at least we can e-mail you if you've got one of your own."

"That's very kind," Lauren's mother smiled. "Do come in."

She and Daniel were drinking coffee in the sitting room, and she poured one for the twins' father while the children puffed upstairs with the boxes and Kim began to set up the computer.

"Do you think your mum would let you bring in a phone line?" asked Keri. "It would be good to think of you talking to us here."

"I expect she'll be glad for me not to be using hers," Lauren grinned. "She does quite a lot of work from home in the holidays when she's not seeing clients or in court. Saves leaving me with Grannie Lloyd all day and she won't believe I'm getting too old to need child minders."

"Could we have one more look at the bracelet before we go?" Keri asked. Lauren held out her arm, and Keri braced herself for the small shock. "Twelve charms. You must be the thirteenth. Do you think that's unlucky?"

"It seems to be at the moment," Lauren sighed. "No one else who's owned it since the first has ever had such trouble!"

"It must be your destiny," Kim said seriously, looking up from the wires he was untangling.

"I don't think I want a destiny. I'm going to have quite enough trouble from those awful girls at school without you two around to help. I don't need to have to worry about anything else."

"Don't take so much notice of them, Lauren," said Keri. "There's nothing they can do to you compared with those People who attacked us. You know what Mum says, sticks and stones can—"

"I know. Words can never hurt me." Lauren had heard her friend quote this too many times, and it had never been much help.

"I wish it was our destiny," Keri said wistfully. "We both feel that real friends would be able to stick by you. It just doesn't seem right to go."

"You can't help it," said Lauren. "Just make sure you keep in touch."

"What other charms have you got?" Keri turned the bracelet around Lauren's wrist, trying to ignore the tingling shock every time they touched. "The spear, a plant, a little bird—that was your Grannie's, wasn't it? Because of all the birds she paints and watches. I wonder who this sunburst face belonged to?"

"Louis XIV, the King of France. Don't you remember our research assignment? I wondered where I'd seen it before. Grannie's grandmother actually knew him—he made her a countess or something. She says I can find out about all of them. But she doesn't want me to do it on my own. She's told me to make sure I keep the bracelet over the top of my pyjama sleeve so I don't get the dreams all the time. When my cousin Max arrives, he's supposed to help."

"I wonder what your charm will be?"

"Do you want me to set up the Internet?" Kim interrupted. "I can install the disc, but you can't do it properly until you've got a phone line."

"OK. Thanks."

Kim carried on fiddling.

They finished all too soon and trooped back downstairs. Their father was anxious to be off; there were still a hundred and one things to do before they left to catch the plane. He drained his coffee cup and stood up.

"Well, I can't say I'm sorry to get them out of the country after all the dramas," he was saying with a wry smile. "America's supposed to be a more violent place but I'm hoping for peace and quiet for my family."

"I hope everything goes well for you," Daniel smiled. "It'll be a big opportunity." He shook hands. The twins looked a question at Lauren.

"Oh, this is Uncle Daniel." She introduced them quickly, not wanting to explain.

"Pleased to meet you," Kim said politely and offered his hand. Daniel gave it a quick squeeze, reclaimed the coffee cup and gave him a friendly grin.

"Have a great time," he said. "I know how much Lauren's going to miss you, but make the most of it. I'm sure she'll be able to fly out to visit you if you'll have her." Lauren looked everywhere except at her friends, embarrassed and angered by his cool assumption of authority over her, as if he was already married to her mother.

"Come along you two, we've lots left to do." Mr. Kirby was already halfway out of the front door.

Restrained by the presence of the adults Lauren rather awkwardly said her goodbyes to Kim and Keri, and blinking away tears she watched their faces grow smaller and smaller as they waved from their car. As soon as they were out of sight she ran back up to her room.

"Her uncle looks all right," Kim said to Keri. "Was that BMW his? Cool car."

"I can't wait to e-mail her when we get there," Keri said. "She can tell us all about him. I liked his ring. It looked really old."

"I didn't notice. What was it like?"

"Well, kind of gold with a sort of twisted design, and a white stone like a frosty diamond."

"I bet it's another family relic," said Kim. "Ask her about it when you write."

As it turned out it was more than a month before they were able to and by then they had completely forgotten.

The next week at school was miserable for Lauren. Tania and Jessica made a point of asking her every morning if she had made any new friends yet and sneering at anyone else who tried to be nice to her. Without Keri's calming presence, maths lessons were a total nightmare, with

Lauren feeling even more stupid and clumsy every time Mrs. Cooper looked at her. Kim's friend Matt had heard nothing from the Kirby twins either.

"I expect they're just busy moving in," he said.

"I expect they've got better things to do than remember you nerds," Tania scoffed on her way past them.

"Don't forget it's us nerds who'll be living in expensive houses when you losers are still hanging round the local bus shelters." Matthew never let anyone bother him, quite happy being top in every subject at school. Lauren felt a pang of envy. Perhaps she wouldn't care so much about them either if she were good at something. As she sat down sadly next to Keri's empty seat the Head Teacher walked into the room with another man, very young looking with a suntanned face and black curly hair that flopped over his forehead.

"Good morning 7B," he said and the class immediately quietened. "Mr. Brown is away ill today. This is Mr. Silva who will be your registration Tutor and will teach Set 1 Maths until he's better." He shook the hand of the strange teacher who thanked him with a one-sided smile, little laughter creases springing to life around his eyes. Lauren stared. Could it be?

"Let him out of college to babysit us?" she heard Tania mutter to her friend Jessica. The new teacher looked amused and raised one eyebrow.

"Let me assure you… what's your name?"

"Tania."

"Let me assure you, Tania, that I'm neither wet behind the ears nor deaf. Can I continue?" Tania went red, and the rest of the class sniggered as he opened the register and began to read down the list of names. He glanced up as each replied, and Lauren was sure he would remember them all. When he came to her name he paused and gave her an infectious grin. "Ah, Lauren. I'm sorry we have to meet like this. We weren't coming down till tomorrow but I phoned the school to meet with your Head about next year and he said he was desperate." It was Lauren's turn to blush. "Lauren's my cousin, and I'll be staying with her for a while," he explained to the rest of the class, who were sitting there with open mouths. *I'll give you a lift home tonight if you meet me in the car park*, he added silently, his mind a warm contact. *It really is great to meet you.* He finished the register and closed it with a snap.

"They say a new teacher should never smile for at least half a term," he said mischievously, "but we haven't got that long left before the summer holidays. And yes, Jessica, I would notice if you put that in your mouth." Jessica slipped the chewing gum back into her bag and glared at her desk while the rest of the class got their books ready for maths. Lauren stood up with the rest of set 2 and 3.

Sorry, gotta go, she thought at him.

See you later, his mind smiled at her as she left.

At breaktime she had hardly stepped outside before Josie ran up to her, blonde hair flying, and grabbed her arm.

"Hey, Lauren! Your cousin's great! We always thought Mr. Brown was a good teacher but he's something else! He seemed to just know when one of us wasn't quite sure of something without us even having to ask. Where's he come from?"

"Canada." Lauren suddenly found herself the centre of an excited group of girls, firing questions at her about her cousin that she was totally unable to answer, never having heard of him until a few weeks ago.

"He's a bit too good-looking for a teacher isn't he?" Tessa laughed. "I'm surprised any of you listened to a word in maths! I was too busy staring!"

"He should've been a film star," said Shanice dreamily. "Pays better than teaching. How about inviting us all back home with you, Lauren?"

"I expect he'd like to get unpacked first," Lauren laughed as they went back into school. "But I'll tell him you asked."

"You dare!" Shanice attacked her with her schoolbag and they ran in laughing.

"But don't forget the rest of us!" urged Josie. Lauren had never been so popular at school and when it was time to go home the three girls escorted her to the car park to get another glimpse of Mr. Silva. He reminded Lauren a bit of a friendly tiger as he walked out of school towards them, a hidden spring in his step making him look as if he was just about to burst into a run, or leap over the cars that were in his way. His grin as he saw them waiting was impossible not to grin back at.

The lift turned out to be in a bright yellow sports car and Lauren was whisked out of the school grounds in front of an admiring crowd including Tania and Jessica.

"Give you grief, those two?" he asked, jerking his head towards them.

"You could say that," she replied wryly.

"Look the type," he smiled. "S and S. Sly and Snide. And that Jessica's built like a battleship. By the by, if you call me Mr. Silva out of school, you and I are going to fall out. I'm Max. You'd better tell me which way to go. There was an ulterior motive in my offering you a lift!"

"Turn right." Lauren sat back in the bucket seat of the car feeling happier than she had for a long time. "Is my uncle—your father—here too?" she asked him shyly.

"Should be by now. He was coming down on the train. We got into Heathrow the day before yesterday and he spent the day de-jetlagging while I bought the car and phoned your Head Teacher." Lauren wondered what her uncle had done to de-jetlag.

Sleep mostly, Max's voice sounded in her head and she gave him a startled glance. *Sorry*, he smiled at her mischievously. *I wasn't really trying to pry. It's just that your thoughts are very loud. If you don't want me to hear what you're thinking, just do this.* He sent a little picture into her mind, and she immediately knew how to keep her thoughts private. She bit her lip and wondered what else she had thought in those few minutes they had been in the car. She gave a jump as she realised they were almost at her road.

"Right! Turn right!"

There was a screech of tyres as Max applied the brakes and swerved into Beechwood Road, narrowly missing a car heading in the opposite direction.

"Sorry," he apologised. "Must remember how to drive on the left again." Lauren laughed a bit shakily.

"We're here. Stop by that next lamp post on the right." He looked a bit more carefully before pulling over, and brought the car to a snarling halt outside her house. "I expect Granny Lloyd's here already. Just ring the bell," she told him. "Mum's not used to me not needing a key yet and she's totally forbidden me to use any tricks when Granny's here." Max pressed the doorbell but the door was not opened by Granny Lloyd. Instead, the largest man Lauren had ever seen filled the opening, smiling warmly through a neatly trimmed greyish-black beard striped with white that made Lauren think he looked like a badger.

"Hi Dad," Max grinned. "You made it, then. This is Lauren." Her uncle bent down and engulfed her hand in his.

"I would have picked you out in a crowd of a thousand!" His voice was soft and rumbled in a deep bass. "You look just like Laura when she was your age. Come on in. I've been making a little snack to welcome you home from school." Lauren followed him in, sniffing the unusual smells of baking in the house.

"Dad's a great cook," Max laughed, "but I didn't expect you to take over the kitchen quite so fast!"

"Heather escaped from the office and met me off the train," his father explained. "I told her how I felt about food and she seemed only too pleased." He looked doubtfully at Lauren.

"She would have been," Lauren laughed. "She's usually so tired when she gets home from work that a microwaved Marks and Sparks ready meal's about her limit."

"Well, have a drink and some shortbread and tell us about how your day's been. And you can call me Uncle El." He relieved Lauren of her schoolbag and as they sat down in the kitchen together she found herself telling her uncle and cousin more than she had ever told anyone about how awful school was without Keri and Kim and how Mrs. Cooper always seemed to pick on her. Max gave her shoulder a squeeze.

"Bet I can talk the old dragon round," he smiled. "You just wait and she'll be crawling to you." Lauren laughed at his accurate assumption of her character and told them both rather sheepishly about the fire incident. To her relief they laughed as hard as her grandmother and Kim had and Lauren began to feel that there'd be a lot more laughter about her house now they were there.

"Got any homework?" Max asked. She made a face.

"Maths, but I haven't a clue what I'm supposed to be doing. Every time she explained, I got more and more confused. Granny Lloyd doesn't really understand about school and Mum can't see why I find everything hard when she always found it so easy."

"Come on then, get it out," said Max. "We'll see what we can do about that."

"Count me out!" his father exclaimed. "Go into the other room and leave me and my kitchen alone together."

Max was indeed a good tutor. Whether it was because of her improved understanding or because his smile had won the old dragon over Lauren found her maths lessons a lot easier for the next few weeks, and faced with Max's raised eyebrow almost every time she aimed a sarcastic remark at Lauren even Tania started to leave her alone. She felt even better when she arrived home one afternoon to find an e-mail waiting for her from Keri.

Date: 7/15/00 8.09:45 GMT Daylight Time
From: KeriK@aol.com
To: Laurensilv@brambles.freeserve.co.uk

HI at last. Total nightmare here. Arrived middle of night and found FAMILY in our house big mix up re- dates so had to camp out in hotel for 3 weeks!!!! Moved in now. House AMAZING, huge rooms and shower is MASSIVE. Everything very exciting—we have been playing tourists with Mum and seen everywhere. Don't start school till September so loads of time. How's things and new uncle? Miss you, K.

A large grin of relief split Lauren's face and she dashed off a reply.

"Thank goodness you're all right now. Everything here is good. Uncle El is like a cross between Gandalf and Prof. Dumbledore but without the long beards—he sort of feels comforting and v. nice. Mum loves him—he cooks us amazing food while we're out at work and school! Cousin Max is great—a bit of a keep fit fiend. He joined the local gym the 2nd day he was here and goes jogging after school!

Mum complains about him coming in looking disgusting in a sweaty T-shirt every night but she likes him really. He thinks I need to get fit too and takes me swimming twice a week! It's great. He's started at school already doing bits of supply teaching, and drives me every morning in his PORSCHE!!!! Tania & co are sucking up to me like mad hoping for an invitation back here—fat chance!!!!! They call him the DDG for Drop Dead Gorgeous. I wonder what they'd say if I told them he's about 50 yrs old!!!! That's what Grannie meant about us being long lived—apparently she never had Dad till she was 120!! She says that our women never can have children till they're over a hundred—where does that leave me I wonder? And Dad shocked them all by getting married to mum when he was under 80! But Max says Dad was always a bit serious. Max is waiting for end of term B4 my real lessons start—we're going to explore the bracelet so that I can relive some of our ancestors' memories. Of course he's never done that, as it's only women that get it so he's keen too.

Sports Day and E.O.T. concert next week so not too much work. Miss Baker keeps moaning about you two not being there for the band. Guess what, I've got to throw the javelin for school in the County Athletics Championships! Hope you're still having fun. Let you know how we get on. Miss you loads. XXXXX L."

"Hey, Lauren." There was a soft knock at the door.

"Come in Max," she called back happily. "Guess what, Keri's e-mailed me at last. It wasn't her fault it's been so long. They've only just managed to move in to their house."

"Great," Max grinned. It was hard to believe he was more than about 20 as both in looks and attitude he was very young. "Hey, got much homework?"

"None. It is the end of term."

"Well, how about some exploring then? Aunt Laura told us you were beginning to learn some of our mind powers and that you were strong in defence but we have no idea what else you can do."

"The same as the rest of you I suppose," Lauren replied. "I thought you would tell me."

"Oh no. Doesn't work like that," Max laughed. "And you should be able to tap into some of the skills of the past owners of the bracelet. Dad thinks I should be able to learn a lot too. He did when your Gran shared it with him when they were young." Lauren spent a moment unsuccessfully trying to imagine Uncle El and Grannie Laura being young. When was that?

"Are we going to do it now?" she asked, suddenly feeling as though her stomach did not belong to her. "What do we have to do?"

Max in teacher mode and with his hair like it was in 2000!

K.R.

Chapter 9
Lord of Storms

Uncle El was waiting for them down in the Sitting Room.

"Right Lauren," he said. Lauren already loved his deep rumbling voice. "The first thing to do is sit here together and take off the bracelet."

Lauren sat nervously on the edge of a chair opposite Max with the bracelet between them.

"Now, remember." Uncle El patted Lauren on the shoulder. "When Laura and I shared the bracelet many years ago it was just for fun. We were very close; she's only a couple of years older than I am and we were never encouraged to mix with human children. We explored just for the sake of discovering and it gave me a lifelong interest in history, especially the secret history of our people. I've been Professor of History in three different countries over the last hundred years or so." He smiled. "Now you and Max have not known each other long. You're still very young and have yet discovered few of your talents."

"Have I got any?" Lauren asked glumly. "I'm just ordinary."

"You don't know yet. Max is older but still a youngster by our standards. Old enough to think he knows it all and still young enough to think he can do anything."

"Dad!"

El raised a hand to still Max's laughing protest.

"You will see things that are disturbing, things that might be distressing, and you will never feel quite like a child again. Do you still feel able to go on?"

"I must, mustn't I?" Lauren said seriously, meeting his eyes. "There's too much at stake to back out now. It's the only way we'll be able to see our history and find out who might want Thor back."

"Good girl." A word of praise from Uncle El warmed her. "Now you must trust each other. Max looks a bit like your father, you know." Lauren nodded. Her mother had already remarked on that. "Treat Max as the father you've never known." Lauren gave Max a tremulous smile, and he squeezed her hand reassuringly. "The next thing to remember is to focus. You're not going to live your ancestors' lives with them, but to find out what they knew about the Enemy in the hope that it will help us now. Think hard about this while you travel and you'll see what you need to. Remember, you'll only know what our ancestor knew. And don't worry, I'll be here watching over you both."

"Do we start with the first charm, the spear?" Lauren asked, trying to ignore the butterflies, or were they cockroaches, that were gnawing away at her stomach. Max nodded, and the two of them held the tiny silver model between fingers and thumbs. The room seemed to fade around them and they were standing in dappled sunshine in a woodland glade, just outside a chattering ring of people dressed in woollen tunics and trousers, obviously partying.

"Lori and Alix!" shouted one. "May they live a long and happy life together!" The rest cheered and Lauren could see a laughing couple in the centre of the circle twining their arms together and drinking from each other's goblets. The woman was immediately recognisable as the spear thrower from her first vision but much younger and carefree. Lauren could just see the silver glint of the spear charm around her neck.

"Lori," she murmured to Max. "Have we always been called this?"

"Probably. Alix, Ax, Max. Dad's El is short for Axiel. Your Dad's an Alex. Tradition's always been big in our family. I sometimes thought that if I had a son I'd call him something different but I'm a bit of a rebel."

"She's gorgeous, isn't she? Well, they both are. Are you sure they can't see us?"

"Of course not. This is just a memory and not a very helpful one by the look of it. Concentrate on the thought of the Enemy, Thor." The scene before them misted and then cleared. Lauren blinked. They were in the same place but this time the clearing was empty. They were able to see more details: the sun slanting through the trees, a little spring bubbling into a pool, and primroses, wild daffodils and wood anemones everywhere.

This is a very special place," Max whispered. "Can you feel the strength of nature here?" Lauren nodded. She felt as if she could pull power from the trees and the very earth if she needed to. The young couple appeared again, this time carrying a bundle. The woman Lori placed it carefully on the ground and unwrapped the shawl to reveal a small baby who lay gurgling in the sunshine. Her husband Alix sprinkled a ring of dried petals around the child.

"Welcome, Axiel, to this world," he said.

"Gain the strength and health of this grove in your spirit," his mother added.

Lauren and Max exchanged glances. They both felt intrusive in this very private moment.

"Let's go on," Lauren whispered. The glade faded again as Lauren's mind tried to focus on questions about Thor and this time cleared again to almost total darkness.

They waited while their eyes adjusted, peering into the gloom. It was very silent, an almost unnatural silence so different from the traffic and sirens of the Southampton nights and even different from the night at Grannie Laura's that was filled with country squeaks and hoots. Lauren jumped as they heard the crashing of footsteps running through the undergrowth and a moment later a man came into the clearing, running, panting, and stopped for breath clutching his side close enough for them to recognise him.

"It's Alix," Max whispered.

"What's happened to him?" Lauren gasped, appalled at the sight. Instead of the laughing young face they remembered he was pale, unshaven and his face was lined. He collapsed to his knees. They could feel him trying to draw power from the magical place but they could tell that panic was making him lose his focus, his eyes flicking around as if trying to see a hidden enemy. Suddenly there was a blinding flash and the ground shook as thunder roared. Lauren screamed. Flash after flash of lightning struck around the grove, the darkness vanishing as flames sprouted from trees around them.

"It can't hurt us," Max shouted above the noise, trying to reassure himself as much as his young cousin. "It all happened more than three thousand years ago!" Lauren grabbed his hand and backed into the trees but everything was flame all around. She screamed again and buried her head in his chest. He held her tight; neither of them could look at the inferno, the brightness too much for their eyes, although they could feel none of the intense heat that would have crisped their flesh instantly if they had really been there. Gradually the roaring died to crackling, and the crackling to the silence of death. Slowly, they opened their eyes. Charcoaled skeletons of trees stood around them, scorched blackness where there had been green grass and flowers, a tumbled wreckage of rocks where the spring had bubbled. And in the centre, a twisted hump.

"Oh no. Oh no." Tears sprang to Lauren's eyes. Her involuntary cry was echoed as Lori flew wildly into the clearing and fell to her knees by the burned mess that had been her husband.

"Lord of Storms," Max whispered. They watched helplessly as Lori stood slowly, her fists clenched, eyes hard and dry.

Lauren was shaking with horror. With a sudden wrench, she found herself back in her own sitting room, her face wet with tears.

"What happened?" she croaked, her vocal chords refusing to function.

"I brought you home." Uncle El was holding their hands and had broken their link to the bracelet. "You both looked dreadful." Lauren looked up at Max's white, strained face.

"If anyone's trying to bring back that devil they must be insane," he muttered savagely through his teeth. "It was like the worst horror film you've ever seen."

"But it was all true!" Lauren whispered hoarsely. "At least in films you know it's all makeup and special effects!" She dropped her head into her arms to hide her tears. "I can't do this any more. I'm just Lauren. I get bullied at school and I'm not particularly good at anything. I'm not some hero!" She stood up suddenly, and dumping the bracelet on the table ran upstairs to the familiar safety of her room. Max half rose to his feet to follow her but his father put a restraining hand on his arm.

"Leave her for a while," he rumbled. "Maybe she just needs some space. Let's get supper on the go and you can tell me what you saw."

"Nothing you haven't told me about before," Max said sadly. "But somehow it made it so real, being a part of it like that. Too much for a twelve-year-old, I suppose."

"Don't underestimate her." His father gave him a piercing look. "She's got a lot of her mother in her. I wouldn't mind betting that a lot of people write Heather off as a fragile, beautiful blonde but she's razor sharp and tough as your old climbing boots."

"She's had to be." Max raised one eyebrow back at El. "Half of it's a pose though, too proud to show she cares. Lauren's usually a lot like her there."

"She'll come through if you give her time," El replied confidently. "You go for your run and I'll keep an eye on her."

Lauren came back downstairs after a while and without saying a word turned on the TV. She sat staring at the screen through cartoons, a childrens' adventure story, the news; she remembered none of it later. Every time she closed her eyes the white, anguished face of Lori filled her vision and all she could hear was the crashing of thunder as Thor hurled lightning bolts at that peaceful grove. The sharp click of the front door opening intruded into her thoughts as her mother came in from work.

"Hello everyone. Had a good day?"

"Fine thanks Mum," Lauren replied automatically as she passed them on her way up to change, then looked guiltily at Uncle El who had come back into the room and was pretending to read the paper while watching her out of the corner of his eye. He raised his bushy eyebrows and she giggled with sudden relief at the normality. "What's for supper, Uncle El?"

"Sausage casserole," he laughed. "Got your appetite back?" She smiled rather cautiously. "You can't change the past, you know," he said seriously. "It's happened. It's part of who we are." She nodded, replacing the bracelet on her wrist.

"I think I could carry on. Another day, perhaps." El beckoned her into the kitchen and dropped his voice to a whisper.

"Don't think that if Max doesn't say much he doesn't feel it too," he warned her. "We're all relying on him a lot here. He's always been the Action Man of the family, but he can't do anything this time without you and the bracelet." She nodded slowly, feeling suddenly old and responsible.

"I won't let you down Uncle El," she said quietly. He dropped his heavy hand onto her shoulder for a moment.

"Good girl," he grunted, and a warm glow seemed to flood through her. At that moment, she would have done anything for that growl of approval.

"Where's Max?" she asked.

"Getting hot and sweaty rushing round the streets as usual," his father said with a snort of laughter. "His way of unwinding. He'd better be back in time for supper."

"P'raps I ought to try it too," she replied, going to look out of the window. "He's not usually this late."

"He's not usually this stressed." El looked out over her shoulder. "I'll go and start dishing up. Coming to help?"

"I'll just go out and meet him if that's all right?"

"Don't go out of the garden." He gave her a warning look. "You never know who might be watching." Lauren nodded and opened the front door, but she had hardly set foot outside when Max jogged wearily through the gate, dirt on his arm and leg and a graze on his cheek.

"Max!" Her startled exclamation brought El out after her with a speed that Lauren had thought impossible for someone of his size.

"Some idiot driver went out of control and shot up on the pavement. I only just managed to hurl myself out of the way in time."

"Are you hurt?" El asked.

"Only a bruise or two. Luckily there was a lamp post in between us." Max grimaced, stretching his arm stiffly. "Lucky there was no one else on the road too."

"What happened to the driver?" Lauren asked.

"Ran off. Joyrider probably, he looked pretty young. I'm so late because I had to give the police a statement. Look, I'll just run up and have a quick shower." Despite the bruises, he still managed to bound upstairs three steps at a time. Lauren and her uncle looked at each other.

"Maybe it was only an accident," El said slowly. Lauren felt as though someone had kicked her in the stomach. Maybe? Did Uncle El really believe someone was trying to kill them? He patted her shoulder again. "We'll make sure he varies his route," he growled. Varies his route, she thought rebelliously as he steamed back towards the kitchen. She never wanted Max to go jogging again. She shut the front door with a bang that brought her mother out of the bedroom, half-changed, to complain.

"Sorry Mum," she called back automatically, realising that at least Max's accident had banished the lightning and flames from her mind. They would keep him safe. She wouldn't let him end up like Lori's Alix, she thought determinedly.

She felt much better after supper and even managed to tell her mother a bit about their experience without worrying her. As soon as she could, though, she slipped upstairs to tell Keri about the whole thing. Somehow, writing down the experience made it seem more like a story, further away from her. Those two short glimpses of Lori and Alix's family life had made her feel so close to them, as if they were her real family now instead of her distant ancestors, and she had felt so torn apart by her emotions when Uncle El had dragged her back without even having a chance to comfort Lori or grieve for Alix. She tried to remember every detail and made sure she saved the file before mailing it off to her friend.

"So we haven't really learned much yet," she concluded, "except how terrifying Thor must have been. Now I think about it, I really, really want to find out how Lori and Axiel managed to kill him."

Chapter 10
The Dinner Party

The next afternoon Lauren met Max in the school car park feeling terrified and excited all at once.

"Are we going back?" she asked as he roared the engine into life.

"Are you sure you're ready?" he asked.

"I think so. You need to. Uncle El explained last night. It's you everyone is relying on. He said that you were young enough and clever enough and he and Grannie were getting too old." Max gave a sudden snort of sarcastic laughter.

"The old so and so! You don't want to be a hero, so you think I'll do instead? Do you suppose Lori or Axiel wanted to be heroes? That's how we think of them now but I wouldn't mind betting that they would never have wanted to be famous; they'd rather have had a quiet life and Alix back. We just have to do what needs to be done because there is no one else. All of us, Aunt Laura and Dad and you too. No allowance for age or youth. We have to know more. We need to see how Lori beat Thor."

But when they returned home they found there would be no time for any exploring that night.

"Your mother's invited Daniel Torsen home for dinner," Uncle El told them as he met them at the front gate with a few bags of shopping. "And a couple of women from work. Obviously thinks we need a bit of socialising." Max read Lauren's expression and raised an eyebrow in his quizzical way.

"You don't like him?"

"It's not that," Lauren tried to explain. "He's really nice, and kind, and generous, and we've known him for ever, and he's been a really good boss for Mum. It's just... he wants to be more... and maybe Dad's not dead. And I really, really wanted to see the end of the story of Lori and Axiel. It's a bit like when you buy a book and then find it's part of a trilogy that's not published yet!"

"D'you want to eat with us, or would you rather escape upstairs?" Uncle El asked sympathetically and Lauren grinned in relief, grateful to be asked although she was sure that her mother would not have expected her to join them.

"Escape," she said firmly. "I don't think I could be normal enough for them tonight. And I bet you'll all be yakking and really boring!"

"Fine," he smiled. "But there's a penalty. You'll have to come and help me chop vegetables." She was also left in sole charge of the soup while the family dressed up for a smart dinner party. Her mother appeared first, looking more beautiful than Lauren had seen her for a long time in a new black dress embroidered with little bead flowers. Max and El joined her in the sitting room and she poured them all a drink.

"To the chefs," she smiled, raising her glass. The doorbell rang and Lauren went to answer it.

"Hello Uncle Daniel." She opened the door wide for him, and looked in surprise at the swathe of white bandages holding his right arm in a sling. He grinned at her and with the other hand gave her a huge bunch of flowers.

"That's what comes of holidays," he explained. "One week in the south of France and I sprained my arm water skiing. Perhaps I should take the hint that I'm getting too old." He shook a carrier bag from his arm down to his hand. "Here, there are some chocolates as well and a little something for you at the bottom."

"Thank you." She fielded the bag, put the chocolates on the coffee table and showed the flowers to her Mum.

"Thank you Daniel, they're lovely," her mother gushed, and Lauren had to look away while she gave him a kiss on both cheeks. "Could you find a vase please Lauren? Daniel, this is Alex's uncle El, and Cousin Max." Daniel glanced ruefully at his sling as Max held out his hand and gave them both a nod and smile in greeting.

"I'm very pleased to meet you both at last. Heather's told me what a help you're both being to her. Built in chef and child-minder, was it?" His eyes glinted with what Lauren thought was a slightly malicious humour, and with a sudden adult insight she would never have had before the bracelet she realised that he probably felt the same about Max and El taking up her mother's time as she did about him. "I hope you're managing to enjoy your holiday as well?" he continued. El laughed his deep rumble.

"Holiday? No chance. This is slavery!"

"We couldn't think of a better child to mind, though," Max broke in with a wink at Lauren. The doorbell chimed again and he went to let in Heather's two work colleagues who had arrived together. Lauren escaped thankfully and went to put the flowers in water before looking to see what Daniel had brought for her. It was a CD, just the very one all the girls at school had been buying. She thanked him politely and excused herself to go and listen to it with a good pretence at enthusiasm. Music? It all seemed a world away and so unimportant.

Upstairs in her room she switched it on and lay on her bed trying to enjoy it, the sounds of laughter and chatter floating up from downstairs. What a waste of an evening, it seemed to her, when there was so much to do and enemies so close. She turned the bracelet around idly on her wrist, looking at the different charms glinting in the evening light filtering through her closed curtains, each charm a life. They couldn't all have had such dangerous lives. Thor had died, after all. She fingered the little plant. Grannie had said that was Axiel's daughter who only wanted to learn healing after having seen the terrible injuries inflicted by Thor in the wars. Then she looked at the little scroll. What could that signify? Someone who liked reading? It looked like a peaceful enough charm. Surely there could be no harm in finding out? She took the little charm firmly between her finger and thumb and let herself drift into the past.

She was in a small, dark room in front of a crackling fire. There was a girl sitting on the floor on a thick sheepskin rug, looking up at an old, old woman in a chair.

"Twelve years today," the old woman was saying. "On my twelfth birthday my father gave me something. It belonged to his mother, my grandmother, many years ago and was very special. I have worn it ever since, waiting for another girl in our family to pass it on to." Lauren looked at the face of the girl on the floor, very like the face she knew from her mirror with wild dark hair, black eyes looking eagerly up at the old woman, teeth a little too large, a bit too thin. "I have waited a long, long while. When the time comes you must do the same thing, pass it to your next female descendant."

"Yes, Great Grandmama," the girl replied.

"This bracelet will guide you in many ways. It retains the memory of my grandmother's life in that little horse, and those of her grandmother before her, the granddaughter of Loriel the Fearless, killer of the tyrant Thor. This little spear is the one that she wore around her neck after her husband was killed and she made a vow to avenge him. She lived a violent life in unhappy times. You know the story." The girl nodded. "Her son Axiel had learned many secret things during his life as one of Thor's slaves. He made this bracelet and bound it with spells. No one will ever be able to snatch it from you by force—it has its own defences. And no knowledge our family learns will ever truly be lost while we own it. The wolf is my charm, in memory of a night I spent in the forest when the wolves cared for me instead of eating me as everyone had expected." The old woman allowed herself a smile of reminiscence as she carefully unclasped the bracelet from her own wrist with old, stiff fingers. "We must pass it on when our heir is past her childhood, but still young, still unsure of her path in life." She fastened it round the girl's wrist. "None of us will ever be truly gone while our memories remain. Use it to find out who you are, Loriel."

Lauren remembered vividly that moment from her own life, and her mind drifted away as she dozed on her bed. She later remembered a confusion of travelling as that Loriel made a long journey with her parents away from their home to new lands. She didn't remember why they left, only that they had fled in a sudden wave of fear and urgency and the old grandmother did not travel with them. Perhaps she had died; she had looked very old. She remembered the small towns they had ridden through, and struggling across mountain passes behind a train of other riders and packhorses. She remembered being attacked by bandits, particularly a robber being flung backwards as he tried to wrestle the bracelet from her arm. And she remembered her first glimpse of Loriel's new home, a great city to her, full of tall mud brick buildings baking in the hot sun, narrow streets filthy with rubbish, the busy harbour with many ships floating on sparkling deep blue water and the feeling of safety that the anonymity of the town gave her. They had been running from something, Lauren felt sure, some danger that her parents had not told Loriel. All night she dreamed that life: Loriel's fight to learn and read and study, the strange shapes she made for writing and then more journeys she had made with her husband and son as she grew older. In the morning she woke to her own life in surprise, for a while unsure who she was. She was still dressed although someone had tucked her quilt over her. Shaking her head, she climbed out of bed and headed downstairs.

"Morning, Lauren." Max's cheerful voice met her as she reached the kitchen. "Coffee?"

"Yuk!" Lauren hated coffee. "Addict!" She opened the fridge and poured herself an orange juice.

"You were dead to the world last night," he laughed. "Your Mum had to tuck you up." She gave him a guilty look.

"I used the bracelet. Without you."

"Lauren, it's your bracelet. You can link with it whenever you want."

"I wouldn't go back—not to Lori and Axiel and Him—not without you. I wanted to see what some of the others had done." She told him all she could remember about Loriel and her travels.

"I liked her, you know," she mused. "She was more ordinary than the first Lori, not so beautiful. A bit more like me to look at."

"Oh, I don't think you'll have any problem in that department when you get a bit older and you grow into your teeth." Max gave her an appreciative look and she blushed.

"Her Great Grandmother told her that the bracelet was protected by a mindspell, that no one could take it from her by force. And do you know, Tania tried to grab it from me once and yelled."

"Which explains why the thieves could not just attack you," Max reasoned. "Why they were watching for you to take it off."

"I'm never going to take it off again," Lauren promised. She changed the subject. "Was it a good dinner party?"

"Well, I'd rather have been exploring the past with you," Max admitted. "Your Mum seemed to think I might get on very well with that girl Sally who came last night but she's not my type. Anyway, I think she preferred Daniel to me."

"I wish!" Lauren said feelingly. "Anything to get his mind off Mum! And he is incredibly rich, and rather good looking in an old sort of way."

"Old?" Max laughed at her. "He can't be much more than 40!"

"Well, that's old," said Lauren, and then remembering added hastily "Oh, you're different."

"Thank you very much!" He was laughing at her still and she threw a drying-up cloth at him. He stopped it with a thought and sent it flying back over her head, which made her squeak and crumple up with giggles as every time she tried to escape it wrapped her up again.

"What are you children up to?" Uncle El appeared dressed in a huge striped dressing gown, and Lauren laughed even harder at Max's expression.

"Children?" he spluttered. "I've just been trying to convince Lauren how old and wise I am!"

"Anyone under a hundred's a child," Uncle El said loftily, pouring himself a coffee.

"You all sound a bit too cheerful this morning." Lauren's mother dragged into the room, eyes still half-closed. "What time did they all leave?"

"About two." Max passed her a mug and she sipped, holding her head with her other hand as if it might fall off.

"Thank goodness it's Saturday. Lauren, how do you fancy a quiet day in town, do some shopping, have a bit of lunch out, see a film? We haven't done anything like that for a long time." Lauren glanced at the two men, saw them nod and smile at her, and grinned at her mother.

"That'd be great Mum. Any chance of a new pair of trainers?"

So it was Monday afternoon before she, Max and Uncle El could get together for their journey to that terrible day when the last battle against Thor took place.

Uncle El reminded Lauren of a friendly badger!
Kev

Chapter 11
The Battle

"Are you sure you're ready for this?" Uncle El asked anxiously as he sat once again with Lauren and Max around the small table in the Silvas' sitting room. Lauren nodded, grimly determined despite feeling so scared her insides seemed to be floating in a numb vortex. "You know what you're going to see. You know Lori will die; you know Thor will, too. You know Axiel will get badly burned destroying the crystal. It will be upsetting."

"It's already happened, a long time ago. There's nothing we can do." She repeated the words as if they were a charm that would keep her from getting involved and looked at Max. She could tell from the strain around his eyes that he was not looking forward to the experience any more than she was but he still managed to give her an encouraging half-grin.

"What we must do is try to learn why he had so much more power than all the Alliance." Max was determined to fulfil their brief. "And how they managed to be strong enough to defeat him in the end. You must know some of this already, Dad."

"I don't want to give you any ideas in case it stops you noticing some little detail by yourself," his father replied. "Laura and I were pretty young when we went back to that time. I was even younger than Lauren. We weren't looking for clues so we could have missed a lot."

"I thought it would be the same for all of us," Lauren objected. "We just see what Lori saw, isn't that right?"

"You've only got to study history to know that any two people experiencing the same event can see completely different things." El smiled nostalgically, remembering his years of teaching history students. "Sometimes it just depends what you're looking for. Just make sure you study every little detail of that scene. Also," he added, "look for anything that might suggest why anyone should think they could bring him back. It's something that never occurred to any of us for three and a half thousand years." They both nodded tensely. "Ready then?"

"Wait a moment." Max raised his hand away from the bracelet. "Last time you brought us back when we got upset. This time, I think you should leave it to us. Right, Lauren?" She looked at him, not quite understanding. "Because we need to see everything, right to the end, in case we miss something vital. Only we can know when to return."

"OK," she agreed apprehensively. "But if one of us shouts 'leave', we both leave together. All right?"

"Of course." He grinned at her reassuringly. "I would never leave you there." They sat together and simultaneously gripped the spear charm.

"Lori, show us how you defeated Thor," Lauren murmured like a prayer, and the room faded to darkness.

"Where are we?" she whispered after a few moments.

"Haven't a clue."

"I think here's something moving over there." They both peered in the direction of the slight movement and jumped as a very small flame sprang into life in the centre of a stone bowl, highlighting a woman's face. They could tell it was Lori but she was changed so much. Her forehead was lined and her expression as hard as a stone carving. Dimly, as their eyes adjusted to the tiny light, they began to see rocky walls and a damp, earthy floor.

"Mother." A very soft whisper came from across the cave. She placed the lamp carefully on the floor and then ran to hug the newcomer.

"Oh Axiel." She held him at arm's length and drew him back towards the light. "You look… you look…"

"I know, Mother. It's been hard all these years. Where are our people?"

"Climbing up the slopes. It's bad out there. There's nowhere we can hide. How can we get to Thor?"

"Impossible by any ordinary means. But I have watched him closer than he knows. He is near the summit where he can control the storms. No one can climb up there. The cliffs are nearly sheer. He has a crystal. Listen, this is important in case only one of us has a chance at him. The crystal must be destroyed before we can even try. It gives him so much power and even an army of us would be no match for him while the crystal exists."

"How can we destroy it?"

"Only with our minds. One of us must block the path between them and then crush it. It will be dangerous and we may not survive the blast. The other must attack Thor himself. Our only hope is surprise."

"How can we get to him?"

"A trick of his own that I have learned by watching him teach his son. He uses a Portal that we can open with our minds. Are you ready to come with me?"

"Wait." His mother crossed the cave and unwrapped a bundle she had left on the floor. "Do you want the spear, or a knife? They were all I could carry climbing." He looked at the weapons in the dim light of the tiny flame and ran a finger over the spear blade.

"You brought the old spear?"

"It seemed right, I don't know why. There was something about it that seemed to call to me as I was about to leave. Perhaps because it's been a treasure of our family for so long."

Her son shrugged, took the knife and slid it into his belt.

"You keep it then. Perhaps our ancestors wish to aid you. Now watch." He made a small circular movement with his hand, like turning an invisible door handle, and the air seemed to move within the space he had made. She gasped and peered into the darkness. "Are you ready?"

"As I'll ever be." She held out her arms again and the two of them clung together in a brief desperate embrace.

"How can we go with them?" Lauren gasped as Axiel moved his hand again and the swirl of air grew larger.

"We're in Lori's memory, remember? Come on, follow them in."

Max grabbed her hand and pulled her into the space as Lori and Axiel disappeared. There was a quick jerk and they felt a change in the air around them, the icy freshness of outdoors blowing around their faces, and it was bright with a blanket of frozen snow reflecting the moon and starlight.

Their eyes were immediately drawn to a tall figure in the centre of the rocky platform standing beside an elaborately carved seat. A white fur cloak fell into soft folds around his feet and he was bareheaded, except for a jewelled band on his forehead that sparkled like frost in the moonlight. White hair blew around his face, very handsome but cruel. Something nagged at the corner of her memory. He reminded her of someone, although no one she had ever known had that hard, ruthless arrogance. Lauren was dimly aware of other figures behind him but could not drag her eyes away from the man, so powerful and compelling.

"Look." Max hissed in her ear. They had emerged in the deepest shadows; they could just see the swirling distortion of air that was Axiel's portal disappear and watched Lori, camouflaged in her white furs, edging away sideways in one direction, and Axiel in the other. All Thor's attention was on the slopes below, and he casually held up his hand like a cup and pulled lightning down upon the heads of the climbing army. As he moved, a large crystal in his other hand glowed and responded to his thoughts. Axiel moved a little too fast, and with a burst of horror Lauren heard a woman's voice cry a warning. Thor whirled around towards him.

"Who brought you here, slave?" he snapped, and sent Axiel sliding across the slippery platform with a twitch of his will. Lauren jumped and could not suppress a small scream. He was so fast. Axiel lay still, gasping. At the edge of her vision, she could see Lori moving silently a little further round the curve of the cliff face. She was too far away. Axiel struggled to his knees, desperate to distract his enemies so that his mother would not be seen.

"Who brought you?" Thor repeated, his gaze pinning Axiel back against the ground. Lauren watched with horror as his face contorted and his back arched in agony.

"They can't do it!" Lauren grasped Max's arm, shouting into the sudden silence as Thor's storm seemed to pause and focus itself into one menacing gathering of power directed at the lone figure on the ground. "He's too strong!" Max suddenly dragged her behind him as unbelievably Thor whirled round to face them and the glow of his eyes was like a fire.

"Who are you?" he demanded. "WHO ARE YOU?" His voice was pushed by his will and it rolled around them like the thunder.

"It's impossible!" Max exclaimed. "Impossible."

"Max! Defend!" Lauren yelled, and pushed up her mental umbrella a second before Thor struck. "Help me!" she screamed. The pressure was unbelievably, impossibly strong and she felt her strength sapping fast. Then, from not one but three other minds, she felt power building to help her. Not enough. She gritted her teeth together and held her ground, every nerve, every muscle in her body shaking with the effort. All Thor's attention was on her and like a nightmare she saw his teeth glint in a smile as he raised his hand to finish it. Suddenly a black shape threw itself onto the crystal, cradling around it, shooting it away from Thor's grasp. Lauren felt Axiel's mind snap away from hers as his will bent towards the destruction of the magical object. Thor twisted towards the new danger and as he did so Lori flung herself at him, stabbing her spear deep into his neck. The lightning he was calling to him flamed like a bonfire around them both, flickering and scorching.

Max sprang away from Lauren and grabbing Axiel's arms lent his mental strength to him as he struggled with the crystal. Beams of light shot out from between his arms as he tried to smother its power. Suddenly he let out a terrible cry as if his whole strength was driving into the battle. The beams seemed to crack and an immense explosion shattered the air. Splinters and dust from the crystal shot across the mountain platform. Something flew past and grazed Lauren's cheek. Max was flung backwards by the blast and landed winded behind Lauren as she was battered to the ground.

Axiel screamed, his clothes on fire. Remembering some emergency rules, Lauren scrambled to her feet looking for anything to smother the flames. Something drew her eyes to behind the throne-like chair where she thought she could see some sort of struggle taking place but it was faint, like a shadow. She grabbed a furry drape and flung it onto Axiel, pressing and rolling and using her mind to try to suffocate the flames until they were gone. Then she had time to look at Lori and Thor. She was still clutching the charcoaled remnants of the spear that had driven deep into Thor's throat but both figures were burned and blackened by the force of the lightning; Lauren had to force herself not to flinch away in disgust and horror as a sudden sickness tore at her stomach and throat. She felt Max behind her, his mental strength warming her as he wrapped both arms around her. She swallowed and held on to his elbows with both hands as if it was the only thing that would keep her from falling apart. Axiel staggered to his knees and crawled across to his mother. Her eyes flickered open, the only white in the blackened wreck of her face.

"For Alix," she whispered hoarsely through burned vocal chords.

"For the world," Axiel whispered back.

"You will never be forgotten," Lauren murmured and the eyes turned slowly, painfully, towards her while the burned lips attempted a smile. Max looked around, trying to fix every detail of that terrible scene into his memory. Then everything began to fade as life slipped away from all that held them there, the memory of Lori. Lauren felt a desperate longing to get home and closed her eyes as they were sucked into a blackness that seemed unending. Then the green carpet of the sitting room swam in front of her eyes and she slowly slid to the floor as mental exhaustion set in. Max fell to his knees beside her.

"It was us, Lauren," he said in wonder. "They couldn't have done it without us."

Uncle El, face as white as the stripe in his beard, had grabbed the brandy bottle and held a glass first to

Max's lips, then Lauren's. She gasped and spluttered, but managed to sit up.

"What on earth happened? You were gone. You completely disappeared." His voice was shaking. Max passed a hand over his face.

"It was impossible, but Thor saw us. It was his distraction with us that made it possible for Lori and Axiel to win. Somehow, we were truly present in that time."

"Oh Max! Your hands!" Lauren gasped. They all looked. They were raw with burns.

"Into your mother's car," ordered El, grabbing a handful of tea towels and soaking them quickly under the tap. "We'll think about this on the way to Casualty."

On the way, Max was beginning to gasp with pain but insisted on telling them both the last of his story.

"Remember those figures in the background?" he asked. Lauren explained to Uncle El about the other people that they thought they had seen behind the hypnotic figure of Thor. "They were there all right," he confirmed. "A woman and boy. I saw their faces, total horror at what was happening. She made an escape portal and they went through, but before they disappeared, the boy picked something up from the ground. Something white. I think it must have been a bit of the crystal that hadn't been blown to dust."

"The crystal?" Lauren could almost hear Uncle El's mind working. "Then that means that a bit of that power might still survive as an heirloom for Thor's descendants."

"What about the bracelet?" Lauren asked. "That man at Grannie's talked about 'the record of time'. That must be why they want it so much. It can actually travel into past lives."

"I think there must be more to it than that," El replied slowly. "Perhaps somehow you were caught up in Axiel's Portal. We need to talk about it with your grandmother as soon as your summer holidays begin. But you must think about this. Thor's woman and child saw you. Your part in his destruction has been known to his descendants for centuries. And at last, now the time circle is complete, they probably know who you are."

Chapter 12
End of Term

"Lauren, I'm going to walk you to school today."

Lauren looked up from her breakfast in surprise.

"I always used to go by myself before Max came, Uncle El," she said. "I'll be all right."

"Sorry. I'm not risking it. Besides, the exercise will be good for me." He patted his large stomach.

"You could take my car, Dad, when Heather's using hers." Max could not work or drive with his hands swathed in bandages. His father laughed.

"You must be joking! I think I'd need a can opener to get me into that little thing!" Lauren giggled, imagining squeezing her huge uncle into the Porsche. He rumbled to his feet. "Come on young Lauren."

He walked her to and from school every day after that and she enjoyed the opportunity of getting to know her uncle better. She was feeling a lot more confident in herself than she had ever felt before, especially since her triumph in the javelin at the schools athletics tournament. The little gold medallion had pride of place on the mantelpiece, but for Lauren the best part of the whole day had been seeing her family across the field cheering her on. Her mother had begged the afternoon off work and met them there, Max looked like some animal, waving white paws in the air in excitement when she won and even Uncle El had broken his usual placid calm to envelop her in a huge bear hug when she came across to them with her medal in her hand.

At school even Dragon Breath Cooper had mellowed, asking her every maths lesson how her cousin was getting on, sympathising with his terrible accident and telling the class how much all the teachers were looking forward to his return next term. Josie, Tessa and Shanice had accepted her into their little circle of friendship, which was not the same as having Keri back but cushioned her from the sarcastic comments that Tania and Jessica still threw her way, and she was treated like a school hero by Miss Reynolds after the athletics championships. By the last day, a notoriously relaxed day when they could play games or watch videos, she was feeling almost sorry that school was about to finish for the summer holidays.

"Hey Lauren, do you want to join us?" Matt called. He had gathered a small group together to play his Lord of the Rings board game.

"OK," she replied happily. As she moved to join them, she heard Tania chanting,

"Boring, boring," in a low voice from across the room.

"What would you know about it?" Lauren called to her before she even thought what she was doing. "The nearest you ever get to any excitement is deciding what clothes you're going to wear to go out."

"Well done!" Matt cheered, as Tania looked like thunder and Shanice and Tessa looked up from the magazine they were sharing and giggled.

"About time you stood up to her," chuckled Josie, the only other girl playing the game.

"Think it's funny?" Tania was not going to take this treatment. She stood up and sauntered over to the table. "Laugh again, why don't you?" She tilted the board and the little game pieces tipped into a heap and rolled around. One fell to the floor and they all heard a crunching sound as she put her foot on it. "Go on, laugh!" she said again. Lauren felt anger rising inside her and quickly pulled her mind under control. She couldn't risk her temper giving away any of her secret abilities. She had been lucky last time that no one had thought the fire anything but a freak accident. Instead, she faced Tania and gave her a push.

"That was criminal damage!" she shouted. She hadn't been brought up in a lawyer's household for nothing. "How dare you think that you can go around destroying other people's things?" She pushed her again. "Get lost! Go on, get lost!"

"Lauren!" Much as he'd been secretly longing for Lauren to stand up for herself all year, Mr. Brown could not ignore an argument like this. "Tania! What's going on?" The two of them said nothing but glared at each other.

"Tania broke Matt's game," Josie volunteered in the end. Matt had picked up the little figure of Frodo and was looking at it sadly.

"Is that right, Tania?"

"It was an accident," Tania whined.

"No it wasn't!" Lauren shouted back, red with anger. "You did it on purpose!"

"Lauren, settle down. Tania, find yourself a book to read and come and sit over here. No, not next to Jessica, sit here at the front. Matthew, is that repairable?"

"I don't think so, Sir."

"Well Tania, I think that at the very least you owe him an apology. What do you say?"

"Sorry," she mumbled.

"I beg your pardon?"

"Sorry Matt," she said louder, very sulkily.

"I wouldn't say no to a replacement," said Matthew coldly, and the five of them turned their backs on Tania to resume their game. Relieved, and secretly shocked at herself, Lauren thought that by next term it would all have been forgotten but she had reckoned without Tania's vindictive nature. It was later that evening after supper when they were all disturbed by a loud knocking at the door. Lauren's mother went to answer it and was met by a tirade of shouting. Lauren strained her ears to hear.

"….think that because you live in a posh house your daughter can treat mine like dirt?" she heard. Max was on his feet at once and at the door.

"Do you realise that your daughter has made Lauren's life a misery since the beginning of the year with her snide remarks and her bullying?" he said hotly.

"Don't think I haven't heard about you and the way you've picked on Tania when you've been teaching at the school!" the other voice shouted. "If you didn't look like an invalid you'd feel the end of my fist!" Lauren was frozen in her chair, suddenly terrified at the loud aggression.

"My turn I think," grunted Uncle El, and heaved himself out of the armchair. Lauren followed him to the front door, where he gently pushed aside Max and Heather.

"Can I help you?" he asked quietly. Lauren had never realised before what an imposing figure he was, especially with the added height of the doorstep.

"Who the hell are you?"

"Name's El Silva. Lauren's uncle." Tania's father, big himself and bristling with aggression, had to look up at him.

"Well, what do you plan to do about your niece?" he asked, his anger beginning to sound forced.

"I hope you and I have too much sense to get involved in the tiffs of silly girls," El rumbled, patting him on the shoulder. "It's always something with kids and usually five minutes later they're best friends again. Let them have a break from each other and they'll soon forget it." Tania's father began to nod, confused.

"Well. Right. I'll have a word with mine, but don't you let yours get away with it," he mumbled, and began to back down the drive. "I don't let anyone mess with my family."

"Very wise," smiled El, shutting the door. He winked at Lauren. "Old Jedi mind trick," he murmured and they all laughed with relief.

"I think I know him," said Lauren's mother thoughtfully. "Well, not personally, but I think he's one of Daniel's criminal clients. He's often in the papers for petty theft, fighting, that sort of thing, had a few months in prison. There was an incident a year or so ago when his wife and daughter were in a refuge because of his violence. I couldn't take her case because of him being an existing client of the firm and then it all fizzled out because she wouldn't give evidence and went back to him."

"Poor Tania." Lauren almost felt sorry for her.

"I can't understand why some women will put up with that," said Max.

"It's surprising how many do," Lauren's mother replied, shaking her head sadly. "Fear, thinking there's a better side to the man, insecurity, even feeling that somehow they've deserved such treatment. Are you all right, Lauren?"

"Yes." Lauren grinned suddenly. "Thank you. Thank you all."

She ran upstairs, eager to write to Keri and tell her that she thought her fear of Tania was gone for ever. She turned on the computer and while she waited for it to boot up twirled the bracelet round on her wrist. That birthday gift had truly changed her life. It was quite hard to be scared of child bullies when you had grown up with past holders of the bracelet and faced the power of Thor. When she loaded the internet, she found a message waiting for her.

Date: 7/25/00 5:32:21 GMT
From: KeriK@aol.com
To: Laurensilv@brambles.freeserve.co.uk
Hi. Most AMAZING things happening here. You can tell it's important as Kim has enclosed doc. detailing adventure. It has to be good to make Mr. Illiterate write!!! Hope you've recovered from your fight with Thor—WOW that was truly fantastic. Love K.

Lauren opened the enclosed message from Kim. As she read, her mouth dropped open and before she had even finished she was at the top of the stairs shouting down to the others.

"Quick! Max! Uncle El! This is important!" she yelled. Max was up the stairs like a leopard, with Lauren's mother and Uncle El following at a more sedate pace. "It's from Kim in Florida! You've got to read it!" The others clustered round the computer.

Lauren. Something hapened to me here that was amazzzzzzing—I hope I havent put my foot in it big time. k and me have been spending loads of time on beach this week and have started to meet local kids im going to go a bit slowly cos this is important. we were joining in a game of beach vollyball and this boy and i were going for the ball together and we crashed. we nokd heads and were a bit dazed i think then this other guy he grabs my arm to help me up and what do you think i felt this huge tingle and i knew he must be one of you guys you know the elder people. i was so suprised i didn't stop to think and i sort of shouted out in my mind at him who the heck are you? he was just as shokd as me and mindyeld back how can you tell so we made some excus that we wanted a drink and sat and bought a soda. his names mark erickson and his family have lived in florida more than 200 years quite a long time by american standards but prob only a generation as your lot go!
I didnt know how much i shoud say so ive just told him that i had a friend in england who was one of his people who sorted out my mind and not any more as you never know if he could be one of the enemy so let me know as i like him and we could have a lot of fun together if hes ok. hes very curius about how i got my mind woken as he puts it i havnt told him keri can do it too or that your a girl. mum and dad woud go MENTAL if they thout we were getting mixed up in anything agen hope you can read this as I cant be botherd to spelcheck mail me back quickly—kim.

"His writing's awful," Lauren complained. "He is so, so brainy but he can't ever be bothered with spelling."

"Doesn't know much about apostrophes either," commented Max the teacher, too puzzled to smile. "Looks like we'll have to get your papers out, Dad." El grunted.

"Come on then. You'll all have to heave." He led the way down to the garage where some large tea chests that had been shipped from Canada had been stored. "Can you help, Heather? Max can't lift with those hands." Between them they struggled inside with the box and used a hammer to remove the lid. It was full of boxes and files.

"Whatever is all that lot?" Lauren's mother asked.

"My history papers," El smiled. "I've been researching the history of the Elder People for a long time. Since I was a child in fact. We may be able to trace his people although it'll be difficult since our family lost contact with all the others after Thor." Within a few minutes he and Max had covered the dining table with papers and were so involved in peering through them that Heather had to ask twice if they wanted a mug of coffee. When she put the tray down on the table she caught sight of a folder of old photographs.

"May I?" she asked.

"Of course." El waved a hand rather distractedly at her and she took it away to the coffee table. Lauren sat next to her on the sofa and leaned on her shoulder to see what she had found.

"That's not Grannie?" she gasped at a brown and cracked stiffly posed portrait of a young woman. "She's really pretty."

"I wonder when this was taken." Heather turned it over. On the back was a handwritten scrawl: 'For Tom, all my love, Laura, Christmas 1916.' "Oh," she murmured. "Such a long time ago. I never asked when your father was born."

"Is that Dad?" Laura had unearthed another photograph of her grandmother and a young boy with a thatch of black hair standing outside what was recognisably Grannie's cottage, but with the porch different. "Isn't he sweet." Her mother was shaking her head slowly, and Lauren was shocked to see her eyes full of tears.

"There's so much he never told me," she whispered and stood abruptly and left the room. Max looked up, sensing Lauren's awkwardness. He wandered over and leafed through the pictures.

"Here's your father as I remember him." It was the same photo Grannie had on her mantelpiece at home and Lauren stared at it, trying to rake up some memory of her father from her childhood before his disappearance. There was nothing, no image of him in her mind. "I only met him once, you know," Max said. "I was about your age and we'd been having a holiday with Aunt Laura. He came home for a weekend to see us and I followed him everywhere."

"May I?" she asked, to her disgust realising she sounded just like her mother. When he gave it to her she resolutely propped it on their own mantelpiece next to her medal, not without a guilty glance towards the doorway in case Heather returned. She had never seen a picture of her father before she'd seen it that time at Grannie's.

"See this one?" Max distracted her by showing her a snapshot, in colour this time, of what looked like an old painting of two people in very rich and old-fashioned clothes with huge white wigs. "Dad and I spent a year in France trying to find the original of this."

"Who is it?" she asked curiously.

"The Marquis de Silvère and his wife, in about 1780. My grandparents, actually—your great grandparents. They were killed in the French Revolution and Dad and Aunt Laura had to be smuggled away by their grandmother. The original cart of cabbages story I think, though I guess her mind powers had a lot to do with it."

"Wow!" Lauren had never imagined that her family had so much history.

"Max, I need you!" His father called him impatiently back to the table and they were soon immersed once more in shuffling papers and sorting them into piles.

In the end, ignored, she left them to it and wandered off to bed. How come, she wondered, had so many of her ancestors been executed when they should have been able to manipulate the minds of humans in order to escape. Why hadn't her family increased over the centuries instead of seeming to survive with only one or two children every few hundred years? She remembered the sensation of being hunted that she had felt when she had tried the bracelet by herself at the dinner party and wondered whether her family had had secret enemies for all that time, ever since the first Lori and Alix. Could Keri and Kim have got caught up with them now, those people who wanted her family extinct? She shivered and let her fingers play with the charms as she cuddled down in bed. What had happened to Loriel the scholar's child? She remembered having that baby as if it was her own, another boy so she would never know his life. The next charm was a little ship, the masts and rigging so delicate that they seemed to have been shrunk from a real one, a little square sail almost billowing out in a non-existent wind. Could that baby have been this Loriel's father? And had he loved his daughter more than his own life, she wondered for a moment, remembering that desperate love and anguish of the medieval Loriel and her father as he died. Should she, Lauren Silva, have felt like that for her father?

No, focus, she told herself sternly. Danger. Enemies. That was what she needed to know, not fathers.

Perhaps this ancestor would be able to tell her something about why her family was always so alone?

Dare she? Her fingers froze on the charm. What if….. no. Uncle El had said the trip to that mountaintop with Thor must have been a freak accident because of the way they had followed Axiel into his Portal. It couldn't happen again. And she needed to help. She couldn't let Uncle El and Max do everything when Kim and Keri might be in danger. She settled her head more comfortably on her pillows, took a deep breath and pinched the little ship between her finger and thumb.

"Why were we always running away?" she breathed as she settled into darkness.

A weatherbeaten face nodded a smiling greeting from the steering oar of a wooden sailing ship, so like the charm it must have been the real ship that the charm had copied. A girl, nut brown from the sun, skipped over to him, at home on the rolling deck.

"Alexandria," the steersman said, pointing at the closing shoreline. "Remember?"

"Of course I remember." The girl leaned against him, breathing in his comfortable smell of wood, resin and salt spray. "That's where you found me. Tell me again."

I knew you should be there somewhere, my little daughter. So I mindsearched every street until I heard a whimper and I knew you were inside that house.

Would I have died?

Maybe. The sickness had killed your mother and uncles and you were very weak because no one had fed you.

Why did you leave?

I was always a seafarerer since I jumped on a ship as a stowaway the day my father and grandmother were murdered. My father told me it was safer that way. Always keep on the move, he said. My grandmother was a famous scholar here in this city and loved it but she stayed too long. I'll never forget her piercing eyes or the way she gripped my hand when she gave me that bracelet of yours. 'It's not for you', she told me. 'One day you must get yourself a daughter, or a granddaughter, and it's for her on the twelfth anniversary of her birth.'

Of course I laughed. What twelve-year-old boy likes to think of getting married and settling down? But then she and my father were knifed in the street by assassins and I ran away to sea. I've had four different names and two hundred years of sailing since then, and a few wives in ports around the world over the years but only you to inherit our special gifts. He looked away at the nearing shoreline, his eyes suddenly bleak. It is sadness to love a wife and have to watch her age and die, but a daughter—ah, a daughter is a delight for ever.

The girl smiled and snuggled up to his warm side as the shore grew closer.

I'll never leave you, she said. Lauren had almost drifted to sleep and her finger slipped along the bracelet and touched another charm.

"Happy Birthingday."

The face smiling down at her was so like the photo of her father that Lauren gasped, thinking for a moment that it must be him before she realised that the clothes he was wearing and his shoulder-length black hair were not those of her century. She couldn't help returning that infectious grin but it was not for her and his eyes twinkled through her as he picked up and twirled that medieval Loriel in a laughing hug. He set her down in a spindly wooden chair and knelt at her feet so that their eyes were level.

I have to tell you many important things today, quickly, while your mother is out. He spoke into her mind and his eyes had lost their twinkle and burned urgently into hers. She does not understand—has never understood—about what makes us different from the others. She is afraid of what she does not understand and I have trusted her with too much. Remember this, Loriel, never trust any human, never.

He reached into his pouch and pulled out something Lauren recognised at once: almost her bracelet but without the last two charms, the sunburst face and Grannie Laura's bird.

What is it? the ancient Loriel asked.

It is a gift from my grandmother, that she gave me on her deathbed and made me promise to give to my daughter on her twelfth birthingday. It has been in my family since its beginning, after the battles you already know of when our ancestors split from the rest of our people.

The rest? There are more of us?

Somewhere. I have never felt any trace of them, but I know that we have not only long lost cousins but also ancient enemies. I believe one at least is here and has frightened your mother with tales of sorcery. I have felt a strong mind working against me. He fastened the bracelet onto his daughter's wrist. *My grandmother told me that this bracelet would give you many answers that even I would never know. She also told me never to settle in one place, never to become too well known, or I would be hunted as my father was hunted, but since I met your mother I was too tempted to try to live an ordinary life. Now it is almost too late. In that sack are enough jewels and gold to help us to start a new life away from here. Will you come with me, before she finds out that you have inherited my powers, before she fears you, too?*

The girl stared through eyes like black holes, frozen to the chair as her father tied a heavy sack to her waist and then pulled her unresisting to her feet while he fastened a thick overskirt and travelling cloak around her. He gripped her hand and they started down the stairs. Lauren almost heard the noise from the street before they did, the tramp of feet and then the sound of the street door opening. A frightened servant scurried up the stairs towards them gabbling words that Lauren could not understand and then the father pushed the girl roughly behind a tapestry wall hanging.

You must still go, his mind hissed urgently. *As soon as you can. Tell no one. Always remember I love you.* Lauren huddled terrified with that girl as the crashes and bangs from the house showed her father was not taken gently. When all was quiet she crept out into an empty house and Lauren felt the sharp stab of anguish and helplessness, her shame she had not done more to help, her fear they would come back for her. She tiptoed once more down the stairs, the heavy treasure dragging at her waist, and ducked behind the street door as feet approached again.

"You will come in?" Her mother's voice sounded from outside and she poised to run out to warn her of what had just happened.

"Not now. But you have done the right thing, for your city and your people. That spawn of the devil has bewitched you for long enough." She shrank back again, peeping at the cloaked figure with her mother, and Lauren desperately tried to think where she might have heard that quiet, warm voice before. "At least this way it will be seen that you were his dupe and not his accomplice."

Even half asleep, Lauren knew she had to escape from the terrible pain that racked that child as she realised her mother had betrayed her father and she knew she could not watch the father burn again. Her finger dragged away from the charm and she pushed the bracelet up her arm, over the warm barrier of her pyjama sleeve. Those enemies were ruthless and they were here, now, for her. She kept her eyes closed but slid her awareness to her own house, and heard the comforting sounds of her uncle and Max down below still poring over those papers. Nothing could hurt her while they were there. And she almost, almost knew what it was like to have a father.

Chapter 13
Holidays

"I wonder if we could drag Aunt Laura away from her cats for a few days?" The next afternoon Max and El looked as though they had never moved from the piles of papers that still covered the dining table and Max was feeling that they needed more help, particularly as fingering papers was difficult with his hands still swathed in bandages.

"I could ask her through the bracelet," suggested Lauren. "Do you think if she came to help Uncle El might let you off for long enough to shave?" She was feeling so much at home with her uncle and cousin since their last adventure that she felt able to tease them.

"And what's wrong with a bit of designer stubble?" Max asked belligerently, fingering his chin.

"Goes with the bloodshot eyes and crumpled clothes, I suppose," she giggled.

"Needs to grow a decent beard," Lauren thought she heard her uncle mutter to himself and glancing over she saw him stroking his own lovingly. "Now now, children, save the insults for later," he continued aloud. "What we need is a list." He looked up from the mountain of scruffy papers for the first time. "Lauren, write this down for us. People who attacked Thor's mountain.
1. Axiel and Lori.

2. Kiel and Erik, brothers, Erik killed.
3. Anika + 3 daughters, 2 daughters killed.
4. Silus, his wife Gila, son Silus, daughter Gisela, all killed.
5. Fredici the farmer and his sister Fari, her twin daughters and her human husband, all killed.
6. Sharra White-hair the archer.
7. Henrik and his human wife, Henrikka and Harri their daughter and son.
8. Human friends and Thor's rebels.

Thor's People.
1. Dani, Thor's wife—??children."

"Son. Axiel said he had a son!" Lauren interrupted excitedly. El smiled down at her.

"You see. You did find out some new things. Carry on.
2. Human slaves.
3. Edis and Erin, brother and sister who he called his right and left hands."

"Erin?" Lauren's attention was immediately grabbed. "Wasn't that…"

"The same name as the woman who kidnapped Kim," Max replied grimly. "Yes. I don't reckon it'd be a coincidence, do you?"

"It's not exactly a common name. Are you sure that was all of them?" Lauren asked.

"No," El replied. "Three and a half thousand years is a long time ago. This is the most we've been able to learn from the bracelet and those few records that survived. But there were never many Elder families, and despite our long lives, there are never many descendants. As far as I've ever been able to find out, Laura and I are the first of our family since the bracelet existed ever to have two children in the same generation."

"So who could the Ericksons be?"

"Possibly descendants of Erik, if they keep the tradition of family names as we have. He may have left a young child when he died."

"Then that means they would be on our side?"

"Possibly. We need young Kim to find out a few things for us. Do you think he could be tactful enough?"

"Definitely. He's a born spy," Lauren laughed. "Well, that was when he was going through his James Bond phase, before he discovered Lord of the Rings! He had all the gadgets."

"Well, write to him and tell him to ask his friend if he's ever heard of Thor. Thor's people always called Axiel "the traitor" because they reckon he betrayed them. We always call him "the hero!" This lad might give away what his family thinks."

"Do you want me to do it now?"

"Well, wait a bit. Write some more notes for us first. Next record:

<u>To do.</u>

1. Try to find out how Axiel worked the Portal.
2. Contact families who might support us now.
3. Find out if there might be any descendants of Thor, or families who supported him."

"Why have we all lost touch with each other?" Lauren asked. "They must have gone through so much together. You'd think they would have been really close."

"Most of the survivors had been through too much. Their homes had been destroyed, their families and friends murdered. I think they moved to many different parts of the earth, to live normal lives among the humans. Our family took human wives and husbands, like Laura and me—and your father—but our genes are strong, and our children inherit the Elder Peoples' talents. But we can never stay in one place for long, or become famous, for not many humans could accept that we have long life and good health while they grow old and sick. Most of us have spent our lives trying desperately to be more human than the humans."

"So they could live anywhere?"

"We do," Max replied. "Dad and I lived one life in Scotland before Mum died and we went to Canada."

"Are you a teacher in Canada too?" Lauren asked him.

"Sometimes," Max replied blandly while El started to chuckle.

"What's the matter?" she asked suspiciously as Max gazed innocently at the wall.

"Well, being a teacher's a bit quiet for Max," her uncle laughed. "In Scotland he was working as one of the first helicopter pilots for the oil rigs and in Canada we started our own adventure school. He's a ski instructor in the winter and takes parties white water rafting and climbing in the summer. Mountain Rescue too."

"But it never hurts to get the qualifications." Max spread his hands. "You never know when it might come in useful. Like now for instance. By the by," he added, eyes bright with laughter and falling to his knees in a parody of pleading. "I've never qualified as a bodyguard. Will you still have me?" By this time Lauren was laughing as hard as her uncle.

"I hereby appoint you as my official knight in shining armour!" she announced in ringing tones, tapping him on both shoulders with a teaspoon like the queen.

"As long as you promise to keep on saving my life at least once a week." Max gave her a rueful half grin and she made a little face in return. El turned back to his papers.

"We need Laura," he grumbled. "What's that confounded row?"

"The front door!" laughed Lauren, running to answer it. "Grannie! You must've known we were talking about you! What are you doing here?"

"I thought I might be needed." Laura gave Lauren that companionable smile that warmed her more than all her other granny's kisses. "I had to go up to London to take some of my paintings to the Gallery so I decided to pop in on my way back."

"Laura!" Uncle El surged out of the dining room and lifted his sister off the ground in one of his bear hugs. "You're a sight for sore eyes!"

"Put me down, you wretched giant!" she puffed. "Let me say hello to my nephew. I haven't seen you since you were Lauren's age. How did you manage to get such a handsome son, El?"

"My favourite Aunt!" Max kissed her cheek, his eyes twinkling.

"I'm your only aunt!" she replied trying not to laugh, and inspected his bandaged hands sympathetically. "You and Lauren did well. Very well."

"Lauren saved my life," Max said seriously. "I was so sure that we were safe, only onlookers. I would never have defended us in time."

"Did you see how Axiel worked the portal?"

"No." Max grimaced. "It was a mind spell. No physical traces."

"It frightened them all so much. Thor and his people came and went where they liked. Axiel wanted all records of it to be lost and no matter how his daughter pleaded with him, he wouldn't teach her." Laura's lips tightened as she remembered the scenes from her ancestor's childhood that she had experienced through the bracelet so many years ago.

"Someone remembered it. It must be how Kim's kidnappers left the cellar."

"Thor's woman and child," Max said slowly. "I saw them escape with a piece of the Crystal. They must be the only people, apart from Axiel, who ever knew that spell. And he was too honourable to teach it to his daughter!"

"There's another who knows," Laura said suddenly. "One of the families was always against mixing with anyone. The archer Sharra."

"Sharra White-hair?" Lauren asked, referring to her list.

"Sharra White-hair, Sharra of the Hollow Hills," her grandmother nodded. "Her family always lived secretly and their homes within the hills and mountains are hidden. The only way in was by using the portals so that no human would find the way unless they were taken."

"They still live like that?" Max asked.

"I'm sure. Sharra was one of Thor's bitterest enemies. He had killed her whole family: husband, parents and children. But she had another child after the wars and somehow persuaded Axiel to teach her what he did not want to remember himself. They're a strange family. I'm sure a lot of human legends about fairies and elves started when people have met them."

"You know them?" Max asked curiously.

"We used to know one quite well. On the Island when we were children, before Grandmère made us move to London. Do you remember Shari, El?"

"Could I ever forget her? Very beautiful girl. A real fairy, Max, white hair, pale skin, moved like she was floating, appeared and disappeared all the time—just to bug us I think. I loved her like mad when I was thirteen. Her mother never liked her mixing with us."

"She's just as bad herself now she has a daughter." Laura flicked her eyes to the ceiling in irritation. "But she does still visit me occasionally and I know how to contact her. She may need some persuading but if she believed someone was trying to raise Thor I'm sure she couldn't just stand by and do nothing."

"When can you see her?" Lauren asked.

"I can try as soon as I go home. Now if you like."

"Certainly not!" El interrupted. "We need you here for a day or two. Look at all these papers!"

"What have you done so far? Let me see that list, Lauren." Lauren held out the paper and her grandmother read it carefully, her expression growing grim. "Of course, you've left off the most important task." They looked at her questioningly while she glared at them for a long moment. Taking up the pencil, she scribbled a few capital letters and underlined them so heavily that the point broke. Two words.

<u>FIND ALEX</u>

They all moved uncomfortably. Of course. No one had really forgotten although Lauren still found it hard to think of her father as a real person.

"The portal must come first," Max said eventually. "They can obviously use it so there's no way we could rescue anyone without knowing how to use it ourselves."

"You'll all have to come back with me I suppose." For a moment Laura looked irritated and Lauren suddenly realised how long she must have been living on her own in that cottage, content with the company of her cats.

"We'll try not to be any bother," she said tentatively. Her grandmother looked down at her, and her stern face relaxed into a smile.

"Lauren, it'll be a pleasure to have you all, especially you. I'd almost forgotten I could laugh since your father disappeared until that day when you nearly set the school alight."

Lauren's mother chose that moment to return from work laden with a take-away Thai meal for supper. When she saw Laura she burst out laughing.

"What's one more?" she gurgled hysterically. "Lauren, where can your Grandmother sleep?"

"You can have my room, Grannie. I can sleep on the sofa," Lauren offered.

"Nonsense. You and I can bunk up, Dad, and let Aunt Laura use my room," said Max. "There's a blow-up mattress in the wardrobe isn't there Heather? I think I saw it."

"I'm not sure that it stays blown up," Heather replied doubtfully. "But thank you Max. That would be very helpful."

The mattress did only stay inflated for about half an hour after Max retired to bed. He woke up feeling stiff and despite being so tired he tossed and turned for a long time wondering whether if he blew it up he would manage to get to sleep before it went flat again. He wasn't even sure he could manage the stopper with his bandages. His father had slept almost at once and was snoring in an irritating monotonous drone that made it impossible to settle. Max tried again for a bit longer and then gave up the battle. If he was to get any sleep that night it would have to be on the sofa downstairs so he crawled out of bed, bundled up his bedclothes and crept out of the room. The snoring turned into three or four startled snorts as he tripped over the corner of the duvet on his way through the door but soon settled back to the old rhythm before Max even had time to close it. He laughed fondly to himself as he tiptoed downstairs, the dim light from the street lamp outside enough to find his way down to the sitting room. One of these days he'd make a recording to play back to his father in the morning as he never would believe that he snored at all. He wondered if Heather or his cousin Alex had chosen the huge beige leather sofa downstairs; it was certainly soft, more comfortable than his bed let alone the useless inflatable mattress, and he plumped up the pillows with a feeling of satisfaction. He certainly needed a good night's sleep. His father had been so involved with the search through his papers the night before that bed had been out of the question. He lay back drowsily and watched the orange flickering of the street light as it shone through the windblown leaves of the trees in front of the house until his eyes began to close.

A sudden noise woke him again with a jump; he tried to spring to his feet, caught his foot in the duvet and crashed heavily to the floor, banging one of his bandaged hands painfully on the coffee table.

"Ah!" He lay there for a few seconds swearing silently to himself, wondering what it could have been that had woken him, before untangling himself quietly, listening for a repeat of the sounds, moving like a cat towards the door. It came again; it was outside but in the driveway, not the street: the scrape of the garage doors and the squeak of the hinges. He was halfway to the kitchen when there was a sudden crash of breaking glass followed by the sound of running feet and the angry snarl of an engine as a car accelerated away up the street screeching its tyres. Breathlessly he raced to the kitchen door and flung it open to see a flickering light reflecting from the open garage doors and to hear the roaring crackle of fire.

Chapter 14
Shari

DAD! AUNT LAURA! LAUREN! Max's mind-shout was deafening and they tumbled out of bed half asleep. By the time they had stumbled downstairs the garage fire was beginning to send a flickering orange glow through the kitchen window accompanied by a subdued crackling roar. They pushed out through the back door into the little alleyway that led from the front to the back garden, already filled with smoke.

"Should I phone the Fire Brigade?" Lauren asked, panicking at the thought of the fire spreading across to the house.

"No use trying normal methods!" Uncle El stood in the doorway behind her and the weight of his heavy hands on her shoulders was like strength flooding into her. "Takes too long! All of you, concentrate on the flames. Like lighting a fire but backwards, Lauren. Think of them smothering, dying." Lauren tried hard to push the flames back—difficult when they were roaring at her, trying to devour everything. For a moment all she could think about was that terrible pyre in her dream that had burned her great, great grandfather alive. Max almost screamed as the heat flaring at them made his hands relive their recent burns. Laura and El gripped each other's arms, their whole beings lost in concentration as they fought the inferno.

Lauren felt her mind meld with theirs and Max's, the combination, like it had been at Grannie's when they fought the burglars, making them much stronger than they could have been on their own. The calmness of her uncle's mind, the concentrated power of her grandmother's and the fierce energy of Max flooded into her and she fought to lend them her strength as they tried to pull the air away from around the fire, smothering, damping. Gradually the flames began to die.

"I think we've saved the building." Laura's voice was shaking with fatigue as they eventually dared to walk into the ruined garage and look around at the smouldering wreckage.

"But all your tea chests!" Lauren cried, looking around at the blackened wreckage of packing cases and trunks. "All your things are ruined!"

"At least we had the most important one inside," said El. "Some of those papers were irreplaceable."

"They must have known our stuff was in here," Max said furiously. "Someone's watching us pretty closely."

"We need to move faster," said Laura firmly. "One more day researching, then you'd better all come home with me and see if we can persuade Shari to help us. Back to bed now, Lauren. We need to get some sleep if we want our brains to work."

Easier said than done, Lauren thought to herself as she climbed the stairs, her mind in a whirl. It took her a long time to calm down enough to sleep, and when she finally did her dreams were full of smoke and heat.

"You're not leaving me behind!" Lauren's mother had discovered the events of the night only when she had got up for work the next morning and was giving them all a hard time for not having woken her. "I know I'm not much help but I refuse to be left out any more. I'm owed some holiday, I haven't got any urgent cases on that I can't deal with on the phone and Daniel will have to let me go. Just give me till the weekend."

"I think Alex knew what he was doing when he chose you for his wife, Heather," rumbled Uncle El. "You're not as ordinary as you try to make out."

"If I'd wanted to be ordinary, I wouldn't have chosen an extraordinary husband," Heather snapped back. Her mother-in-law gave her a sharp look of sudden approval. Lauren looked at her grandmother, feeling guilty that she could have thought for one moment that her mum could have betrayed her father like that medieval Loriel's mother had.

Do you think she could have her mind woken like Kim and Keri?

She's older than your friends. It would be harder. The men both nodded thoughtfully.

"What?" Heather asked, half laughing through her anger. She knew she was the focus of attention. "What?" Laura drew her back into the kitchen.

"Do you think she'll want it?" Lauren tensed with worry. All of a sudden she really needed her mother to be more involved with their world and not a suspicious outsider. "Why do you think Dad didn't already share it with her?"

"Your grandmother is particularly clever," El replied. "Not all of us could alter minds without causing any harm. I can in a small way, like with that ranting fellow the other day. But to open a person's mind to their possibilities—that is a rare skill and one not to be shared lightly. Your father probably thought there was no rush. After all, they'd only been married a few years when he vanished. And how do you tell your wife that you and your children will probably outlive her by at least two hundred years?" His face was suddenly totally expressionless. Max gave him a tight look and squeezed his arm briefly.

The two women returned and Heather picked up her briefcase ready for work.

"I will do it," she said quietly to Lauren. "But not yet. Not until we're away at Grannie's and I've got time."

Persuading Daniel that she could have a fortnight's holiday at such short notice was much harder than she had expected.

"We need you here." His hand was on her shoulder, his face very close. "I feel I'm losing you."

"I'll have my phone." She edged away slightly. "And I can take the laptop in case there's anything urgent, but my diary's fairly free for the next two weeks. Nothing Sally can't handle."

"I don't like it. You need your friends around you with everything that's been happening."

"I know you want to be kind, Daniel, but I really need a break. I've had no holiday since the two days at Easter."

"It's such short notice. I was hoping you'd come to the Greenwich conference with me while there's someone who can take care of Lauren."

"I need to spend some time with my daughter!" she eventually almost shouted. "We've been burgled, set alight, Lauren's friend was kidnapped! We need to get away, to spend some time just having fun! Don't you understand?" She felt unhappy lying to such an old friend but he was really getting too overprotective.

"Do you want to go to the St. Tropez Villa?" Daniel eventually realised he could not win this one. "It's free all summer. You really enjoyed it last time, and I could fly out for the weekend."

"Thank you Daniel, but we'll just pop over to the Island and stay with Alex's mother. Country air, beaches, all we need."

"On one condition," he finally capitulated. "I'll come over at the weekend and take you both out for a sail. Storm Queen's berthed at Cowes at the moment. That's if your husband's relations will let you out of their sight?" Recognising the jealousy in his voice and breathing an inward sigh of relief, she gladly agreed.

"A sail would be lovely. We'll buy you dinner afterwards." She smiled and gave him a little push away from her. "Now you'd better get on. You're due in court in ten minutes. Thank you Daniel."

"That man is so rich!" Lauren commented when her mother returned home that night and told them about it. "Villa in the South of France, yacht, fantastic house in the New Forest, those gorgeous horses! Why aren't you earning that much?"

"Well, it is his firm," Heather laughed. "But I think he inherited a lot from his family. They've always been wealthy. I think they've owned their manor for centuries."

"Oh well, I suppose a day sailing will be fun for you," Max said. "We can't be working all the time. Shame Lauren's friends can't come too."

"We almost forgot about the great week we had at half term after the awful ending," Lauren said wistfully. "I wonder if the little house we made is still there in the forest."

"You'll have to show me," her mother smiled. "It's a beautiful area. We used to go over every year, on your grandfather's birthday. Does Grannie still leave flowers on the spot where he landed?" Lauren hadn't heard that story, and felt unaccountably sad at hearing that her grandmother had fallen desperately in love only once in her long life, with a young pilot who had crash-landed on the Downs next to her garden. They had only been together for a few months when he had been shot down over France and killed, before her father had even been born.

They found time for a walk after a couple of days settling in. Lauren had found the first night difficult, sharing the room with her mother that she had shared with Keri on that terrible night. Every noise woke her with a jump, especially when it was so quiet in the countryside after the busy city noises at home. It had been even harder at first to pass that spot at the bottom of the stairs. There was no trace now of the horrific events of her last visit but every time she half-closed her eyes she could remember the shocking silence after the two deafening explosions, the splashes of blood everywhere, and Kim trying not to cry.

The weather was hot and she felt a lot better after two very normal days on the beach with her mother and Max, who could not hide his frustration at not being able to enjoy a swim with his hands still in bandages. It was almost like being an ordinary family and she pretended for a moment that it was her father there with them. They went for a walk up to the forest on the Tuesday afternoon. The little house was still there but a couple of empty crisp packets and a bit of rearrangement showed that it had been taken over by local children.

"Litter bugs!" snorted Lauren, picking up the rubbish and stuffing it into her pocket. Her mother laughed.

"Since when did you become so environmentally friendly?"

Since you brought me up that way, Lauren retorted in her mind. Heather had still not fully adjusted to the new way of communicating.

It needs a bit more waterproofing on the roof if you wanted to stay dry in a storm. Max walked round it critically. Lauren stuck out her tongue at him.

It was only a game, not a home! she complained.

Might be a bit of fun to try it, though.

WHY DON'T YOU? Lauren's mother thought at them, her inexperienced mind so loud it was like a shout. *IT'S A BIT OF A SQUASH AT LAURA'S. IT MIGHT BE PREFERABLE TO LISTENING TO YOUR FATHER SNORING ALL NIGHT!* Lauren and Max laughed.

"Shout that loud and you'll have the whole country knowing you're here!" The new voice, silky smooth and bored with a clipped accent that made Heather think immediately of a South African client of hers, made them jump as it sounded from above them. They looked up. Lying along the branch of a tree in a pose that reminded Lauren strongly of a cat was the most beautiful creature she had ever seen. She wondered later why 'creature' had been the first word that came to mind and decided that it was because despite the beauty there was something alien about the girl. Long white blonde hair threaded with blue beads hung around a heart-shaped face the colour of coffee beans from which huge green eyes looked down at them under arched eyebrows. A slender hand stretched out, made a small gesture like turning an invisible doorknob, and the three of them jumped again as she appeared next to them on the ground. Her clothes were as bizarre as her hair, like nothing Lauren had ever seen or imagined, and seemed to be made mostly of thin strips of a translucent leaf-coloured fabric hanging over a very tightly fitting white bodysuit.

"Mother didn't tell me there was anything quite so tasty," she purred, a finger touching Max's arm while she looked at Heather. "Is he yours?"

"My husband's cousin," Heather said rather coldly after a moment of surprise.

"Max," he introduced himself. "This is Heather and this is Lauren." She nodded a greeting to Heather, a small smile on her perfect mouth. Lauren, ignored, thought crossly that she had never seen Max with such a soppy grin plastered on his face.

"I was looking for you." The strange girl addressed him as if there was no one else present. "You were very easy to find. Mother wants to meet you." She took his bandaged hand in hers, repeated her small gesture, and with a slight eddying of the air around them they vanished.

"Huh!" Lauren exclaimed.

"She's got to bleach that hair," Heather muttered. "No one with skin that dark could have hair like that." Come on Lauren, I guess you and I will have to go back the hard way."

They found the others in the garden with an older woman, obviously Laura's old friend Shari. She was very like her daughter but pale-skinned, tiny and slender still, with the same bright green eyes under thin dark eyebrows and her luxurious white hair arranged in an elaborate net studded with what looked like real jewels.

"I don't know what you fed this one on," she was saying to Laura while looking up at El. "He was such a skinny little fellow when we were girls." Lauren and her mother flopped into deck chairs, puffed from the long uphill climb, reluctant to interrupt. Max and the girl were sitting together on the grass at the feet of their parents.

"He always fed me," Laura replied shortly, her tension showing in the stiff set of her shoulders. The silence throbbed between the two women.

"Well, Laura," Shari nodded at last. "I can't let you prize our last secrets away from us."

"I wouldn't put it quite like that," replied Laura. "You know I wouldn't ask if we weren't desperate."

"To lose a child is the worst thing that could have happened to you," the woman agreed. "But you have not convinced me how anyone could use your son Alex to bring Thor back. And for anyone to know how to find us after all these centuries of safety would be a betrayal of everything my family ever worked or fought for."

"We know they are using the portals." Laura's voice was quiet but firm. "Who are you more afraid of, them or us?"

"Come back with me," her friend replied. "We need to talk, and try to learn whether what you say is possible. Axiel, come with us."

"Axiel?" Lauren almost exclaimed, and then as her uncle grumbled to his feet remembered that of course Axiel was Uncle El's real name.

"Amuse yourself for a while, Sharla," Shari ordered. Her daughter smiled her mysterious smile and raised her eyebrows at Max.

"I expect we could think of something. Come for a walk and tell me about why you're bothering us. I'll find us somewhere interesting. And while we're about it, I'll try to do something about those hands of yours." Without waiting for Max to stand up she touched his bandage and they vanished again.

"I think it's expect us when you see us," Laura said with an apologetic look over her shoulder. "Make yourselves at home, Heather. Oh, I'd be grateful if you'd feed the cats." She and El clasped hands with Shari, and were gone.

"Huh!" snorted Lauren again. "Can you lend me your laptop so I can e-mail Keri?"

"I suppose that leaves me as chief cook and cat feeder," her mother laughed. "To think I tried to introduce Max to Sally from work when this one was waiting for him."

"Huh!" Lauren stamped inside, plugged the computer into the phone socket, and relieved her feelings a little by writing a long screed to her friends. It was probably only lunchtime in Florida, she thought. Perhaps they might reply later tonight?

Chapter 15
Sharla

"Come on then." All the glass beads on Sharla's hair rattled as she gave an impatient jerk of her head at Max who was trying hard not to look as disconcerted as he felt by the rapid transport from one place to another.

"Come on where?" he asked sarcastically, looking at the metre and a half of slippery downland grass around him on the narrow end of a clifftop peninsular. The wind pushed against him, flapping his shorts around his knees and flattening his shirt to his back as he twisted carefully to look along that narrow causeway to the security fence and safety. "How far have we come already?"

"Not far." She slid down so that she was sitting right on the cliff edge, feet dangling. "We're still on your Isle of Wight. There are the Needles." She pointed downwards and Max could see the top of a line of chalk rocks leading outwards into the sea, a red and white striped lighthouse at the end, fringed with white surf in a deep green sea. "Come and sit here." She patted the grass next to her, laughing up at him with a mocking challenge in her eyes. Memories of children at school calling him chicken when he refused to play tag on the railway line suddenly jumped into his mind. He was not averse to a bit of danger—every mountain climber knew that it was the danger that made it worthwhile—but he preferred not to take stupid risks.

"I don't think so," he drawled lazily. "Chalk cliffs are known for crumbling if you get too close to the edge."

"Oh, come on." Her eyes taunted him. "You don't think I'd let anything happen to you, do you?" He felt a reluctant smile rising in his own and cautiously sat down next to her, forcing himself to look down at the little band of white foam that was the waves breaking on the shore far below. She took his hands and he winced as she unwound the bandages, the sight of his still raw flesh almost as bad as the pain. "Hasn't anyone ever taught you how to heal minor injuries?" she asked incredulously. "I don't know how your family ever managed to survive!" He watched her face as she closed her eyes in concentration, her mind a caress on his throbbing fingers, soothing the pain as she concentrated. He would never have expected her to be so gentle and sensitive. He dared not look at his hands until she looked up through her preposterously thick eyelashes with the more usual wicked glint in her sea-green eyes. "Well, any better?" she asked. He flexed his fingers trying not to show his amazement.

"A bit red still," he said critically after examining them closely.

"Does this hurt?" She grasped his hand firmly, and before he could reply or recover from the tingling shock of her touch on his bare skin she had kicked herself forwards and pulled him after her off the cliff. He heard himself yell with shock as they fell, his stomach left behind him at the top as he saw the stony shore rushing upwards towards them. He squeezed his eyes shut, braced himself for the killing impact… and fell gently into warm water. He surfaced, spluttering, his hand still imprisoned in a grip that felt far too strong for the slight figure of his companion. She was laughing at him, little rivulets of water cascading down her face.

"I did that to a human once off the Victoria Falls when I was fourteen," she said nostalgically. "Mother had to spend two weeks modifying his memory before they let him out of the mental ward in the hospital." Max swallowed the indignant remark he had been about to make and gave her a reluctant grin.

"You really are the most…" He shook his head, lost for words. "We must do it again sometime. But it probably wouldn't be the same without the element of surprise." Strangely, the experience had made him feel more alive than he had for a long time in the confines of the city and classroom which had begun to suffocate him before their escape to his aunt's cottage, and he grinned and shook the water out of his hair like a dog. She laughed again.

"Try this one then." He glared at her suspiciously, wondering what she was up to this time, and she suddenly twisted him around. The menacing triangular fin of a shark was circling them; as he watched it dived below the surface. He ducked his head underwater and pushed out with his mind as the open jaws arrowed towards them. The shark stopped, confused, and nosed around the ring of force that Max had created. Sharla sank down to his level, her beaded hair floating upwards, a stream of small bubbles rising from her mouth sparkling in the sunbeams slanting through the water and gave him a quick thumbs up of approval. Another buzz shot up his arm as she grasped it, the water was gone, and they were lying dripping on soft grass with evening sunlight dappling through trees.

"What's here then?" Max asked distrustingly. "Man-eating tigers?" She gave him a disarming smile and shook her head.

"You've passed my tests of whether you're a fun person to know or not. No one else has even passed the cliff test, let alone the shark. And you finally stopped thinking like a human. Now try this." He looked at her warily, trying to be ready for anything, and as he watched she shimmered out of sight.

"Sharla?" he asked, peering at the spot where she had been. "Sharla?" He could almost see something, the vaguest whisper of a ghost, a slight thickening of the air. He reached out and touched it; it felt solid enough and he grasped her wrist. "You are still there." She shivered back into sight.

"Another notable failure of the famous Silva family," she scoffed. "Can't mindshield?" Max sighed.

"Can you show me that?"

"No problem. All you do is try to blend in with everything around you, then kind of shrink inwards in your mind. Here." She sent a vivid picture into his brain. "Try it." Max tried. When he thought he was truly invisible, he rolled athletically to his feet and tiptoed around behind her, ready to clap his hands over her eyes. She vanished and his hands clasped nothing.

"Ah!" he exclaimed, laughing as his shield collapsed. Sharla reappeared swinging from the branch of a nearby tree and dropped laughing to the ground.

"Not bad," she admitted.

"Where are we?" Max looked around, sensing something about this place that seemed familiar. He crouched down and as his palms touched the ground, power and strength seemed to flood into him. He sprang to his feet, staring around in surprise.

"You're the first of our people I've ever met apart from Mother so I thought you should know something about your heritage."

"I already know this place. It's the grove where my ancestors Lori and Alix were married and dedicated their baby. But I saw it destroyed by Thor when Alix was murdered here."

"You saw it?" she asked suspiciously. "How?"

"Perhaps **you** need to know something about our heritage," Max replied, trying not to sound smug, and told her about their journeys into the ancient Loriel's memories and the amazing outcome of their last visit. She listened in silence.

"My mother will need to know this," she said when he had finished. "I thought she would never agree to your aunt's request, but this may make a difference."

"I'm sure Dad and Aunt Laura will have told her. You could teach me, couldn't you?" He looked at her pleadingly but she shook her head firmly.

"Never without Mother's permission," she replied. "Not even when you look as cute as that. My ancestors spent more than three thousand years making sure that no one could ever find us and I don't care to be the one to ruin that. You'll never find this place again by yourself without knowing but I thought you should see it at least once. Come and look around. We restored it after the wars." She pulled him over to one side of the glade and gestured towards a tall, squared off stone. "You'd definitely like to see this." His breath caught in his throat as he looked where she was pointing and realised what was on that pillar.

About the size of the palm of his hand, sparkling as though it had just been made, was a grey flint spearhead.

"Lori's spear?" he whispered. "The spear that killed Thor?"

"None other." She looked delighted at having surprised him at last. There's something about this place that preserves things. Even fruit doesn't go mouldy as fast here as in the outside world. It still looks like new, doesn't it?" He shook his head in awe.

"Thank you for bringing me," he murmured. "I wish Lauren could see this too."

"Maybe someday." She looked considerably less pleased at this and looked away as if she had suddenly lost all interest in him. "I'll take you home now. If you need me, just concentrate hard and call my name. Far hearing is one of my better skills." As she silently opened the portal that would take him home, Max tried hard to probe her mind without success. However she did it was impossible to tell. She laughed a bell-like laugh at his efforts and blew him a kiss as she left him in Laura's garden and disappeared.

Lauren almost forgave him for his desertion when he came running in calling her name.

"Lauren! Lauren! Are you there?" His eyes were shining with excitement. "You'll never guess where Sharla took me!" She signed off from the computer and looked up trying hard not to smile at him.

"Go on then. Where?"

"The Grove!"

"What—not that place where Lori and Alix were married? Where they took Axiel? Where..." she couldn't bring herself to talk about that third time when they had witnessed Alix's murder. "I thought it was destroyed."

"Shari's family restored it and have been tending it all these years. It is beautiful again. If they decide to teach me how to use the Portal, I'll take you. And you won't believe what they've got there! The spearhead of that spear that killed Thor!"

"Lori's spear?" Lauren gasped.

"On a tall rock, like an altar or a museum. Did you realise it was made of stone?"

"Stone?"

"Well, a worked, glassy sort of stone, flint probably. I hadn't really thought about how long ago it must have been."

"Where is the grove, do you think? Is it in England?"

"I have no idea," Max said in surprise. The thought had not occurred to him before. "Somewhere very private and quiet. It was summer, or warm, but not tropical. Same time of day as here. Did you know that they think of our family as deserters for trying to forget our past when Axiel's grandchildren moved away while they preserved the memories and traditions of the Elder People?"

"I think you and I just changed all that," Lauren said thoughtfully. "When we were born and travelled back to help with Thor's defeat."

"I hope they realise that," said Max seriously. "I really need her to teach me how to use the Portal. It's not only for your father now but because I realise how much we have lost. We have to know. I have to know." He sat in his still damp clothes staring at nothing until it grew dark, feeling completely blown away by his experiences that day, a different person than he had been only a few short hours ago. He had never met anyone like Sharla. Surely there could be no one else like Sharla but he hadn't quite decided whether that was a good thing or not. She made him feel like a fool, a child who knew nothing of his heritage, with her superior looks and her casual handling of her mind powers. But he could learn. He had to learn. After today, his family's rejection of everything that made them different was not good enough for him any more, or for Lauren. His cousin deserved to know how to live like a true Elder. Lauren watched him for a while, half listening to the busy sounds of her mother clattering dishes in the kitchen, and then slipped unnoticed away to bed.

Laura had known Shari on and off for nearly two hundred years but their relationship had never been one that involved favours on either side and she was finding it hard to beg now.

"This is no game, Shari," she sighed eventually, feeling that she had exhausted every argument. "It's my son's life I'm pleading for."

"You're only guessing." Shari leaned back in her chair, face hard. "You have no proof that he's still alive even, let alone that someone will use him for such an unlikely purpose. How could anyone be resurrected after three and a half thousand years?"

"They said it, not us," El growled. "They were desperate enough to kill to prevent Laura knowing that."

"My ancestors spent all their time and energy for generations creating this place for our family," Shari said angrily. "You expect me to waste the labour of all those years by giving away our secrets to the first people who ask without any proof that there could be danger to us?"

"If Thor returns, those years will certainly be wasted," Laura replied grimly. "In his time, there were no secrets that could be kept from him, and no lives that were safe."

Shari made an impatient snorting sound.

"If it wasn't for Lauren and Max, your ancestors wouldn't even have survived," said Laura wearily. "And they'd never have known how to use the mind portal if

Axiel hadn't taught Sharra the archer all those years ago." Shari shrugged, her face closed. "You've never seen, have you?" Laura said suddenly. "Never seen your ancestor's battle against Thor, the death of most of your family. Let us bring Lauren here, and the bracelet. You should see what your ancestors went through and maybe you'd believe that they would have wanted you to help us."

"Maybe," Shari conceded. "I'll have to think about it. I've had enough talk for today. You'd better go home." She touched both their hands and without another word took them back to the cottage. When she had disappeared again Laura let out a low growl of frustration.

"I don't know when I've ever been so close to wringing someone's neck!" she exclaimed. "Well, not since Alex was fifteen, anyway. We'd better get some sleep. I think Lauren will be our only hope. If Shari bothers to come back."

Sharla surprised them all by walking into the middle of a family conference around the breakfast table the next morning.

"I don't know what you said to Mother yesterday but you certainly upset her," she said accusingly to Laura. "She wants me to take you back, with the young one." Heather's hand flew protectively to Lauren's arm but Laura gave her a very faint shake of the head.

"All right, Lauren?" she asked. They had already discussed sharing the bracelet's memories with Shari and Lauren was only too pleased to be able to help instead of being ignored.

"Wait here and I'll come back for you later," Sharla ordered Max. "Perhaps we can find a better cliff to jump off."

"Have you ever thought 'volcano'?" he asked coolly. The others all stared at him. He hadn't told any of them about yesterday.

"Cliff?" Lauren asked him incredulously but she was pulled into darkness before he could do anything but twitch his eyebrow at her.

She arrived into the most amazing place she had ever been. It must have been underground as the rock walls and ceiling were natural stone and not built of blocks but a row of lamps near the high ceiling created shafts of light that sparkled on multicoloured jewels set into the walls in mosaic-like patterns. Every other face of rock she could see was carved or painted with African animals and strange plants. She stared around in wonder. "Oh, it's beautiful!" she gasped.

"You're the only living person to have been here apart from your grandmother and uncle." Sharla looked down at her through drooping eyelids. "It's much better since they invented solar electricity. It was very gloomy before."

"Just you two live here?" Lauren asked. "What about your father? Any other relations?"

"Just the two of us," Sharla replied airily. "My father was some human mother had a fling with. We don't believe in long-term relationships in my family." Lauren and her grandmother exchanged glances. They weren't exactly an advertisement for relationships themselves. Lauren, like Sharla, had been brought up by her mother, and Grannie had managed alone with her son after her airman had died. "Actually, he was a Zulu chieftain in the days before the Boers and British ruined our culture, and he thought she was some supernatural spirit. You can call me princess if you like." Sharla continued, tilting her head and fluttering her lashes at them, "but all I inherited from him was the colour of my skin. Better than Mother's pale ivory, don't you think?" Lauren nodded, willing to agree with anything this rather frightening person said.

"Do you work or anything?" she asked.

"Never tried it," Sharla replied. "Living in an undiscovered diamond mine does have its advantages. When we run out of cash we just pull another stone out of the wall. The humans seem to love it." Lauren just gaped.

"You must be Lauren." Shari's curt voice sounded from behind her and she jumped. "Sharla, I need some space now. Laura will keep an eye on us. Go and play with your new friend."

"I was hoping I might be able to try the bracelet too?" she wheedled.

"What do you think this is? A playground?" her mother snapped. "They're trying to prove a point and they're going to have to try very hard before I'll believe them."

"If we work this out there'll be plenty of time to share it with you too," Lauren said generously, which made Sharla look at her properly for the first time.

"Perhaps I'll take you for one of my walks sometime," she said thoughtfully. "Call me if you want me, Mother."

Shari beckoned Lauren over to a roofed alcove strewn with thick brightly-woven rugs and as she clicked her fingers three chairs slid up to the low table in the centre. Lauren felt much, much more nervous than she had ever felt with Max. Shari was so intimidating and she felt as if the whole burden of their search now rested only with her. As she automatically went to release the catch of the bracelet a truly frightening thought crept into her mind that turned her stomach cold. What if Shari was one of the enemy, gone over to Thor, and this was all a trick to make her take it off.

"What do I do?" Shari sat stiffly next to her.

154

"Just hold this little charm with me between our fingers and thumbs so we're both touching it." Lauren left it firmly clasped on her wrist. It would be uncomfortable, but that was better than risking it being snatched. "Grannie, you don't think it might turn out like before, so we're really there do you?" she whispered. Her grandmother smiled reassuringly.

"I think El must have been right, that it was somehow Axiel's portal that caught you and dragged you back in time. Just think of Sharra the archer and her family, and you'll link into Lori's memories of them." Lauren swallowed and closed her eyes, wary of the sudden joining of Shari's unfamiliar mind. She felt her surprise as they drifted into a mist and found themselves standing in the biting cold of a winter landscape.

"It's as if we're actually there!" the older woman murmured. "I hadn't expected it to be so real." Two women were kneeling on the ground beside a freshly covered grave.

"We can't allow all of our people to be picked off one by one." The speaker was Lori, talking urgently, her hand on her companion's shoulder. The other woman looked up, a young face ravaged by grief, white hair straggling out from under a fur hood.

"He was only twelve!" she cried. "Only twelve!"

"Since when did Thor respect either youth or age?" Lori said impatiently. "Listen, tomorrow I meet Axiel for the first time for five years. If he has a plan, will you join us?"

"I'll do anything," the archer Sharra hissed through her teeth. "I have no one left now. If I give my life in the fight there will be none left to mourn me."

"I would." Lori said, her eyes boring into her friend's in a way that reminded Lauren of her grandmother. "We're not here to sacrifice ourselves, Sharra; we're here to win, and to rid the world of this evil."

"Win?" Sharra gave a mirthless crack of laughter. "Against this?" She waved her hand around at the blackened trunks of trees and the grave mounds in front of them.

"Trust Axiel," Lori urged. "He has given so much to find out Thor's secrets. I know he will find a way."

"It's been so long I can't remember a world without him."

"We used to laugh. I remember when your parents and Alix and I and the others would dance all night in the Grove before you and Axiel were born. Your grandmother was such a musician we felt as though our feet had wings. We will find a way to bring our laughter back. Go and gather our people, Sharra. Gather an army if you can and we will defeat Thor. Evil can't win for ever."

"Even if it does, I'd rather die fighting than running like a frightened mouse while that man tries to be the only Elder left on Earth." Sharra looked up, determination in her face. "Death or victory, Lori." Lori clasped her hand.

"Death or victory, or maybe both," she replied. The scene began to fade as Lori walked away, and Lauren thought desperately of what else she knew that could help to sway Shari. She took them to the mountaintop as Lori died, and heard once again her exultant dying whisper,

"For Alix," and Axiel's ragged reply,

"For the world."

"Death or victory," Shari murmured as their consciousness returned to her home. "Lori found both. Laura, I need your brother to bring all the evidence he has here and let me study it. You'll both have to stay till I've decided, one way or another. Wait here while I take your granddaughter home and collect him."

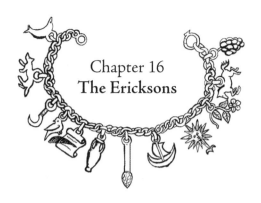

Chapter 16
The Ericksons

"Wow, poor Lauren seems a bit upset," Kim sympathised as he read the long message from their friend the next morning.

"I'm not surprised. She must be feeling really left out."

"I don't suppose the Silvas mean to. It's that Sharla. I expect she fancies Max."

"Bound to I should think," conjectured Kim. "Lauren said he's very good looking and all the girls at school did."

"Even old Dragon Breath Cooper!" Keri giggled, although even her laughter had an edge of nervousness that morning.

"Send a reply and tell them where we're going."

Keri clicked on 'reply' and started.

"Hi Lauren. Hey that sounds a bit American! Thought we should tell you what's going on here. Mark's parents came round to meet Mum and Dad and fixed for us to go out to their place for the day. Kim tried to get some info out of him but he sort of clammed up. I just hope you're right about the Ericksons being on our side because I expect they want to find out what we know and we're pretty nervous. Gotta go as Dad's waiting to drive us over on his way to work. Keep your fingers crossed!" She sent the message, and shut down the computer.

"Come along you two!" Their father's voice floated upstairs. They had never felt less like talking during the short car journey but tried to be normal in front of him, having their usual argument about whose turn it was to sit in the front seat. In reality both had a sick hollow in their stomachs that grew bigger the nearer they got to Mark's home.

"Nice house," Bob Kirby commented as they arrived. "Bound to be, I suppose. The Erickson Corporation is one of the biggest companies in the States, let alone Florida. Be good and don't forget your manners. I'll pick you up on my way home."

"Yes Dad," they chorused, exchanging glances. Mark was on the doorstep to welcome them.

"Hi guys," he said with a wide smile on his freckled face, waving cheerfully at their father as he drove away. "Come on in." Keri took a deep breath as they walked through the door and it closed behind them. It was not just the Ericksons who were waiting on a shady veranda by a swimming pool; there was a whole crowd of men and women of different ages, too many to be just one family.

Sorry about this, Mark whispered in Kim's mind. *You really got the wind up them with your questions and the whole tribe wanted to meet you. Mom cut it down to these few.*

Few? Kim muttered to Keri.

Mark's mother stepped forward to greet them with a handshake that tingled up their arms.

"Welcome to our home," she smiled. "I hope you don't think we're too intimidating meeting you like this, but it's been a long, long time since any humans who are not members of our Family have known about us."

"And to have had your minds woken at such a young age when you are not Family is not only unheard of but also gives away the skill of your trainer." Mark's father, a tall fair-haired man, spoke.

"We have to find out if you are a threat to us." An older woman spoke next, something about her deep-set wise eyes reminding them of Laura.

"We're not." Keri was the first to speak. "We didn't expect to meet you. But our friends have terrible enemies and we can't tell you anything that might harm them."

"I'm sorry, but we must know one way or another. If needs be, we can modify your memories so that you remember nothing."

Keri and Kim exchanged frightened glances and edged towards the door. Mark was standing with his back to it.

"Sorry guys, but either you're OK or you'll never remember any of this," he said. Keri thought angrily that he didn't sound sorry, not the least little bit!

The old woman came close, took her shoulders gently and looked deeply into her eyes.

"Nobody will harm you, I promise," she murmured. Panicking, Keri shrugged off her hands and tried to shout mentally to Kim. She could see Mark's father holding Kim's arms, Kim struggling wildly, but somehow she could not break away from that terrible gaze that sapped her will and froze her resistance. Then everything went dark.

Lauren showed the message to Max when she found it that evening.

"It's a big risk," she said worriedly. "Do you think they should have gone?"

"Too late now." He shook his head helplessly. "They won't have a chance at hiding anything they know if the Ericksons are half skilled. I need to tell Dad and Aunt Laura."

"Can you?" The two older members of the family had not been seen since the day before.

"I'll call Sharla." Max closed his eyes for a moment, and within seconds the strange girl was beside them.

"You called?" she purred, leaning on his shoulder.

"Have you seen Dad and Aunt Laura?" he asked. "We need to get them a message. It could be urgent."

"Come with me," she ordered, and before Max had time for more than a crooked apologetic smile at Lauren they were gone.

"Oh no, not again," Lauren grumbled and went to find her mother.

They got the chessboard out after a supper that was spoiled as they'd kept it warm for hours hoping the others would come back. Neither of them wanted to go to bed before at least one of their relations returned. Lauren was no competition for her mother's fast brain and lost quickly.

"I wish Grannie had a TV," Lauren sighed as she packed the pieces away after refusing a re-match. One of the cats rubbed against her legs and she pulled it onto her lap. "I'm too worried to think."

"The worst thing is there's nothing we can do except wait and if there's one thing I've always hated it's being helpless," her mother sighed crossly. Lauren looked at the clock for what seemed like the hundredth time since eleven, and checked the computer again to see if her friends had replied. Her mother looked up decisively.

"Come on, bed. The only thing we can do is be fresh and alert in the morning," she said firmly.

Max returned very late and woke them up by knocking hard on their bedroom door.

"Sorry," he said with a rueful grin. "I just thought I'd better let you know I'm back. Dad and Aunt Laura don't want you to be alone here at night."

"What did they say?" Lauren blearily wrestled herself out of the duvet and sat up.

"They're worried. Shari nearly went mad when she found out Keri and Kim knew about her. Is it OK if I use your e-mail to see if they've written yet?"

"Yes of course. I'll check again in the morning."

"When are they coming back?" Heather asked.

"Don't ask me. I'm afraid I've got to go back tomorrow with more of Dad's papers."

"Don't mind us," she replied sarcastically. "We'd be having a lovely holiday if we weren't so worried. And you might even get a meal if we knew you were getting back for supper. At least the cats appreciate us!"

"I'm sorry." He hovered in the doorway, silhouetted by the landing light. "We are doing our best, you know."

"Do you really think there's any chance?" she asked wearily. "I've been trying to remember, to think what Alex could be like after seven years."

"If there is a way, we'll find it," he promised, closing the door.

Keri remembered tossing and turning fitfully, as if in a dream. Someone kept asking her about Lauren and all she could answer was "She's my friend. She's my friend."

Max checked the computer for messages. There was nothing. He quickly typed in one of his own.

"What's happening? Let us know." and sent it. With nothing else to do, he went to bed.

Keri's mother was surprised to have a phone call from her daughter in the late afternoon.

"What's up? Are you all right?"

"Fine Mum. We're having a great time. There's a pool and everything. Can we stay a couple of nights? Mark's parents are having a barbecue tomorrow and we're invited."

"Well, yes, I suppose so if you're not going to be any trouble. Perhaps I'd better speak to his mother."

A short conversation with Mrs. Erickson relieved her worries, and she called her husband to tell him not to pick up the twins.

The next day, Friday, brought no message from them. Lauren was becoming really worried, more so when she saw how tensely Max asked about it during his brief visits home.

"Do you think we should go sailing tomorrow?" she asked anxiously. "Perhaps we should stay here."

"You can't do any good," he tried to reassure her. "They're probably just having such a great time. Don't worry. I'll keep checking."

Kim was woken, as if from a dream, by someone shaking his shoulder. He blinked hard, trying to remember where he was.

"Hey, drink this." It was Mark, holding out a glass chinking with ice cubes. Kim's throat suddenly felt parched so he drained it in one swallow.

"What happened?" He began to remember, and looked around wildly. *Keri! Keri! Where are you?*

It's OK Kim. I'm here and it's OK."

"You were sure strong!" Mark was laughing. "You mindchucked Dad and Uncle Rick into the pool when they tried to hold you." Remembering, Kim struggled to his feet, angrily clenching his fists.

"Kim, we really are truly sorry for our treatment of you." Mark's mother came forward. "Please let me explain." To his relief, Keri appeared and perched on the side of the sun lounger. He reluctantly sat down again, and the others pulled up chairs to join them.

"We see that you know the story of Thor. My husband's direct ancestor, Erik, was killed in that battle but his brother came back and looked after Erik's baby son as if he were his own. He was determined that the Elder People that survived should bind together and never lose their sense of community. Since that time when we have married we have rarely married humans and our families have grown to the several hundred that run this Corporation." Keri gasped.

"You mean… all your employees are Elder People?" Mark's mother nodded.

"My own family is descended from many of the original survivors of that great conflict. But Erik's brother Keil quarrelled with Axiel and that argument followed down the generations. Axiel refused to be the hero Kiel wanted to remember or to share any of the secrets he had learned from Thor and Axiel's daughter lived a solitary life caring for her beloved herbs. Axiel always maintained that they would never have defeated Thor but for the help of some strangers, but no one ever believed him."

"That was true, though, wasn't it?" Kim was beginning to regain his temper. "It was Lauren and Max."

"That is the most incredible part of your story," the old grandmother broke in. "All these centuries and in reality the real battle has only just happened. Time is truly an amazing thing."

"There are only four families who broke away from us," Mark's father continued. "Axiel who moved to distant lands and lived only with humans, Sharra the archer who was always very strange and solitary after her son was killed, and the families of Dani, Thor's wife and his henchmen Edis and Erin. They were never seen after Thor died."

"Erin!" Kim almost shouted. "That was the name of the woman I—" He couldn't quite say 'the woman I killed', and changed it quickly to "The woman who kidnapped me." Keri squeezed his arm.

"We thought that your friend could have been a member of any of those families," continued one of the old men. "So we had to be sure."

"And we are truly disturbed at what is happening over in England," Mark's mother finished. "We would like to help."

"Do you know how to use the Portals?" Keri asked. They shook their heads. "Then what can we do from over here?"

"We may have some information that could help shed some light on how Thor could be restored," Mark's father said. "Would you ask your friend to ask her Uncle El to contact us? He sounds like the historian amongst the bunch."

"We could do it now," said Kim. "If you've got a computer."

"Got a computer?" Mark grinned. "Dad invents them!" His equipment was indeed state of the art, and Kim sent off a short note to Lauren in his usual spelling.

"All well here Ericksons keen to help ples get your uncle daniel to get in tuch asap love Kim"

Chapter 17
Storm Queen

Lauren woke early the next morning, feeling a combination of excitement at the thought of her day's sailing and worry about her friends. The first thing she did was turn on the computer and was mystified by the message. She wrote back:

"Uncle Daniel? What's he got to do with anything? Glad Ericksons are OK, any help welcome as Uncle El and Grannie have not been seen for days and Max is still hanging out with Sharla non-stop. Uncle El is AxiEL not DaniEL—is that what you meant?" Happily, she sent the message and ran in to wake her mother ready for their day out. She left a scribbled note for Max next to the kettle as they slipped out quietly, not wanting to wake him after his late night.

"What did you say?" her mother asked, negotiating the car carefully around the bends of the rutted track.

"Told him to look at the e-mail," she replied. "Do you think Uncle Daniel would take us round the Needles if I asked him?"

"I expect so," Heather smiled. "I've been on the boat before, but only for a little party last year for the fireworks at the end of Cowes Week. Do the gate for me Lauren, please." Lauren concentrated for a moment on the latch and the heavy metal gate swung open in front of the car.

"Is the yacht big?"

"It's got a good sized cabin. I think it was one of the larger boats in the harbour when I saw it. You know Daniel. He always likes to go for the best."

"Can he sail it on his own?"

"I don't know," her mother laughed. "Wait till we get there and you'll find out!"

It seemed to Lauren ages before they got to Cowes, parked, and found the marina where they looked down from the high quayside and picked out the tall white yacht waiting for them with brass gleaming and flags waving in the light breeze. Lauren ran eagerly down the steps to the floating pontoon, followed a bit more elegantly by her mother carrying the bag with their spare clothes.

"It's a perfect day for landlubbers and new sailors." Daniel was smiling warmly down at them from the top of the cabin, smart as always in white shirt and trousers and deck shoes. Lauren felt very grand as his two crewmen handed them aboard and they climbed down into the little cockpit. "Come and sit over here while we get out of harbour, and then you can take a turn at the helm," he said to her as he stepped lightly down to join them. He took the wheel and started the engine while the two men cast off the ropes that had moored them to the floating decking.

"Where are we going?" she asked.

"Well, not too far in a day. I thought we'd go along the coast a bit, stop for a picnic lunch we've brought, take you for a look at the Needles from the sea and then get back here in time for that dinner your mother promised me."

"Perfect," Lauren smiled.

Max woke later that morning, the sun streaming through his window making it impossible to sleep longer despite his late night. He stretched lazily and padded downstairs for a coffee, smiling to himself as he imagined Lauren teasing him as she did every morning about not being able to start the day without one. Finding her note by the kettle, he made his drink and took it into the next room where the laptop was plugged in to the phone socket. As he read, a frown began to crease his forehead. Why on earth would the twins have thought his father was called Daniel? For once he was ready for Sharla when she appeared on the sofa next to him, and handed her the second cup of coffee he had made.

"What's the matter?" She was not as insensitive to other people's moods as she liked to make out.

"It's still the twins. It looks as if the Ericksons haven't harmed them—in fact they're offering help of some sort—but I can't make out what's happening. Could you take me to a place where neither of us has ever been, and find some people neither of us has ever met?" She looked at him helplessly and shrugged.

"I don't know how I could. Maybe we could get to Florida?" Max hit the table in frustration making their coffee jump in the mugs and took to prowling the room, pausing every few seconds to check the computer. "Look, they'll reply in their own time," she continued. "It's probably still night there. Why don't you come back with me? I think Mother's weakening, you know." Max pressed his lips together.

"Your mother is the most stubborn woman I've ever met and that's saying a lot when you look at my family. Why can't she realise that we're not doing all this for fun?"

"I believe you." She looked up at him, the playful tone suddenly gone from her voice. "If she lets me, I'll help you as much as I can."

"Thanks." He was too tense even to attempt a smile at her. "I don't even know why I'm so worried now but there's something, something nagging against the back of my mind. Some clue I've missed." He resumed his pacing, unable to be still. "Come on, Kim," he murmured to himself. "Come on."

True to his word, Daniel allowed Lauren to take a turn at steering, or helming as he called it, and her mother watched with amusement as she concentrated fiercely on keeping the course with her tongue caught between her teeth while Daniel instructed her from behind. His eyes met her mother's in a smile.

"She's a quick learner," he nodded and Lauren glowed at his praise. "Perhaps she'd enjoy a dingy sailing course this summer? Lauren, this is where I thought we'd stop for lunch. Let me take over for a moment and I'll run her into this bay." She smilingly relinquished the wheel to his expert hands and looked out eagerly at the little cove lined with a concrete promenade, an old iron pier jutting out towards them. The two crewmen were busy rushing around furling the sails and dropping the anchor and then one of them at a sign from Daniel went below to organise lunch.

"Ever swum off a boat before?" Daniel asked her, pouring a drink for her mother from a tray held by the other crew member. There was even ice chinking in the glass. She shook her head. "Well, there's nothing like it for working up an appetite. Got your costume?" Lauren had indeed dressed in her swimming costume under her clothes as her mother had insisted on several layers in case the evening turned cool. She quickly pulled off the lifejacket he had insisted on her wearing and her shorts and shirt and looked cautiously over the side at the water that looked very clear, deep and green.

"Do I have to dive?" she asked doubtfully.

"Don't worry, there's a ladder." He opened a little door in the railings at the stern of the boat. "Should you swim with that pretty thing?" he asked, pointing to the bracelet. "You wouldn't want it to get lost. Why don't you give it to your mother to look after?" Her hand hovered over the catch for a moment. Perhaps she should? No.

"It'll be OK," she replied.

"Oh, it's got a strong fastening," her mother called out from the cushion where she was relaxing with a gin and tonic in her hand. "Have a good swim."

Lauren climbed down the ladder and slid gingerly into the water, coming up gasping at the cold. Daniel dived from the deck, hardly raising a splash as he cut into the sea.

"Race you round the boat!" he called as he surfaced, setting off at a fast breaststroke. He let her have the inside track and with a lot of splashing she reaped the rewards of Max's swimming lessons and managed to beat him back to the ladder. Laughing, he climbed back up. "You win. All I'm fit for is a large gin with your mother." She swam around a bit more, enjoying the sun and looking at the little fish swimming underneath her, and then climbed back up to join them. It was not as easy to get up the ladder as to get down it but one of the sailors had been watching and offered her a hand to swing her up the last few rungs.

"Have a canapé?" The other offered her a plate of food as she sat down dripping in the sun with her mother and Daniel and she selected an assortment of mouth-watering delicacies. It was like being a princess, she decided. If things had been different and her mother had married Daniel this is what her life would have been like. She caught herself with a gasp as she felt like a traitor to her real but unknown father. Had Grannie and Uncle El managed to persuade Shari to teach them how to use the Portal yet? Would they ever?

Lunch was delicious but long and Lauren was beginning to get a little bored by the time her mother and Daniel had finished.

"Fancy a swim to shore for an ice cream?" he asked.

"Give it half an hour for lunch to digest," Lauren's mother lectured, half asleep. "And put on some more sun cream."

Lauren climbed out of the cockpit and padded along the curved deck round the edge of the cabin to the front of the yacht where she sat with her legs dangling over the side wishing she had brought a book to read. The white cliffs of the Needles just peeped around the rocks at the end of the bay they were in and behind her Hurst Castle on the mainland looked close enough to jump to.

"Dangerous channel when you don't know it." The sailor spoke from behind her with a pleasant Isle of Wight accent. "The whole Spanish Armada couldn't get through here with the wind and tide against them."

"Are there lots of rocks?" she asked.

"Well, some, but it's the current that's so dangerous. Runs like the fastest river with the tide. Do you want to learn some sailors' knots?" Lauren spent the next half hour happily learning how to tie knots and was almost sorry when her mother roused herself.

"Well. I definitely need some exercise. How about that ice cream?"

"Where do you put the money in that bikini?" Lauren chuckled.

"Round my neck in this little pot." Her mother gave her a superior look and the two of them swam off together leaving Daniel on the yacht getting ready for the afternoon sail.

"This is really great, Mum," said Lauren as they wandered along the promenade licking ices. "Where are we going for dinner?"

"I've booked us in for a meal at a hotel just along the coast from Cowes," she said. "We can go in the car and it won't be too far to drive Daniel back to the ferry afterwards. Laura says they cook very good food."

"Yum," Lauren mumbled, finishing the last bit of cone.

Heather looked past the end of the beach and the low cliffs to where a bank of cloud was beginning to build from the horizon.

"We'd better head back," she warned. "It looks as if we might've seen the last of this lovely weather."

"Race you back to the boat." Lauren grinned and ran back down the beach into the water.

The freshening wind was ruffling the waves into little peaks and troughs by the time they were back at the yacht and they started to shiver with cold as they climbed back on board. Lauren was very glad her mother had made her pack her coat and jeans. They dried and dressed down in the cabin, which was beginning to bounce around in the most alarming manner. Lauren squealed as the yacht began to lean into the wind first one way and then the other, making them fall around and forcing them to hang on to the handrail really tightly as they climbed back up to the deck. She looked out and could only see green swirling waves too close to the edge of the railings as the boat heeled over.

"Wind's getting up!" Daniel was laughing into it, eyes sparkling. "There's your Needles, Lauren." The huge rocks rose steeply out of the water, looking too close and threatening with white breakers crashing on them and foaming up the near-vertical chalk cliffs. Lauren thought the red and white lighthouse at the end looked like a weird bird's nest with its helicopter pad on top.

"How did this blow up so fast?" Heather asked, clutching at the back of her seat as the yacht reared up over a wave.

"The sea's like that," Daniel grinned. "Always exciting and never your friend. Hold on!" He spun the wheel and Lauren lost her footing and lurched over to the other side of the cockpit as the boom swung over her head and the yacht turned and leaned on its other side. They bounced frighteningly and she suddenly had to shut her mouth tightly and climb up to the side where she leaned over and lost all of her lunch. He laughed again at her wan face as she clutched at her mother. "Good job you did that with the wind!" he called. "Better take her below again Heather, and give her a bowl." Hanging on to every handhold, miserably terrified she would lose her grip and be flung overboard, Lauren allowed herself to be herded back down by her mother and lay on a seat feeling terrible. She closed her eyes and despite being thrown around the bunk felt herself drifting to sleep with her mother's arm comfortingly around her. She half woke as the hatchway opened with a howl of wind and rain and Daniel's voice shouted down,

"It's a pretty bad squall! We're going to head for the mainland Heather—we won't find it easy to make it back along the Solent."

"If you think it's best," Heather replied weakly, beginning to feel queasy herself in the stuffy cabin and the door slammed shut again.

"What is it Mum?" Lauren asked sleepily.

"It's all right love. Just a storm but Daniel knows what to do."

"Storm Queen," Lauren mumbled as she drifted back to sleep. "She'll know what to do."

Max had sent his father's papers with Sharla, not wanting to go far away from the computer, but five cups of coffee later there was still no reply. He walked from one end of Laura's sitting room to the other feeling he knew and hated every cat on the walls, glancing through the window at the sun-drenched garden and wishing he dared to wait outside. At last the computer gave a little bleep and he instantly sat down and retrieved the incoming message.

"If el is axiel whos uncle daniel I no hes one of you elder people cos my hand buzzed wen we shook hands."

"No," Max breathed, his face suddenly draining of colour. He tapped a quick reply.

"Daniel Torsen is Mrs. Silva's boss. Could be trouble—Lauren's sailing with him—I need your friend's address in Florida quickly—Max."

Kim was evidently still at the computer as the address came back immediately.

"He's back?" Sharla had returned in her usual sudden way and perched herself on the back of the sofa.

"A picture. Could you find them from a picture?" Max snapped at her, beyond being surprised by her sudden appearance.

Possibly, she thought. Max typed back.

"Has your friend a photo of his house you could send as we may be able to use the Portal?"

There was a wait. Max resumed his pacing while Sharla watched him in increasing irritation. Eventually she grabbed his shoulder and forced him to stand still.

"What is your problem?" she asked angrily. "You're stalking about like a trapped lion."

He was almost too anxious to explain.

"The man who's taken Lauren and Heather sailing—we never imagined—he's one of us. But he's hidden it for years—he's known Lauren's family since before she was born. He must be responsible for everything!"

For once Sharla was completely serious.

"I think I should tell our parents," she said. "Lauren and Heather must be in terrible danger and he has the bracelet."

She disappeared.

Cowes harbour
Ken R.

Chapter 18
The Portal

How did we not realise?" Back at the house, Laura was muttering angrily. "Daniel, son of Dani? Torsen, Thor's son?"

"And the bandaged arm, Max, when he came to dinner. He didn't want to have to shake hands because he knew we would find out his secret!" El joined in the recriminations. Max was by the window, looking out at the darkening sky and hearing the first big raindrops begin to lash against the glass. He picked up the phone and dialled Heather's mobile number for the tenth time. It was still switched off or out of range. He leafed through the directory and tried another number.

"Hello, harbourmaster? Can you tell me if Storm Queen's back in berth yet? We're a bit worried as some friends are overdue…. not yet? Thank you…"

As he replaced the phone hopelessly Shari came over to him, took his hands and gave them a searching inspection.

"Not a bad job, Sharla," she said. "He repairs well." Laura made an impatient sound in the back of her throat and Shari reluctantly met her eyes. "I'm sorry Laura, I should have listened. I think I'd better teach you what you need to know."

"Oh Shari, thank you!" Laura was too tense to smile her relief.

"Not just you, Laura, all of you," she said decisively. "But you will need clear minds. If you want us to help your relations you will have to stop worrying about them for an hour or two."

"Max, if Lauren were in immediate danger I think she would contact me through the bracelet," his aunt tried to reassure him. "She always has before." He nodded slowly.

"Come around here and sit in a circle holding hands," Shari instructed. "Empty your thoughts and listen only to mine."

It was all so simple, Max thought later. Too simple. It was all in the wish to be somewhere else, in imagining it well enough to be there, a kind of longing in a special part of his brain and not in the conscious mind at all. If only he'd offered to drive Heather and Lauren to the harbour he would have seen the boat and could have transported to it immediately. If only they had persuaded Shari to teach them this sooner, Lauren could have learned as well.

"If onlies are a real waste of your life," Sharla said scornfully, reading his mind again.

"We have done this," he murmured, "when we came back to Lauren's house after the battle with Thor, but we never realised it. It must have been her longing to be back home that saved us then. If only she wants to come back enough, she could do it herself."

Keri sat tensely at Mark's desk, her turn on 'computer watch'. They had mailed off two photos: one of the family with Kim and Keri round the pool that they had snapped instantly with the digital camera and one of the house from the road. They had no idea if either would be of any use. Mark's mother came in and put a hand on her shoulder.

"You're a really great friend, you know," she said. "I don't think most of our own People could have held out against our questions so well for the sake of friendship. I'm sure Lauren will be all right." Keri looked up, tears hard to hide.

"What do they want to do to her? Why is the bracelet so important?"

"We think it's something to do with the spear charm Axiel used to create it and its contact with the crystal. Somehow, that moment in time when Thor and Lori died was frozen into the spear around Lori's neck. We think that because they died locked together not only Lori's memory is preserved there but that Thor somehow realised its power and saved some essence of himself when he knew he was lost. The rest of his power came from the crystal. If Dani his wife managed to hear his last frantic mindscreams and her son saved a piece of the crystal as Max and Lauren seemed to think he did, they may have been planning one thing all these centuries. To rejoin the charm and the crystal."

"But why wait all this time? Why now?"

"Because the circle was not complete until now. I think from what you've told me your friend's family must have been watched and hunted for many years despite their attempts to escape their past and pretend they were no more than human. It wasn't until Lauren was given the bracelet that Daniel Torsen would have recognised her as one of the mysterious figures that distracted his ancestor Thor from his killers. Then I think there was a desperate attempt to get hold of the bracelet and prevent that from ever happening."

"Could they have changed history?"

"Maybe. But thanks to you and Kim that didn't happen and instead he lost two people, who we think were descendants of Thor's most faithful servants. And then history fulfilled itself when Lauren and Max jumped back over three thousand years by accident and helped Lori and Axiel."

"But what's happening now?"

"Your friend is in great danger. Maybe we are all in great danger. And we can't do anything without the family of Sharra White-hair. Nothing except wait." She pursed her lips and sat back, eyes like Keri's watching the computer screen and waiting for something, anything, to happen.

Down in the stuffy cabin of the yacht, Heather was desperately trying not to panic. Holding her sleeping daughter with one arm, the other had to cling on tightly to the side of the bunk as the boat pitched and bounced and tipped from one side to the other. Her stomach kicked through her throat as they swung over to one side like the most hair-raising ride on a roller coaster and then she felt pressed to the floor as it lurched up towards her. Her lunch had gone the same way as Lauren's; she had only just made it to the small bathroom in time to be very sick and her head was swimming. She realised why so many people afflicted by seasickness felt they just wanted to die and was glad Lauren was so soundly asleep. How the tiny boat was to survive this battering she could not imagine. The door opened again with a scream of wind and a shower of spray that splashed down the steps.

"Are you still all right down here?" She could see Daniel's teeth gleaming in an unbelievable smile in the dim light.

"Are you still all right up there?" she riposted weakly.

"Not long to go," he grinned. "We'll be out of the channel in a bit."

"Daniel Torsen, I believe you're enjoying it!" she exclaimed.

"Only a little squall. You should try a real storm in the Pacific." He laughed again, raised a hand in a mock salute and swung back outside. It was like a radio being switched off when the door slammed behind him, the cabin a relative haven of peace. If only it would stop moving.

She had almost dozed herself as she knelt by the bunk holding onto Lauren when there was a sudden change of motion as the yacht turned at last into a river channel. There were sounds of feet on the deck above her and a pale shaft of sunlight gleamed through the rain-spattered window as the squall began to pass. Daniel, wet with rain but more alive with excitement and power than Heather had ever seen him before, opened the cabin door once again.

"Want to come up on deck? We've made it to home waters. You should see my house in a minute."

"I can't leave Lauren."

"She must be exhausted, poor girl, after all the swimming and then the seasickness. Let her rest." He looked at her white face and added, more sympathetically, "Come on Heather. You'll feel a lot better in the fresh air." Heather looked for a moment at her sleeping daughter and tucked the blanket around her before climbing back on deck. They were motoring up a river between banks of trees, a few yachts at anchor bouncing on the still choppy water, clattering ropes that gleamed white as a watery evening sun began to break through the scudding clouds. She looked at her watch.

"It looks as though you won't have to buy me dinner after all," Daniel smiled. She made a face.

"Don't mention food or I'll be sick again."

"You'll be all right when you get your feet on dry land. We can get cleaned up back at my house and then decide what to do." She nodded agreement, a mistake as it made her head whirl again, and leaned on the rail taking great gulps of fresh air. They turned up a side creek, so narrow that she was afraid the yacht would be grounded.

"Don't worry, it's deep enough now it's high tide," Daniel smiled. "There's my jetty." One crewman jumped off the boat with a rope to tie them up and held Heather's hands while she stepped thankfully onto the wooden landing stage, her legs shaking with the aftermath of her sickness and relief at being on dry land once more. The other, at a sign from their boss, climbed down to the cabin and reappeared with Lauren still sleeping in his arms. The back of a sprawling house set above terraces and gardens was visible at the top of a sweeping slope of lawn.

"Carry the girl up to the small green bedroom," Daniel ordered the man. "You can go with them Heather, and settle her down."

"It's not like Lauren to sleep like this," she said worriedly.

"Well, if you're still concerned when she's tucked up in bed we'll telephone for the doctor to come out and see her. But I expect she's just exhausted." He gave her a warm smile. "It is a rather drastic way of getting you to visit my home at last, but you are very welcome."

"It's beautiful." The old stone walls of the house gleamed a mellow gold in the evening sun as they walked across the wide lawn and through a formal garden heavy with the scent of lavender and old roses.

"It could all be yours, you know," he murmured, so quietly that she almost thought she had imagined it. Rather thankfully, not daring to meet his eyes, she left him in the hallway and followed the sailor and her daughter upstairs.

His mind still ringing from another hour's heavy tuition, Max was drinking a tenth cup of coffee and was again trying to contact the others on the phone. The harbourmaster had agreed to ask the air-sea rescue helicopter to try to get a sight of the missing yacht and Laura had found the telephone number of the restaurant Heather had booked. She tried it but was told they had neither appeared nor cancelled.

"I really need to go to Florida to get help from the Ericksons and talk to Kim and Keri. Do you think it would be possible?" Max asked Shari, who was looking even more exhausted than her three pupils.

"It's a big risk," she said. "Impossible for you, you're too new to it." He looked at Sharla and she stared back, green eyes wide.

"I could try," she said eventually. Her mother moved to her, face worried.

"Sharla, you have no idea where you are going. No one has ever tried to Portal to somewhere they've never been. You could end up in nothingness."

"Is it worth the risk, Max?" she asked without taking her eyes off him.

"Lauren is worth any risk. If you'll take me, I'll go." She swallowed once and gripped his newly healed hands so hard that he winced.

"Well, goodbye folks," she said lightly. "I hope we will see you again." They took one more long look at the photographs on the computer. On impulse Max put both arms around her and they gripped each other tightly.

"Come on then," he murmured.

Kim was taking his turn on computer watch when the next message came in.

"Expect Max and Sharla" was all it said. He raced outside to tell the others. They were all still there; another family had joined them with a couple of very young children. Mr. and Mrs. Erickson were busy flying trayloads of snacks and drinks around the garden, stopping them for their guests to help themselves, and all the adults were talking seriously together in hushed voices. Mark and his older sister Sandy were trying to organise all the children into teams for a game of no hands water polo.

"Hey, Kim!" Mark greeted him. "Coming in my team?"

"There's a message," he panted. "Someone's coming. Max and Sharla. The message said to expect them." The whole garden had hushed as he spoke and Kim turned bright red as he realised that everyone was staring at him.

"Expect them? How? Where?" Mark asked.

"The Portal. They must be using our photos to try to get here."

"Clear a space round the poolside," Jim Erickson ordered, and they all waited, almost holding their breaths, wondering where the two would appear.

"They're sure not rushing," one of the smaller children commented after a few minutes.

"Maybe they had a few things to collect first," his mother replied. "Wait a bit." But nothing happened. After about a quarter of an hour Mrs. Erickson shook her head to dispel the tension.

"Well, there's no sense standing here watching empty space," she said. "Kim, why don't you go back inside and ask them when, and where, they're planning on arriving?" Kim and Mark went back indoors and typed out an equally brief message.

"Expect max and sharla when?"

El read it out slowly to the others when it arrived. There was no way it could take longer than a few moments to travel, even as far as Florida. Laura's eyes squeezed closed in pain as she held out her arms wordlessly to Shari. Her old friend was shaking with disbelief. El screwed up the papers he was holding and lost his usual calm as he threw them savagely across the room.

"Curse Thor, curse Daniel Torsen and curse me for letting them go!" he shouted, before his own voice broke and he had to slump to a seat, his head in his hands.

Chapter 19
Daniel

"Oh, Mum, I'm so tired," Lauren grumbled, half asleep, as her mother ruthlessly pulled off her jeans and sweatshirt.

"You can go back to sleep in a moment, when you're undressed. Perhaps it's a good thing you wore this awful baggy T-shirt after all." Heather eyed it with distaste. "At least it will do instead of your pyjamas. You really ought to eat something before you go back to sleep."

"Ugh." Lauren yawned. "I'll be all right Mum. Just go downstairs and do the polite bit, please."

"I don't like to leave you."

"Oh Mum, what can happen to me here? Stop fussing." She curled up into a tight ball and closed her eyes again. Heather stood looking at her worriedly for a moment and then went into the ensuite bathroom to do what she could to freshen up, feeling a bit like a nervous teenager on a first date with someone she didn't want to get too close

185

to. It would be difficult to keep her old friend at arm's length in his own house, particularly when he was being so kind and thoughtful. She spent too long combing her hair and touching up her mascara, aware that she was putting off that moment when she had to go back down.

He was waiting for her at the foot of the stairs, changed, the only sign of his battle with the storm his still damp hair. His smile dispelled her awkwardness as if it had been a dream.

"Welcome again to our home." He bowed her into a large drawing room and she thought not for the first time how gracious but old-fashioned his manners were. "Heather, I would like you to meet my mother." She felt a quick burst of relief that she would not be alone with him and held out her hand to the woman coming towards her, a tall, handsome woman, very like her son. The shock of their touching shuddered up her arm and she gasped aloud.

"Ah," Daniel said softly. "A complication."

Laura was the first to force herself to recover rather shakily from their outburst of grief.

"There's nothing we can do for Sharla and Max", she said, her voice flat as if all her energy had drained away with her tears, "but we must not forget Heather and Lauren."

"If they survived the storm," El said thickly, "where would he take them?"

"His home?" Laura suggested. "Perhaps Heather has his address somewhere." She ran upstairs, every step reminding her of how Max would leap up two or three at a time, and reappeared a few moments later with a diary in her hands. "Lucky she's travelled light for their day on the water," she murmured as she leafed through the book but there was no record of a private address for Daniel. They tried the telephone enquiry service only to be told the number was ex-directory and eventually with no other ideas they sat down in hopeless silence watching the daylight fade outside, silently remembering their lost children. They were roused from their thoughts by the urgent ringing of the telephone. Laura picked it up and they saw a sudden change in her expression as she clutched the phone to her ear.

"Max!" she exclaimed. "Oh Max!"

Max and Sharla had shot from the darkness of their journey into brightness and noise. Motor horns blared and as they blinked, dazed, the driver of a car leaned out of the window and yelled a sentence of unprintable American at them. Max staggered and pulled Shari off the highway onto the pavement where they leaned against a traffic post, panting.

"Well, it doesn't look like Mark's house, but we're still alive!" Sharla gasped. They both burst out laughing in relief, and swung each other round in circles at the side of the road. Max grabbed at the first person that passed them.

"Where are we?" he asked.

"Get outa here you freaks!" The reply was shouted. They burst into hysterical laughter again. Max realised that he had become so used to Sharla's bizarre appearance that he had forgotten how strange she would look to ordinary people. Her clothes today consisted of what looked like a red bikini covered by a semi-transparent ankle-length dress embroidered with leaves and red ankle boots with preposterously high heels. She had dyed her beaded hair a startling shade of green to match the leaves on the dress. People were beginning to stop and stare at them from a safe distance and she began to make faces at them. The third man Max asked called out,

"Downtown Jacksonville," avoiding their eyes. That almost set them off again.

"Right city, wrong area. I don't suppose you brought any dollars with you?" Max choked.

"Not even any British money!" Sharla gurgled. "No pockets even! I don't really do money. How about you?"

"Nothing," Max replied, sobering up. "Not much use, are we? I guess if we don't want to go home with our tails between our legs we'll have to use our wits." He smoothed his hair in an attempt to look more respectable and tugged at his shirt, wishing he had changed into something more formal than his old trousers and trainers. "Do that mindshield thing, Sharla. I don't think Downtown Jacksonville's quite ready for your fashion sense." She looked around thumbing her nose at any curious passers-by; when it looked as if no one was watching she faded into invisibility. Max stood her behind some traffic lights while he hailed a cab and they were soon speeding out to the suburbs.

"You're not totally useless," Sharla commented, closing her eyes and resting her boots delicately on the back of the driver's cab. "I'd never have remembered that address."

"I just hope the Ericksons don't mind paying for the taxi!" Max murmured.

Someone shaking her by the shoulder woke Lauren with a jump and recognising the woman who came to help clean their house she blearily tried to remember why she was not in her own bed.

"Mrs. Cleaver! What are you doing here?" she asked. "Where am I?"

"Mr. Torsen's house," the woman replied shortly. "Here, this is for you. You need to get some food inside you after being seasick."

"Where's Mum?"

"She's having dinner with the boss. Adults only. Come on, sit up." Lauren struggled upright and took the cup. It was tomato soup, not too hot. She gulped it down, feeling suddenly hungry, but even before she had finished the last sip she felt her eyes beginning to close again. She emptied the last dregs into her mouth, handed the cup back to the waiting Mrs. Cleaver and settled back on the pillows. She never even heard the door close.

Kim and Keri were feeling more helpless than they had ever felt in their life. They had never met Max but Lauren's e-mails had made him feel like an old friend and they knew how much she had come to rely on him. The Elder families, joined by yet more people as the word spread, were sitting rather glumly round the pool, shocked by this outcome of their offer of help.

"Walter's going to call out the company jet," Mrs. Erickson told her husband heavily. "Are you ready to go?"

"Guess so," he replied unenthusiastically. "That poor kid still needs help."

"Lauren never talked about him much but I remember her saying once that her mum's boss wanted to marry her," Keri whispered to her brother. "Surely he wouldn't hurt them?" Kim made a disbelieving face.

"He must've lied about everything else. Maybe he lied about that too."

They were roused from their silence by the urgent ringing of the doorbell.

"Who else are we expecting?" Jim Erickson asked impatiently and went to answer it.

"Mr. Erickson?" The young man on the doorstep was standing there apologetically, looking over his shoulder at the driver of a city cab who was having a shouting match with someone in the back seat. A girl who looked as if she was dressed for the circus stormed out of the vehicle, slamming the door so violently behind her that they were surprised the window remained intact.

"If you expect people to pay for a ride in your tin pot little cab when all you can do is insult them, you've got another think coming!" she screeched.

"I ain't seen much sign yet of you payin', lady!" the driver shouted back, leaning out of his window as she stalked up to the front door. A sudden smile creased Jim Erickson's sun-tanned face. "Don't tell me!" he laughed. "Max and Sharla?"

"How do you do?" Sharla spoke through her teeth. "I hope you're not going to pay that foul-mouthed idiot. Do you know what he called me?"

Max tried to make shushing gestures with his hands that Sharla totally ignored, and Jim hastily shoved a handful of notes through the window to the driver who revved his engine and reversed quickly back out of the driveway. Sharla turned and glared at the cab as it accelerated up the road and seconds later there was a bang and screech of brakes as a front tyre exploded. Max grabbed hold of her shoulders and mouthing a silent apology to his host marched her into the house, still complaining loudly. Once the front door was shut behind them she calmed down and allowed Jim to lead them through the house to the pool. The assembled families broke into a ripple of applause as the couple walked through the garden doors. Mark snapped away with the digital camera.

"A historic moment," said Erickson. "The first time all the families of the Alliance have met together for three thousand years or more." Max allowed himself to be hugged and his hand to be shaken by everyone while his eyes searched for Keri and Kim. He picked them out, standing shyly back from the crowd, recognisable because they looked so alike.

"We need to pool our knowledge," he said. "This feels too much like a party while Lauren's in danger."

"We've thought about that." Erickson clapped him on the shoulder. "Three of us should come back with you. If you can manage the transport?" Sharla broke off from complaining to the oldest aunt about the manners of modern taxi drivers, who was nodding wisely despite being almost stone deaf and completely unable to understand a word of Sharla's fast South African accent.

"Whatever," she said ungraciously.

"I'll come, and Annie here, a direct descendant of Anika of the Alliance. She has a particular skill of mindsearching. If she is within a few miles of your family she should be able to track them." A serious looking woman in her middle years lifted a hand in greeting. "The other is my wife's father, Lou Henrikson. He's spent three hundred years studying every record we have about Thor. Come inside with us and we can make some plans."

"You can't go without us!" Kim leaped forwards. "If Lauren's a prisoner, we have to help. Please, please?" He had grabbed hold of Max's arm and was clinging like a leech. Keri stood still, huge pleading eyes fixed on Max.

"We can't take children," Sharla said firmly.

"I'm afraid we all stopped thinking of these two as children a long time ago," Max said, with a half smile at Keri.

"Your minds are as strong as many of ours," Mark's mother agreed. "But I don't know what I could say to your parents."

"Let me phone them," Kim begged. "I'm sure they'd let us stay another day or two." Max clapped a hand to his head.

"Phone!" he exclaimed. "If you don't mind, I'd better phone our parents. They must think we're dead!"

Heather was trying to hide the cold fear that had filled her when she had touched Daniel's mother's hand and realised that she was one of the Elder People and therefore so was her son. Everything Daniel had ever said and done was now filled with sinister purpose and she found it difficult to recognise the handsome figure sitting opposite her at the dining table as her old friend. She pecked at course after course of the meal with no appetite, running plans for escape through her mind. Daniel's mother had said little but hardly took her eyes off Heather, an uncomfortable stare. Daniel kept up a relaxed conversation without answering any questions, trying to pretend everything was normal.

"I have been hoping for a long time, Mother, to bring Heather back here as my wife," he said suddenly. Heather choked on the wine she was sipping.

"You know why that could never happen."

"You can't think that derelict of a husband of yours will ever come back?" The mask was almost slipping, anger lurking behind his eyes.

"I think you would know that better than I." Heather showed that she could give anger back. "I don't know what you've done with him but I will never forget him, or forgive you."

"Forgiveness?" Daniel's mother broke in. "What do you know of grief for a murdered husband after your feeble seven years? My husband would have made me Queen of the world. What do you know of revenge? I will never be satisfied until all your miserable family lies dead at my feet!" Suddenly realising the full implications of this, Heather jumped up, tipping her chair to the ground with a crash.

"You are Dani, and you have never died from that moment to this," she whispered. "And you..." she looked at Daniel. "You are the boy Max saw on that mountain top." Daniel, Thor's son, spread his hand so that his ring burned brightly as it caught the light.

"Preserved by the power of the crystal I saved that night. And now at last I have everything I need to bring back my father. I have not one but two of Axiel and Lori's heirs, I have Lori's amulet on the bracelet, I have access to the Grove of Power and the spear that killed him and tomorrow night the sun, moon and planets will be in the same position as they were that night." He raised his arms to the ceiling and his gesture was echoed by a peal of thunder from outside the house. "Tomorrow the Lord of Storms will return!"

"You will not kill them until I have the rest of their family," his mother spat. "I will not be satisfied until I have slaughtered every descendant of that traitor Axiel. They will not come without these two as bait."

"You can't hurt Lauren!" Heather gasped. "She's only twelve!" Daniel turned back towards her, madness in his eyes.

"I remember being twelve. I was only twelve when I saw my father murdered in front of me on a mountain top." His hand reached out and rested gently on her shoulder. "Don't worry. You'll soon forget them. I can help you forget anything."

Heather screamed her daughter's name.

Lauren heard that scream in her mind and struggled as if through deep water to try to get back. She was somewhere different, not in the green bedroom. But it was too much for her and she collapsed back to sleep.

Kim and Keri had a few problems persuading their mother to let them stay with Mark for the rest of the week. She insisted on bringing them some extra clothes and taking back their dirty underwear.

"Oh Mum!" Kim protested.

"Well it's all right for you. I suppose Mark could lend you things. But do think of your sister," she grumbled. Kim finally saw the funny side.

What heroes, about to embark on a great quest, ever had their mothers chasing after them with clean underwear? he spluttered to Keri in his mind.

Remember what a smoothie Daniel Torsen was that time we met him and we thought he was Uncle El? she replied. *I wouldn't want to meet him looking grimy, even if it is only to fight him.*

Mrs. Erickson insisted on their mother staying to eat with them, the barbecue excuse coming true as none of the assembled guests wanted to leave before they had news of Lauren and her mother. The oldest aunt found her quickly and was holding her arm.

"Very talented children, yours," she was saying loudly. "I haven't seen such talented humans since 1652." Mrs. Erickson came over swiftly.

"Come along Auntie," she shouted into her ear with a wink at Mrs. Kirby. "Lizzie needs you to help cut up some sandwiches." She took her away and Kim and Keri exchanged a relieved look.

"Well, it's good to know that other people have embarrassing relations," their mother whispered quietly, laughing.

"Great pool, isn't it Mum?" said Kim, trying to make her look away as one of the tiniest children pointed at a bowl of ice cream which started to wobble towards him through the air. His father grabbed it and gave it to him quickly.

"Whoever is that girl?" Mrs. Kirby asked, catching sight of Sharla muttering impatiently with Max and Jim Erickson in a corner near the house.

"Steak sandwich, Mum?" Keri handed her a plate, sure she was about to pass a comment on Sharla's weird appearance that might make her lose her very volatile temper if she happened to be mind reading.

"Thank you." Jo Kirby took a bite. "Mmm, this is good. Americans really know how to barbecue." Kim tried not to let his jaw drop open as Mark winked at him from behind her back and juggled two burgers with his mind before tossing them into rolls he was holding open and handing one each to the twins.

"Good to have you here Mrs. K," he grinned ingenuously.

"Well, it's very kind of your parents to invite me," she replied. "But I mustn't stay. Kim and Keri's father will be wondering where I've got to."

"I think I need some ketchup," Keri muttered, giving him an evil look out of slitty eyes. Mark twitched a finger for the bottle of sauce.

"Right beside you," he laughed.

"Well, I never saw that!" Mrs. Kirby exclaimed happily, taking some herself.

Rat! Keri couldn't help giggling. Kim tried to copy Mark by reaching out for the mustard.

"Kim!" His mother suddenly grasped his shoulder. "Make sure your sister doesn't get left out. There aren't any girls her age here." The mustard dropped into the pool as Kim stammered,

"Of course Mum," and Keri echoed,

"I'm fine, Mum. Mark's really nice."

By the time she was ready to leave, both twins felt as though their nerves were in rags and escorted her to the front door with great relief.

"Now, don't forget to clean your teeth," she warned them as she left. Keri closed the door and leaned against it raising her eyes to heaven. Max was laughing from beside the stairs.

"Mothers!" Kim exploded.

"Just be glad she's here to care," he replied with a lift of one eyebrow, suddenly serious.

"Come on," Sharla said impatiently. "Max can take you two and I'll manage the adults."

"You're guinea pigs," Max smiled at them. "I haven't tried this with passengers before. Get some coats. When we left the weather in England was awful."

"Wait," Mr. Erickson said firmly. "It's afternoon here, pretty late in England. "We need a few hours sleep. We'll be no good to anyone half dead with tiredness. Get upstairs. My wife will wake us in five hours." Reluctantly they all saw the sense in this and allowed themselves to be led to bedrooms where they managed to sleep while Saturday ended in Florida and Sunday morning began in Britain.

Chapter 20
The Manor

Lauren half woke again, too sleepy to panic as she found herself sightless in a very dark room. As she stared fuzzily into blackness a rectangle of window began to gleam white as the moon scudded out from behind a thick blanket of cloud. She yawned, trying to keep her eyes open. There was some reason why she should struggle, some reason…

She opened them again. A low morning sun was slanting through the window silhouetting thick metal bars, bathing the bed in dazzling yellow light. She had thought it was the moon. She narrowed her eyes against the brightness and tried to clear her thoughts but somehow couldn't remember why she was there or even where she was. She looked at herself and wondered vaguely why she was wearing a T-shirt instead of her pyjamas and then her eyes closed by themselves again.

She was being shaken. Protesting, she forced her eyes open again. A very pale man was kneeling by her bed shaking her shoulders; she had never seen anyone so white, as if he had not been out in the light for years. She tried to turn over and go back to sleep but he wouldn't let her.

"They've brought us some breakfast. You should wake up." She blinked again. His speech was slurred, he had a horrible long, straggly beard and he smelt awful. She choked and turned her head away, foul-tasting bile flooding into her mouth. If she hadn't been so tired she would probably have screamed.

"Who are you?" Backing as far away from him as possible on the narrow bed, Lauren managed to speak although it was difficult to move her mouth.

"I… I… I'm me," he mumbled. Can't remember. Who're you?" She had to think for a moment.

"Lauren. I'm Lauren." He pushed a piece of dry toast into her hand and she nibbled, realising she was very hungry.

"Lauren." he repeated, the word slurred, like a slow motion recording. "Pretty name. Pretty girl. I think I knew a Lauren once." His hand brushed against hers as he passed her another piece of toast. It buzzed a bit. That was supposed to mean something, wasn't it? She was too tired to chew. She had to go back to sleep. She pushed him away and tried to settle back.

"Mother's bracelet," he said. "You've got a pretty bracelet like my mother."

Grannie… she thought vaguely as she drifted back to sleep.

Laura sat bolt upright in bed, certain she had heard her granddaughter's voice. *Lauren!* she called in her mind. But there was nothing else. A dream, maybe? She looked around. The summer day was dawning brightly. Time to get up. She dressed and went downstairs where she found Shari already waiting for her.

"Better wake up that idle brother of yours." She raised her thin eyebrows. "If you can. Someone should do something about his nasal passages. He sounds like a grumbling volcano."

"Sharla and Max will be back soon. They said around sunrise." Laura poured the coffee she needed to be able to start the day properly. "We have to make some plans. We don't want another fiasco like those two children setting off for America with nothing in their pockets. And we still need to find Daniel's address. EL!" she shouted upstairs, pushing her voice with a heavy nudge from her mind.

The volcano gave a loud snort and quietened, and soon afterwards El came down.

"Come on Sharla," her mother muttered to herself, looking out of the window to where she expected her to appear. "We need to get on now." A moment later, as if they had heard her, the garden was full of people.

"Kim! Keri!" Laura called out in surprise, and ran outside to greet them. "Now I know we'll get Lauren back!"

"This is Jim, Anika and Lou." Max escaped with difficulty, wincing, from the hard hug and thumping on the back his father was giving him. "Dad, Lou's got about as many old history files as you but they're all on computer."

"Hmmmph." El eyed the other man through bristling eyebrows. "Not so much of a dinosaur as me, eh?"

"Oh I was," Lou laughed, his face crinkling up like an old elephant's hide. "But our families have always tried to move with the times and Jim here's brought our company into the heart of the computer industry. I didn't have a prayer!" El chuckled back, pulled out a chair for his new friend and they all sat round the large kitchen table to plan.

"Daniel's address?" Max asked in surprise when they told him their problem. "I suppose you tried the laptop? It is Heather's work computer." The older generation exchanged glances.

"Well, we were around for a while before they invented the things," El rumbled looking embarrassed.

"About a hundred and seventy years," Laura muttered.

"I'll look," Kim said eagerly. "Where is it? Sitting Room?" He disappeared, to return a few minutes later waving an address scribbled on a piece of paper. "Got it."

"New Forest," Laura said. "Old West Dean Manor. Someone will know where to find that."

"Make sure we take some money this time," Max reminded them dryly.

"Definitely," agreed his father. "Portal or no Portal, we'll need a taxi to help us find the house."

"Maps," added Laura. "It's bound to be on a map."

"Telephones," said Lou. "Make sure we've got each other's numbers in case we get separated." Max nodded.

"And Heather's, just in case she can finally answer." His eyes went suddenly bleak. "I just hope they're there."

Lauren suddenly woke to complete recall. She was sitting up on a bed, sunshine flooding through the window, with Daniel next to her holding her arm so that the bracelet glinted in the sunbeams. Her first smile at him froze as she saw his expression, no longer friendly and relaxed but intent, his silver-grey eyes hard.

"I need you to take this off now, Lauren," he said. She tried to pull away.

"No. No. Why am I here? Where's Mum?"

"Oh, she's having a lovely time. Quite the lady of the manor. She's having breakfast with my mother. Now, Lauren, take off the bracelet."

"No!" she whispered. He was much too strong for her to get free.

"Don't hurt her." The straggly man pawed feebly at Daniel's arm. "Don't hurt pretty girls." Daniel grinned like a wolf.

"I see you've met your father. I hope you're impressed. Your mother wasn't. She quite thinks she's made a mistake waiting for him all these years. Now, TAKE OFF THAT BRACELET!" Lauren was gasping with pain as he twisted her arm. Frustrated, he grabbed the bracelet himself to pull it off her hand. A shock like a soundless explosion threw him backwards and he reeled away clutching his hand under his arm. The rage on his face as he turned made Lauren shrink back on the bed, trying to flatten herself against the wall as his face pushed closer to hers. He hissed a breath, fighting for control.

"Don't worry, one way or another that bracelet will come off your hand. It would have been a lot easier for all of us if you'd given it to your mother on the boat—you would just have had a nice painless swimming accident." Lauren's body turned to ice as she remembered how nearly she had taken it off for that swim. "Now you'd better go back to sleep." His eyes seemed to bore into her for a moment and she felt hers growing heavy again. The last thing she remembered was the pale man, her father, stroking her arm gently and repeating over and over,

"Don't go back to sleep pretty Lauren, don't leave me alone. Don't leave me alone…"

Her grandmother had her arms wrapped round her ears and her face looked suddenly old and crumpled. "It's Lauren. She's screaming. She sounds terrified!"

"Ask her where she is!"

"Too late. She's gone. Completely gone."

"She's all right?" Max gripped her arms so hard that she winced. "She's not…" He couldn't bring himself to say it. Laura shook her head helplessly.

"She's just gone," she said. "Come on. It's time we got over there."

"Lauren! Lauren, wake up." Someone was shaking her again, and calling her name. She forced her eyes open. The shock of seeing someone completely unexpected made her wake up more fully.

"Tania!" she exclaimed. "What on earth? Where are we?"

"You're at Mr. Torsen's house. My dad works for him. What are you doing here? What's he doing to you?" The questions were too much for Lauren, and she started to drift away again. Tania slapped her face. "Stop it Lauren. You've got to get out of here. Wake up!"

"I can't. Go away." Everything was dark, just an annoying something keeping her from complete oblivion. Tania stopped in frustration.

"Hey, you!" She poked Lauren's father, who was sitting with his hands round his knees, rocking to and fro. "Old man! You've got to get her out of here!"

"Me?" He looked up. She poked his shoulder.

"Yes you. Help me get her out of here!" She pulled him up. "You've got to save her."

"Me save pretty girl?" he slurred. She almost had to force his arms around Lauren but eventually he had lifted her off the bed. "Where do you want us to go?"

"Anywhere. Away. GO!" She pushed him out of the room and along a passage towards a back door and as he stumbled up a few steps into the garden she relocked the door of their cell and threw the key hard into the bushes.

"There Mr. High and Mighty Torsen," she snarled to herself. "That'll take you a while to find."

Alex Silva wandered aimlessly across the lawns not knowing where he was, or who he was, or that it was his own daughter he carried in his arms. He found a path leading through a small wood and staggered a little further before collapsing at the bottom of a large oak tree.

"Safe here," he said, pulling her head on to his lap. "Safe now, Lauren."

It was lunchtime when Torsen's men discovered they could not get into the room with a meal for the two prisoners. In a panic, for they knew his temper, they looked through the window and could see no one. They knew their duties and one of them went straight away to tell him.

"When I find out who is responsible, he or she will be sorry they were ever born," he said coldly. "Search the grounds."

There were guards everywhere. Kim and Keri were trying to peer through the huge iron gates guarding the entrance to the old manor house without being seen by the searching men kicking through the undergrowth. Some were carrying guns, some two way radios.

"There are too many of them." El saw no point in risking discovery if they were to rescue his niece.

"Is she even here?" Laura worried. "We can't waste time if she's not."

"Let me try," Anika offered. "Which of you knows her mind best?"

"Keri, I should think," suggested Max, looking at his aunt to see if she agreed. Laura nodded.

"Keri, would you link minds with me to see if we can find her?"

"Anything if it's for Lauren." The older woman held out both her hands and Keri took them cautiously, not sure what to expect.

"Now, think hard of your friend. You'll feel my mind with yours. Try not to let it disturb you." Keri closed her eyes and built up a picture of Lauren in her mind. Suddenly she felt Anika's thoughts inside her head and almost broke the link. It felt wrong.

"Please let me do this," Anika said quietly. "It's the only way we can find her." Keri swallowed hard and tried to pretend it was Kim with their familiar twin connection. She tried again. The picture she had in her mind of Lauren began to change. Somehow she was wearing only a dirty T-shirt that was nearly as long as her knees and she looked asleep. "Yes," Anika whispered. "She is there, somewhere in the grounds. But she sleeps." She let her mind slip away from Keri's.

"We must get inside," Keri pleaded with the others.

"We can't break through in force," said Jim. "We could try to hide ourselves from humans by creating a mind shield but we don't know if all of them are human and if Torsen's there he could break it easily.

"We can't get past this fence at all without letting off alarm bells," Laura said grimly. "He has Wards on his boundaries like mine at home but ten times stronger. Anyone who crosses uninvited would trip them."

"But she looked so awful." Keri was nearly in tears. "We can't just leave her there. And there was someone with her. A really horrible-looking man."

"Don't worry, we'll find a way," Max's irrepressible grin was reappearing; he was so relieved that Lauren was still alive that nothing seemed impossible. "Why don't we all spread out and look for anything that would help us?"

Kim and Keri decided to stick together and started to walk along the wall of the estate. After a while, the wall turned into a barbed wire fence that curved towards the river through a tangle of brambles and they could see the mast of a large sailing boat sticking up over the top of thick bushes at the edge of a huge sloping lawn.

"Hey, Kim, look!" she whispered suddenly. A familiar but completely unexpected figure was kicking through the short wet grass.

"Tania! What the hell's she doing here?" Kim exclaimed and before Keri could stop him he had put his fingers to his mouth and let out a piercing whistle. She turned and looked in their direction. There didn't seem to be any of the men about so he stood up waving; to his surprise she came running across to the edge of the fence.

"Thank God someone's come!" she cried. Her face was grubby with tears and she had a black eye.

"What are you doing here?" Keri asked.

"Dad works for Mr. Torsen. Mum's in hospital. He beat her up and then he made me come here with him so I wouldn't tell the police. Listen, you've got to help. There's something bad going on here. That man's had Lauren and a funny old man locked up in there and I think he's drugged them or something because they're really weird, and I think he's going to do something awful to them. I heard him talking to Dad. I let them out and they're all looking for them and if he finds out it was me I'm dead!"

"You always hated Lauren!" Keri exclaimed.

"Oh, that's only school. She used to be such a wimp with that boring hairstyle and it was so unfair that she always had money and a smart mum and no father. And Dad told me I had to be horrible to her and he'd give me a new stereo if I managed to nick her bracelet. This is different. I think old Torsen's really going to murder her or something. And they've got the boat shed stacked full of drugs they've smuggled in on that yacht of his and Dad's really angry and I don't know how Mum is." Tania wiped her nose with her wrist and sniffed hard.

"You'd better come with us, Tan. Lauren's family's all here, looking for her. You've got to help." Kim stepped on the bottom wire while Keri pulled up the middle one to help Tania crawl through. *I hope that didn't set off their alarm!* he said silently to Keri. *I think we're on to a winner. A phone call to the drugs squad might distract them for long enough for us to get in and find Lauren.* Laura and Jim agreed.

"No one will track us getting in if there are police cars everywhere," Jim said excitedly. "Young what's your name… Tania… d'you feel brave enough to tell the cops what you know?" She nodded.

"If you can keep my Dad off me."

"Don't you worry, young Tania." Uncle El was already pressing buttons that seemed too small for his huge fingers. "You stick with me. I'll make sure no one harms you." He spoke urgently to the emergency services and then to the police while the others all watched, tension in their faces. He rang off and looked down at them. "Now all we have to do is keep our heads down and wait for the cavalry," he said.

Chapter 21
The Chase

It did not take the team of searchers more than an hour to find the two escapees. Lauren was still sleeping on the wet grass and her father had forgotten why they were trying to leave so the men picked Lauren up and dragged Alex straight into the large drawing room where Daniel Torsen was drinking tea with his mother and Heather.

"Not on the carpet!" he drawled and dismissed his employees with a wave of his hand, leaving the two grubby prisoners lying on the polished wood floor near the door. Lauren awoke at a snap of Daniel's mind.

"Oh, hello Lauren," her mother said in surprise. "Have you been having a nice game?" Lauren sat up blinking, barefoot in a dirty T-shirt and with hair that had not been brushed for two days.

"Mum!" she wailed.

"That's nice, dear," Heather said calmly. "Would you like a cup of tea? And your friend?" Her husband pulled himself to his hands and knees, staring through half-closed eyes and his filthy straggle of black hair.

"Heath… Heather?"

"Sit down!" Daniel snapped and he sank back to the floor. "No Heather, they don't want tea. They're too dirty. In a moment, I'm taking them on a little trip."

"That's all right then." She arranged herself back on the sofa and sat sipping from the elegant china teacup. Lauren's sudden hope at seeing her mother died like a pricked balloon as she looked at her sitting there in a new dress, beautiful and distant as a statue.

"Mum. Please, please take me home," she whispered through starting tears, trying to crawl over towards her. Daniel's eyes flickered in a sudden amused smile and he twitched one finger at her that made her tongue freeze in her mouth and her legs and arms turn to jelly.

"Where are the others?" Dani's deep voice broke in. Her son shrugged.

"They're obviously too stupid to trace our address, even when I made sure Heather had it on her laptop."

"You can't take these two away until the others come."

"I have to take them when the time is right. You know that. We can't risk anything going wrong. Your revenge will have to wait. Perhaps it would be a greater revenge for them to lose these members of their family and to have to live with their failure." Dani was not convinced. She pursed her lips and glared at the two prisoners. Suddenly, Daniel felt the shock of one of his Wards being broken. A smile of triumph lifted his mouth but did not reach his eyes.

"They're here," he said.

Max? Grannie Laura? Lauren struggled harder than she thought possible against the weakness that filled her. She had to stop them falling into Daniel's trap. She staggered to her feet and made for the window but only managed a few steps before he stopped her with a thought.

"Oh no, you're going nowhere."

She fell to her knees and stared at the window in helpless panic, waiting for them to come, knowing that even their joint mindpowers would be useless against Daniel's Crystal-enhanced strength.

The silence was suddenly broken by the sirens of police cars as they came screaming down the drive. Daniel exclaimed with anger.

"I haven't got time to deal with all this," he snapped. "I'll take them to the Grove now." His mother grabbed his arm.

"No Daniel! Not yet! I won't let you." She clung to his arm and he had to drag her along with him as he crossed the room to look outside. A fleet of police cars swung round the bend and pulled up with a scrunch of gravel.

"There are too many! We can't waste the time." Still dragging his mother behind him, he grabbed a handful of Lauren's shirt and Alex's grimy collar.

"Not yet! They're coming!" his mother kept screaming. "You can hold the police off!"

"You stupid woman!" he exclaimed. "You'll risk everything for the sake of your pathetic vengeance. When Father is back, he will show them what vengeance is!" There was the sound of running feet and hammering on the front door and then a few gunshots from down towards the river. Dani grabbed her son's arm.

"No! No! I can't face Thor while any Silvas are left alive!" Lauren never knew where the knife in Daniel's hand had come from; she gasped in shock as he let go of her and delivered a swift stab to his mother's body. Her grip relaxed and she reeled away to collapse on the sofa next to Heather. Released, he regained his hold on the two prisoners and looked down at her for a moment, his face expressionless.

"She's been irritating me for centuries," he muttered and cast a burning glance at where Lauren's mother was sipping her tea, completely unconcerned. "Wait for me, Heather. I will come back for you, when you're no longer this man's wife."

Too frozen with horror to move, Lauren felt herself vanish into blackness.

Max had rushed ahead of the others with his usual impatience and followed the police cars down the drive, keeping out of sight behind the line of bushes, and then sprinting across the gravel mentally raising the vision shield that would make most people unable to see him. If Lauren was there, where would she be? He sent out a pulse of awareness, searching desperately for some trace of his cousin's thoughts behind the ancient stone frontage of the huge house at the end of the long gravel drive but finding nothing. He ran to the tall front windows and grabbing the stone sill he managed to balance his toes on a ledge in the wall so that he could just see through into a richly-furnished drawing room. He was in time to see Daniel apparently push his mother away from him and grab hold of Lauren and a ragged skeleton that could only be his cousin Alex. About to crash through the window, he remembered a quicker, less destructive way and opened a Portal into the room. Too late; he swore bitterly to himself, slamming his fist against the wall as he realised he was a fraction of a second too late and the three had vanished. He looked around in a hopeless search for some clue to where they had gone.

"Oh, Max." Heather, sitting on the sofa, gave him a bright smile. "How nice to see you. Would you like a cup of tea?" He stared, horrified, at her normality amongst the crashes, bangs and shouts of a police search with the body next to her, mouth still open in a last scream, sightless eyes glaring, the knife handle sticking out of her chest.

"Where's Lauren?" he snapped.

"Oh, she's just popped out for a moment with Daniel. I think they said they were going somewhere called The Grove."

"You'd better come with me before the police find you here," said Max grimly, grabbing her round the waist. He opened a Portal and in a heartbeat they were back with his aunt outside the grounds. "I don't know what we can do with this one, but I couldn't leave her there!" he panted. Heather smoothed her clothes and looked around vaguely.

"Hello Laura. You're here too. I don't know what Max has done with the teapot."

"Where's Lauren?" Laura ignored her daughter-in-law. They could try to help her later.

"The Grove. With Daniel and Alex."

"What!" Shari all but shrieked. "All the centuries we thought we had it protected and that devil knew all the time?"

"The Grove? It still exists?" Jim Erickson grabbed Shari's arm in excitement.

"I hope so," she replied grimly. "Come on. There's no time to waste."

Lauren could still not move or use her mind powers when they arrived in the Grove but she felt she knew that place intimately and lay helplessly on the soft grass remembering the three times she had been there before in Lori's memory. It was almost unchanged, the burning and destruction of her last visit only a three and a half thousand year old nightmare.

Daniel left the two of them crumpled on the ground as he strode into the centre of the glade and fell to his knees, drinking in the energy of that magical place. His eyes shone; even his hair seemed to crackle with power and the crystal ring blazed dazzlingly on his finger. He looked invincible. Lauren knew that she too could use that power but somehow the mindspell Daniel had bound her with stopped her being able even to try. He stood up and searched around unhurriedly with his eyes, then held out his hand and Lori's shining stone spearhead, still perfect after more than thirty centuries, flew to it. He extended the other hand and was grasping a thin wooden shaft, split at the end and coated in some sort of resin, which he bound on to the spearhead. Then he crossed back to his prisoners, pulled Alex's hands roughly together, and fastened them tightly behind his back. He tied his feet.

"I would really like you to have your mind back, to savour your last moments." Lauren thought he was growing more and more wolflike. The caring friend, always with the perfect smile and the perfect clothes and the perfect present, was completely gone—as if he had never existed. She bent all her will to the bracelet to try once more to make her grandmother hear her but it was no good. She was too weak. As Daniel grinned triumphantly showing too many teeth the vagueness in her father's eyes began to clear and horror took its place.

"Meet your daughter, Silva," Daniel laughed. "She thinks you smell." Alex looked down at his unkempt and thin body and a small smile managed to twitch his mouth.

"I'd have been a bit worried about her if she didn't notice." His voice grated as if from disuse. "I'm sure she realises who's to blame." Lauren tried to give him a smile back to show her support.

"I think I should make sure they know I've been here," Daniel muttered to himself and twisted a hand upwards towards the sky. A bolt of lightning crashed down, smashing the pedestal that had held the spearhead into a thousand pieces that flew across the glade like bullets. The shock of the strike threw Lauren and her father backwards.

The grass sizzled and burned. Daniel laughed in delight. "One more journey to make—your last, I'm afraid. You'll need some clothes." One thought, and Lauren's pile of clothes from the bedroom at the Manor appeared on the ground beside her. He released his hold on her body long enough for her to scramble into them before the Grove faded away.

Only nine of them had decided to transport through the portal to the Grove. Shari had taken Laura and Lou Henrikson and Sharla had taken Jim and Anika. El was still trying to release Heather's mind from Daniel's control and as it had been he who had contacted the police he had decided reluctantly that he should stay with Tania. Max held out a hand each to Keri and Kim.

"Only fair that you two should be with us."

"I hope we can help," said Keri, very nervous.

"There's one chance we have and that's surprise." Max prepared himself for the journey, looking at the others, making sure they were all ready to leave as one. "He doesn't know we can use Portals. He won't be expecting us." He nodded a signal and they all transported together.

They arrived into an eruption of smoke and dust. For a moment they all stood staring, disorientated by their short journey and trying to make sense of what they saw. Shari spat out a few words, some of them in English, that Max hoped Kim and Keri were not listening to. He saw Sharla's eyes full of angry tears and slid an arm around her. She flung it off furiously, spitting out a sentence that he was sure was untranslatable Zulu, hammered her fists on the nearest tree and then hid her face on his shoulder.

"It was such a beautiful place." Her voice was muffled by his collar.

"It will be again." He tried to be positive, patting her back helplessly, his mind full of wild fears of what that man could have done to Lauren. He had seen the Grove looking worse but he remembered only too well what it had been like to be there with lightning striking all around. No one could survive. His eyes searched fearfully for anything that could be her body, his mind refusing to admit what he was doing even to himself. Jim Erickson had moved away from them and was stamping on the smouldering grass with his big boots.

"I think we can safely say they've been here." Anika said grimly. "Keri, come sit by me again and help me try to find your friend." Keri, pale-faced, took both her hands and thought desperately of Lauren. Once again she experienced the intimacy of another mind sharing her thoughts, only not as disturbing this time as she knew what to expect. She could feel nothing.

"I don't think she's here, if they ever were," she said.

"Oh they were," said Shari angrily. "Only one of Thor's descendants would repeat the destruction to this beautiful place."

"Why would he have wasted time coming here just to do this?" Max cried.

"What was kept in this grove?" Lou Henrikson spoke for the first time. "There must have been something here that he wanted."

"This is where we kept the spearhead—Lori's spear." Shari spat out the words, her face hard with anger. "It was on a pedestal, over there. He's blown it to pieces."

"Are you sure?" Lou asked. "I thought all along that if he was to have a chance of reversing his father's death he would need that spear. Perhaps it's just the pedestal that he's disintegrated." They all stared at him for a moment, and then started searching the ground for any shards of flint that could have been a part of the spear.

"Unless it's dust, I think you must be right," Laura agreed after a while. "Where would he have taken it?"

"There's only one place where he would go," said Lou. "The mountain. It all leads to the mountain."

"Where is the mountain?" Max asked.

There was a moment's appalled silence as everyone realised that no one knew.

Chapter 22
The Mountain

Lauren lay in a crumpled heap on the snow-covered mountain platform where Torsen had dropped her, only able to watch as he dragged the bound body of her father across to the spot where she remembered Lori lying in a heap on top of the corpse of her enemy Thor. A quiet gasp of pain escaped Alex's lips as Torsen heaved him against the platform and delivered a savage kick to his side as he stepped up himself and with a glow of the Crystal ring cleared three millennia of snow from the mound that had been his father's throne. Freed from their icy shroud the strange carvings were as clear as she remembered them from three and a half thousand years before. Her father lay gasping at its feet. Her father. She looked at the ragged clothes and foul, tangled hair. How could this helpless wreck be her father?

"Yes, your mother felt just the same," Daniel sneered, eyes sweeping his helpless enemy with scorn. Lauren felt a wave of hatred sweep over her, banishing the confusion and fear. He was only what Daniel Torsen had made him over seven years. She watched him try to ease himself into a sitting position and willed him to manage as the agony contorting his face made him gasp again. Then his eyes met hers, full of pain and love, and she felt her own flood with tears of guilt.

Dad? she mindwhispered.

My little daughter. You are my little daughter. How long…? His mindvoice trailed away as he stared and stared at her. Lauren crawled over towards him, thankful that Torsen seemed to be lost in contemplation.

I'm so sorry. Her father's voice in her mind was just like her memories of their ancestors. *I'm so sorry that I have missed your growing. I'm so sorry that I should meet you now only to lose you again.*

Oh Dad! She buried her face in his filthy shoulder and sobbed as if her heart would break.

"I'm sure there's a reason why he was in such a rush to take them today." Lou was still thinking aloud, pacing the grove almost as restlessly as Max. "Laura, Max, you both saw that day when Thor died. What do you remember?"

"It was night," Laura volunteered glumly. It had been about two hundred years since she and El had shared that bracelet experience. Max tried to calm his thoughts enough to picture that scene and felt his hands burn as he relived that moment when the crystal had shattered. He swallowed hard and tried again.

"It was a peak in a mountain range. High. The air was thin—not thin like Everest but certainly as high as the Alps. There was a flat platform that was only accessible through a Portal. Axiel said no one could climb to it. That was in those days of course—with modern equipment, perhaps…" his voice died away as he realised that none of the rest of them were climbers and anyway they couldn't climb anything when they didn't know where it was. Or fast enough. Oh Lauren… he couldn't think straight while she was in such terrible danger. "There was a carved stone chair in the centre of the ledge. Like a throne. Thor was standing by it when we first saw him. The woman and boy were over by the cliffs on the right hand side. We didn't see them at first in the dark. I remember the moon was very bright, full and rising behind them so they were in shadow. It was quite low and huge. There was a very bright star as well; it could have been one of the planets. Lori and Axiel slipped into the shadows but Lauren and I didn't realise—we stayed in the full moonlight in front of him, which was why he could see us first. I think we must have been very near the edge." He shivered a little as he remembered being blasted backwards across the slippery ice. So close to the drop.

"I think the moon's the clue," Lou said excitedly. "And the planet. The time of year must be crucial. Torsen must need everything to be as similar to that night as possible. The anniversary. I'm no astronomer, but I guess it wouldn't happen every year that the moon and planet were the same. Maybe not even every century!"

"But where?" Max groaned. Already the sun filtering through the smoky dust of the clearing was sinking. If they were to save Lauren, time was running out.

On the mountaintop Lauren and her father were shaking with cold, only the evening sun slanting across the range of mountain peaks making the temperature slightly bearable. When she put her arms around him to share warmth he tried to smile at her, teeth glinting like a beaver's in the tangled black of his beard.

It was warmer when we were dry.

Oh Dad! She was about to apologise for her tears when she realised he was trying to joke and hugged him harder. She wondered if she could loosen the ropes that tied his hands under cover of her coat.

"No, you can't," Daniel gloated, still linked to her mind. "And don't think you can contact that interfering grandmother of yours either. I have shields round this peak that would repel a nuclear bomb. But do make the attempt. I enjoy your struggles." He sat on his father's carved throne like a spider, watching them. Lauren had to try; she held the bird charm tightly and thought desperately of Grannie. But there was nothing there. Daniel laughed. Lauren tried to hold her head high and pretend she didn't care.

You look just like your mother the first time I ever saw her. She heard her father's voice in her mind, together with a sense of his pride in her that washed around her like a warm glow. *She was being threatened by some rough types. She must have been terrified but she wouldn't give them the satisfaction of letting them see it. That was when I decided I had to know her better.*

The sun was beginning to set, turning the snow on all the jagged peaks around to gold and pink. Miles and miles of mountains.

If this is the last thing I see, I'm glad I could share it with you, her father thought to her. She hugged him closer, closing her nose to the smell.

"Touching," laughed Daniel. He could violate their every thought. The sun dropped behind the furthest mountain, a thin sliver of red, tinting the tips of the mountains with blood as they glowed in the twilight.

"Time to prepare, I think." He slid off the throne like a cat gliding towards its prey, power in every movement. "Now, I need that bracelet." He pulled her away from her father onto the ice and knelt roughly on her shoulder, stretching her arm out along the ground. She yelped with pain. Alex lurched at them but only fell over, able to do nothing while his hands and feet were tied. "Last chance, Lauren. Take it off now." Everything was swimming with pain. She screamed again with real terror as she saw the axe in his hand.

"No! I won't! I won't!"

"Either you take it off, or I take your arm off." She moaned and writhed against his grip. Dimly through the roaring in her ears she heard her father's voice shouting hoarsely.

"Take it off, Lauren! Take it off! You can't do anything! Take it off!" She screamed again, hysterical, only aware of the shining axe blade above her arm, and groped the other hand across to try to release the clip. She felt the weight on her shoulder ease and tried again, her fingers shaking so much she could hardly make them do what she wanted them to, fumbling desperately at the catch until the bracelet slipped off her wrist. With a huge sigh, Daniel grabbed it in both hands and cradled it for a moment as if it was the most precious thing in the world. Lauren crawled back towards her father, still shaking with sobs, feeling as though part of herself had been torn away. She turned and glared at Daniel.

"To think I once thought I would like you for a father! I prefer the real one, and so does my mother!"

He hit her savagely with his fist so that she fell backwards, hitting her head hard on the icy ground. She lay there stunned.

He had the spear in his hand; he pulled the ancient ring from the other and slipped it over the thin haft. It spiralled down until it hit the stone blade with a soft thunk. Then he carefully bound the bracelet around it so that the spear charm lay against the crystal which began to gleam with life in the gathering dusk. He pushed Alex face down on the ice and stood with a foot on his back with the spear poised above him, waiting, as the sky darkened.

Lou was still trying to work out how Daniel would be intending to bring Thor back.

"The bracelet must be the link," he muttered. "Somehow that spear charm was there twice, once when Lori stabbed Thor and once when Max and Lauren found themselves truly at that event. Somehow, the two times merged, and the present affected the past; Lori and Axiel could only do what they did because you and Lauren were there, Max. And now it's there for a third time, with the crystal shard and with the spear. Perhaps he can merge the two times and draw the spear from the past into the spear from the present. Instead of stabbing Thor, Lori would join with him to kill the sacrifice, her own descendant. Alex or Lauren." The others listened, faces tight with fear. Max clenched his fists and stood straight.

"Well, it looks like it's up to me. If I can visualise that place well enough, perhaps I can get there."

"You must take us." Laura and Sharla spoke together and the others all joined in.

"Too risky." Max backed away from them. "If I don't make it, you'll be all that stands between the world and Thor. Wish me luck. Give Dad my love." His crooked smile lit his face for a moment as he prepared himself for the journey, only his fourth using the Portal and already the second that he was not sure he would survive. Laura thought she would remember that little toss of her nephew's head as he flicked his hair out of his eyes for as long as she lived. Kim and Keri did not even have to look at each other. Minds as one, they leaped to catch Max's coat as he disappeared. In the blink of an eye, all three were gone.

They were floating in nothingness. All their senses were blind; they could see nothing, hear nothing. Max stifled his first reaction of panic as he felt the others with him.

You're a pair of idiots, aren't you? He couldn't quite keep the smile out of his mind. They shifted their grip from his coat to his arms and the contact was comforting. They floated in the dark.

The first thing Lauren was aware of was pain nagging at her, waking her; as she forced her eyes open it seemed to explode across her face, blinding her and dragging a weak moan from her dry throat. She struggled to sit up and remember where she was. The moon had risen over the mountaintop and she could see the silhouette of Daniel, draped in a long furred coat that made him look even more like his terrible father had looked all those centuries ago, standing spear in hand over a dark mound that must be her father. Only the wind ruffling his hair showed that he was not a statue he was so still.

Dad? Her mind cried out in a sudden panic.

Still here, Lauren.

As she watched, she could sense Daniel pouring strength from his mind into the crystal ring. It began to glow until brighter than the moon it cast his shadow behind him like a huge black predator. She could not take her eyes off the sparkling spear point. Perhaps if she thought really hard she could move it away from her father's back. She felt Alex's mind with her pushing but even together they were no match for Daniel and the crystal. He was laughing, enjoying their weak struggling, but she kept trying in helpless desperation.

The bracelet shone
Keri K.

All of a sudden she began to be aware of a change in the atmosphere; something was happening. She half twisted around. Like a ghost, the thin and transparent figure of Thor was beginning to emerge in front of his throne as the power of the bracelet and crystal began to bring back that moment before he had died. Once again she saw him pull thunderbolts from the air and send them raining death and terror down the mountainside. He grew more solid as Daniel's power drew the past towards them. Lauren knew what she would see if she turned right round and didn't dare. She heard the huge voice rolling and echoing around the mountain peaks as Thor saw what must be herself and Max as they had appeared before on that mountain top.

"Who are you? WHO ARE YOU?" Thor's voice, magnified by the power of the crystal, echoed once again through the icy wastes.

Max, Kim and Keri exploded from the air and skidded to their knees just as Axiel threw himself onto the crystal.

Lauren? Max reached out, searching for her before he had even stopped sliding.

Max! Max! Oh please help Dad! Their eyes took only a fraction of a second to adjust to the moonlight after the intense darkness of their journey. Keri threw herself at her friend and Lauren clung to her, strength from her mind and warmth from her body flooding into her. Max grabbed the spear haft and stood eye to eye with Daniel, fighting for control. All their minds and his strength were not enough to move it.

Kim suddenly knew what he had to do. He stood up and strained his eyes for the other shadowy figures from the past under the cliff. The crystal exploded under Axiel's body; Kim threw himself flat on his face as the blast shot pieces of dust and grit across the platform. He dimly saw the other Max slithering across the icy ground. The explosion lit up the cliff face for a few seconds and Kim saw what he was looking for: a tall woman frozen with horror and a boy of about his own age running forwards, reaching for a glowing shard of the crystal. He launched himself in a flying tackle that would have amazed all his sports teachers and grabbed the twelve-year-old Daniel round the knees. They both skidded across the icy rock. He glanced round. The crystal was still lying there. The other boy jumped back towards it. Kim grabbed at his clothes and they fought, kicking and punching, as he desperately tried to stop him. He clung on to Daniel's arm as he reached out again for that sparkling fragment; Daniel swung his fist wildly and Kim yelled and let go as it connected with his eye. Daniel lunged towards the Crystal and Kim grabbed frantically at his leg and brought him crashing to the ground. He managed to lie across the other boy, using his weight to hold him still as he kicked and struggled. Then Daniel suddenly stilled beneath him and as Kim looked up, horrified, he saw the crystal starting to move, sliding as the

224

young Daniel's mind began to pull it towards them. Kim struck out with all the mental energy he had. It glowed brighter and then exploded with a little puff of dust.

"NO!" The shout of anguish came not from the boy that had been Daniel but from the man as the crystal ring was suddenly gone from the spear and Daniel's strength was no more than normal. Max felt the spear begin to respond as he pulled.

Get Alex away! He grunted with the effort. Daniel was still very strong. Keri and Lauren crawled across and pulled the stiff body of her father away out of danger and Keri, fingers not as numb as Lauren's, tried to pick at the tight knots that bound his hands behind his back. Lauren looked around—something was still going wrong. Lori's struggle with Thor was not as it had been the last time that she had seen it.

The bracelet! Max shouted into her mind. *It's still pulling the spear away from the past. I must get it off!*

Too late! Lauren knew there was no time to win the spear away from Daniel's last desperate attempt to prevent his father's death. *Keri, Kim, Help me!* With tears of loss gathering in her eyes she sent a thought of pure destructive heat at the bracelet. Tiny curls of smoke began to drift from the wood around it. She felt Keri and Kim strengthening her as she fought to destroy the precious thing that she had loved. Max and Daniel sprang apart as the spear haft burst into flames and the bracelet fell away from the head, a tangled, melted heap of silver. The platform seemed suddenly empty as the past vanished back to the past and the six people left panted quietly in the silent moonlight.

With a roar of loss and rage Daniel launched himself at Lauren. Max was there first; somehow he grabbed his arm and rolling over the ground used his feet to throw Daniel over his head. He slid on his hands and knees right to the edge of the cliff. Max sprang back upright and braced himself ready for the counter attack but Daniel knew when he was beaten. For a moment he crouched there glaring at them, a snarl of hatred disfiguring his face, and then without taking his eyes off Lauren he straightened and stepped slowly and deliberately backwards off the cliff. She screamed with shock. Max rushed to the edge and stared down into the black depths below but there was nothing to be seen and no sound to be heard except the eerie hissing of the wind around the mountain peak.

Lauren found the spearhead and used the still sharp edge to saw through the ropes that bound her father. He managed a ghost of a smile through chattering teeth.

If I could move my arms, I'd give you a hug. He was too stiff with cold and cramp to speak. Max walked slowly back to join them.

"Let's get out of here," he said. They were all too exhausted even to feel elation at their victory.

Do me a favour. Alex still tried weakly to joke as Max clasped his arm to pull him up. *Get me to a bath before I have to meet my wife.*

Chapter 23
Homecoming

"Will you be all right, Lauren?" Max asked anxiously. She found she was clinging to his hand and had to peel her fingers away from his comforting warmth. She nodded tightly. She had to be strong for her father, this stranger, who was looking around disbelievingly at the home of his childhood, his head shaking slowly. "Alex." Max took his arm again firmly. "Come upstairs to the bathroom and I'll show you where my shaving gear is."

"Thank you." Her father's voice was quiet, husky, and he allowed himself to be led upstairs like a pet dog. Lauren waited until Max bounded back down again, two steps at a time, sniffing carefully at his arm to make sure he had not picked up any of the unpleasant aroma; his cousin was at that moment not pleasant to be too close to.

"I ought to say thank you too." She looked up at him, eyes so huge and black that he could hardly see where her pupil ended and the iris began, looking quite unlike herself with one side of her face swelling to twice its usual size.

"I should say sorry I took so long. I should've been there before he hurt you." He looked down at her and squeezed her shoulder, so thankful to see her safe and home that his voice failed. He cleared his throat hard and tried to give her a grin. "I wish I'd been able to hit him harder."

"Are you bringing Keri and Kim back here?" she asked.

"I'd better take them home to Florida before their parents miss them."

"Well, tell them… you know… thanks and everything. And I'll see them soon, won't I?" she stammered, really wanting to plead with him not to leave but knowing her friends had to be taken off that mountain quickly.

"I'll see you later." Reluctantly, he tore himself away. "I'll need to find Dad and the others. They don't even know you're all right yet." She gasped, suddenly remembering the rest of the family.

"Mum?" she squeaked.

"She's all right. They all are. I'll send them back as soon as I can." She nodded again, and stood silent for a moment in the emptiness of his going. Then she showered quickly in the downstairs cloakroom, her numb fingers and toes throbbing under the warm water, and changed into some clean clothes while her father disappeared into the bathroom for what seemed like hours. Eventually he came downstairs, the beard gone, wrapped in his mother's huge blue fleece dressing gown and holding a pair of scissors, looking taller than he had looked in his filthy rags, his hair dripping down his back. He stopped in the doorway.

"Your poor face." He reached out a finger and touched her cheek gently.

"It's OK." Actually it was throbbing like a pneumatic drill, but she couldn't talk about it.

"How's your hairdressing?" he asked her, his eyebrows twitching at her pleadingly.

"Never tried it." She tried to smile back despite the pain it caused her but suddenly felt so flat and drained that even talking seemed too much effort. She took the scissors from him and inexpertly began to cut his matted hair, noticing with relief that it was no longer lank and straight as it dried but began to fluff out around his head like a bush. Every time she glanced at him she found him staring at her as if he could not get enough of looking. She felt like pinching herself to prove he was real, saying to herself 'this is my father; this is **my** father; this is my **father**' over and over in her head. She had hugged him on the mountain when they'd thought they were going to die. She wanted him to hug her back now he could move his arms. She wanted it really, really badly.

"D'you want some soup?" she asked, suddenly shy of him and not knowing how to make conversation.

"Thank you. Let me do something." He took the tin from her and started to open it but she had to finish the job when his hands started to shake uncontrollably.

She was nearly crying herself as she tried to concentrate on saucepans and stirring, wishing desperately that she felt able to help, while he leaned on the table and buried his face in his arms, shoulders quivering. She was suddenly terrified of how her independent, undemonstrative mother would react when she met him again after seven years. What if Daniel was right and she hated what he had become? What if they never became a family again? He had recovered himself by the time the soup was ready and they drank it in silence, both tense. The sudden noise of their relations' voices in the hallway made them jump.

"Lauren!" She heard her mother's voice calling and the door burst open. For once Lauren didn't mind being ignored as she stopped still in the doorway with eyes only for the man sitting at the end of the table.

"Alex!" she whispered, an unconscious echo of his ancestor three and a half thousand years before. "Oh Alex, you look… you look…"

"Disgusting? Repulsive? Skeletal?" His face lit unexpectedly in a self-mocking grin as he tried to help her find the right words. She gave a slow shake of the head, eyes glowing softly in a way that Lauren had not seen before.

"Never," she whispered. "Not while you can still smile like that." He held out a shaking hand towards her and Lauren slipped away from the table and bolted for the hall where her grandmother was waiting with a tear sparkling on her cheek, content just to see her son home safely. Uncle El enveloped Lauren in the huge bear hug she needed, but somehow it didn't comfort her like she had thought it would and she found herself shaking with sobs as she clung to his huge chest while Laura softly closed the kitchen door.

They had to wait nearly an hour before Lauren's parents came back out of the kitchen, both red-eyed but with arms wrapped around each other, and Lauren finally allowed herself to believe that they would be a proper family at last.

"Oh Lauren!" Heather pulled her close while her husband went across to greet his own mother. None of them could speak for the emotion that clogged their throats. Then, finally, her father turned to her holding out both arms and the hug she walked into was everything she had dreamed a father's hug should be.

A week later nothing had quite returned to normal. Lauren, her face still swollen and bruised from Daniel's fist, although no longer painful after Sharla's healing touch, was sitting on soft grass in the Grove beside Keri with Sharla sitting cross-legged next to them, dressed in what appeared to be nothing but beads with bare feet resting on her knees, her toenails and fingernails painted with bright red, yellow and green African patterns. Trust her not even to sit like anyone else, Lauren smiled to herself, finally beginning to enjoy Sharla's strange behaviour after a couple of nerve-racking expeditions. It had been a good job Max had prepared her in advance and she still hadn't dared tell her mother about them.

"Keep very still," Sharla was instructing them. "Just feel out gently with your minds. Think thoughts of friendship, and hold out your hands." They slowly reached out their handfuls of hazelnuts. Keri held her breath as the little red squirrel put one foot on her wrist as it stretched out for the offered food. Very gently she moved her other hand and stroked its back. Her smile was pure delight.

"I always liked these little creatures. They're so different from the wild animals back home," said Sharla, tossing her hair back so that all the beads rattled. The squirrels ignored it. "You'll find you can tame most creatures if you're patient enough and speak into their minds. My favourite was a lioness I knew from a cub who would hunt for me."

"There was a Lori once who knew wolves," Lauren remembered, feeling suddenly sad that she would never know some of her ancestors' lives now the bracelet was gone. "And one who fell off a boat and was saved by a dolphin." She suddenly giggled as she watched Keri sitting with a squirrel on each shoulder, squeaking as one nibbled her hair. "Where is this Grove? Has it a place in the real world?"

"Of course it has, but we have spent centuries shielding it so that no humans will ever find it," Sharla replied. "Unless they're invited, of course." She shot a wicked smile at Keri. "It's actually in the forest quite near your grandmother's house. Where else would you find red squirrels? If you climbed the trees you could see the sea now though apparently in the old days when our ancestors first came here you couldn't."

"On the Isle of Wight?" Lauren was almost dis-believing.

"A magical spot, though of course it was probably not an island either in those days at the very beginning. The Grove was special to our people for thousands of years before Thor—they must have done something to this piece of ground to make it so magical and powerful but we have no idea what. The first time I found you, in the forest, you were within a bowshot of it but you would never have known it was there. I'll walk you here one day without using the portal."

"Do you mind? About the rest of us knowing, I mean?" Lauren asked. Sharla thought for a moment.

"No. It's what it was meant for. We should all be able to come here together as we did in the old days for our celebrations, births, marriages. It is a very special place."

"Will you and Max—" Keri spoke without thinking and stopped as soon as she realised how tactless she was being. But Sharla just laughed her tinkling laugh.

"Oh no! He'd drive me nuts in a week—he can never, never keep still, not even for five minutes. And I know I embarrass him when I say what I think. We'll never be anything but the best of friends after all we've been through but there's no romance." She lowered her mind-voice to a very private whisper. *Besides, I'm sure he doesn't know it yet but I think he might just wait for someone else to grow up, if she grows up sparky enough to be able to cope with him.*

Keri's mouth dropped open; she glanced at Lauren obliviously feeding the squirrels next to her and then she grinned at Sharla.

I wonder if Kim might have anything to say about that! Over at the other side of the glade Kim, his own black eye now fading from the lurid purple stage to a tasteful blue and green, was mindlifting stones with his friend Mark Erickson and Max. They were restoring the stream and pool to the way it had been at Max's first visit, under the stern supervision of Shari. As they watched, Max straightened and ran a hand through his hair, still wondering how Shari had managed to pull the water up through the underlying chalk rock against nature.

Or young Mark over there? Sharla's smile was full of mischief. Keri narrowed her eyes.

She'd better keep her hands off him! she sniffed, and Sharla laughed.

The pool finished, Mark and Kim wandered back over to the girls.

"I guess I'd better get you guys home before your parents miss you," said Mark. All the Elder People could now use the Portal; 'saving a fortune on the company jet' was how Jim Erickson had jubilantly described it. The children had all been lectured fiercely by Max about the danger of trying to go anywhere they didn't truly know. He thought the reason for their long stay in the darkness was because he had visualised the moon over the cliffs so clearly that they could not arrive until it was in that spot. He shuddered to think what would have happened if it had never been in that spot.

"Wait a moment." Laura spoke from where she and El were working cutting scorched branches from the bushes and flying them into green bin bags. "Alex has got something for them." They all looked towards Lauren's parents where they sat together under the trees holding hands. Lauren didn't think they'd let go of each other all week; she was not sure whether it was her mother not wanting to let him go in case he disappeared again or her father clutching at the lifeline that made him able at least to pretend to be normal. Alex was still pale and thin, his old clothes hanging loosely on him and his shock of black hair showing a few strands of grey from his seven-year ordeal. He reached into his pocket.

"No one has ever had better friends than we have had," he said softly to them all. "I wouldn't be here now without anyone—your family Mark, Shari and Sharla, and our family." He looked at Laura and El. "Especially Mum who never gave up on me. But you four are special. Kim, Keri, you're probably the best and bravest friends that anyone could ever have." He smiled at them and Lauren finally realised what her mother had meant about her father's smile as it lit his narrow face deepening the creases in his cheeks, completely transforming the haunted look in his eyes to one of warmth and humour.

"Max," he continued, "I'll never know whether I'll be more grateful to you for saving my daughter's and my lives or lending me your razor that day. Lauren, what can I say?" He was suddenly serious as he reached out and hugged her against his side. "It's quite a shock waking from some nightmare and finding your baby daughter all grown up and saving your life. I will never, never forget the way you stood up for me on that mountaintop. Not to mention your hairdressing skills." Everyone laughed. His ragged haircut had been a family joke all week, but he had not allowed anyone to touch his daughter's handiwork. He raised his hand and they all fell silent again. You could tell he'd been a lecturer, Lauren thought proudly.

"You four did something that no one in the world outside will ever know about, but which probably saved the lives or freedom of every one of them. The first thing I want to do is replace this." He held up Lori's spearhead, walked over to the pool and laid it gently on the stone by the little waterfall. "It's a puzzle," he continued quietly. "It looks like Solutrian work. Upper Paleolithic. Beautiful example of bifacial retouching."

"Uh?" Kim and Mark gave Lauren a mystified look.

"Don't worry, it's what he does—did," Lauren muttered out of the side of her mouth. "Archaeologist."

"It must have been ancient even in Lori's time," Alex mused. "The Solutrians were the people responsible for some of the earlier cave paintings in France around twenty thousand years ago but three and a half thousand years only takes us back into the Bronze Age." He put a hand on Kim and Max's shoulders and gave them one of his self-mocking smiles. "I never saw it when it was stuck into my back. Wouldn't've been a bad end for an archaeologist, stabbed by a Stone Age flint spear!"

"Dad! Alex!" Laura, Heather and Lauren all shouted at him at once, still not quite used to his ghoulish sense of humour.

Alex turned to look at them. "Your bracelet Lauren—and Mum—was ruined. But a jeweller Heather knows has melted the remains down for us. He made these. He pulled four little chains from his pocket. "No spells, no magic, but maybe they will remember they were once part of the bracelet and retain some link." He handed them one at a time to his wife and she solemnly clasped them around their necks. From each chain hung a silver copy of the leaf-shaped Stone Age spearhead. Heather gave the twins a huge hug.

"Come and see us again soon. We'll be back in Southampton next week."

"Will you be back at work?" Keri asked. Heather shrugged. She still didn't know if she had a job to go back to. After the drugs raid on Daniel's house the office had been closed down while the police searched his papers for any more evidence.

"I'll find another job," she said firmly. "Perhaps it's only when you lose something you realise how much it means to you." She let her eyes rest briefly on her husband and daughter. "But I'm not in too much of a hurry. We've all got a bit of catching up to do."

"What happened to Tania?" Kim asked.

"She's in care till her mother comes out of hospital," El said. "But it won't be long and that father of hers is safely in prison. She's a major witness in the drugs case."

"No wonder that man was so rich." Lauren still could not bring herself to say his name, and Heather felt sick at the memory of how close they had once been.

"What do you think happened to him?" asked Kim.

"He's still alive somewhere," said Max seriously. "He hasn't got the power of the crystal any more, but he's still got a stronger mind than most of us. We're going to have to do something about that."

"He's had more than three thousand years to practice!" said Uncle El.

"He won't be immortal any more now he's lost it, will he?" Laura mused.

"He won't like that." Alex shook his head slowly. "But his whole long life was dedicated to bringing his father back. To murder his own mother because her bitterness was getting in the way of that…" There was a long silence, while they all remembered his desperation. "There's no telling what he'll do now. He's bound to have wealth hidden away."

"What are you going to do, Max?" Keri asked. He shrugged, his little half-smile sarcastic.

"Teach myself to be a true Elder instead of a mutant human?" He beckoned Lauren and Mark over. "Watch this. We've been practising!" He slapped palms with both of them and they stood in a row grinning at the others. "Now you see us, now you don't!" Lauren winked at Kim and Keri and the three of them began to fade in and out of sight. Then Max appeared on a low branch of a tree above them, and they began swapping places round and round like a human juggling act. The twins and Lauren's family convulsed with laughter as Max and Mark finally collided on the branch and fell in a tangle to the ground on top of Lauren. Even Shari allowed herself a lift of her thin eyebrows.

Beginners! Sharla said without moving her lips.

"I see what you mean about Elders not growing up properly till they're over a hundred!" Heather said to Laura when she was able.

"Hey, I've just had the most brilliant idea!" exclaimed Kim. "You could make a fortune organising a ghost walk, ghosts and all!"

"Don't give up your day job," Sharla muttered.

"Well, I did promise next year to Lauren's school." Max pulled the others to their feet and dusted himself down without embarrassment. "But after that I don't know. Dad and I have the Adventure Centre to worry about—we can't leave poor Steve in charge indefinitely but we won't go back until we're sure Torsen's not a danger to us all any more. Maybe one day I'll go to America, refresh my pilot's licence, and see if I can join the Space Program." They all laughed. Knowing him, he probably would.

"You need a spaceship?" Sharla asked him incredulously out of the corner of her mouth, and Max's face went suddenly thoughtful.

"Come on," Mark nagged the twins. "You had enough trouble explaining all those bruises to your olds. I don't want them thinking I've kidnapped you as well as giving Kim a black eye!"

"I'll see you three soon." Lauren smiled at them from the shelter of both parents' arms. "And don't bother about the e-mail any more! Oh—Uncle El!" She grinned at him wickedly. "If you write about this in your History of the Elder People, don't forget to put in the bit about Kim's mum and the clean underwear!"

Mark pulled the twins away back to Florida before Kim could give her a second black eye.

GOLDENWING
by Jordin Everrey

Keri woke at dawn, her hair damp with dew and freezing cold. Shivering, she found her trainers and pushed her feet into them before walking across the wet grass to go to the tent and dress. The others looked very peaceful, three heads half-buried in damp pillows and under sleeping bags. She made a face; she had known she wouldn't really enjoy the experience and she pulled on her clothes quickly, wishing for a hot shower.

Wimp. Kim's voice laughed in her mind.

Oh, you're awake are you? I suppose you enjoyed every moment! Her mindvoice dripped with sarcasm.

Just look around! Kim was enthusiastic. The sun was just beginning to send golden beams slanting through the trees, sparkling on dew-laden cobwebs. A few birds were singing in a bored summery way, and Sharla's red squirrels could be seen running around the upper branches.

Well, I suppose it is rather pretty, but I think I'd rather look at it through a window. It's too early. Shall we wake up the others and go and scrounge some hot porridge from Lauren's house?

Better not wake them up yet. Hey—I've got some chocolate in the tent. Bring it here, and you can have half. By the time they had finished the fruit and nut bar and washed it down with a swig from a bottle of squash the sun had dried the dew from the plastic covers. Kim pulled his T-shirt and shorts out of his tent and dressed quickly, looking round furtively in case Sharla should suddenly be waking up in her hammock.

It's going to be another scorcher, he thought. *Max and Lauren'll be disappointed. No chance for any surf.*

"They're being very boring." Keri spoke aloud in the hope that it would wake their friends. Kim gave Mark's shoulder a shake.

"Come on, time to wake up." Mark did not stir. Suddenly worried, Kim shook harder. "Come on, wake up!" Keri felt a cold hollow in the pit of her stomach and yanked the plastic sheet off the two sleepers.

"Wake up Lauren!" She shouted in her ear and shook her hard but her head just lolled back like a doll's. She put her ear to Lauren's mouth. "She's breathing. She's just... asleep. Something's wrong." She looked anxiously at her brother. "Quick, we'd better get someone."

"Max!" Kim had run across the Grove and was shaking his arm but there was no sign of movement from him. "Have they been hurt?"

"How? We've been right next to them all night!" Keri cried, running across the clearing to look at Sharla, still curled around her knees in the hammock looking like a sleeping hamster. Kim looked at his sister, panic in his eyes.

This book can be pre-ordered by visiting the website
www.thestonespear.co.uk

THE STONE SPEAR saga.

Book 1   The Charmed Bracelet.

Twelve charms, each charm a life.

When her strange grandmother gives Lauren Silva an heirloom bracelet for her twelfth birthday present, she begins to develop unsettling mental abilities and to have terrifyingly real nightmares.

Could a series of attempts to steal the bracelet have anything to do with the mysterious disappearance of her archaeologist father seven years before? Soon she, her friends Kim and Keri and her cousin Max are plunged into a desperate adventure where she has to bridge time to save her family and the world from an ancient enemy.

Book 2   Goldenwing.

Thousands of years ago, on a distant world, a young boy and his father risk their lives to capture the egg of a wild Goldenwing, their only chance to escape poverty. The giant bird brings Rik his first friends, but their world is under threat from monstrous creatures that attack and devastate their world. Their only chance is flight, helped by the discovery of a powerful crystal.

Max and Lauren find out more about the struggle of their ancestors to escape, but their enemy will try to use this knowledge to bring the ancient evil to attack the Elder People on Earth. Lauren has to travel space and time to stop him.

Book 3   The Third Crystal.

The ancient enemy of the Silva family is declining into revengeful madness and plots savage attacks on them. While escaping from him, Lauren, Max and the Kirby family are pulled into a secret refuge of the Elder People that has been hidden for millennia, and where the inhabitants have been taught to hate and fear humans. Lauren and Max have to find the way out before their enemy kills them, and before the twins and their parents are executed.

Book 4   The Red Crystal.

The Saga of the Elder People continues to unfold as Lauren and the twins travel back in time to the Ice Age with her ever-curious archaeologist father, and find out more about the ancient, terrifying menace that forced her people to flee their Homeworld. They are faced by new ruthless enemies that only want to find a way to steal the riches of Earth in the present day.